DEADLY
CURRENTS

BETH GROUNDWATER

DEADLY
CURRENTS

MIDNIGHT INK
WOODBURY, MINNESOTA

FIRST EDITION
First Printing, 2011

Book design by Donna Burch
Cover design by Lisa Novak
Cover image © Ann Manner/Photodisc/PunchStock

Midnight Ink, an imprint of Llewellyn Worldwide Ltd.

Library of Congress Cataloging-in-Publication Data

Groundwater, Beth.
  Deadly currents / Beth Groundwater. — 1st ed.
    p.   cm.
    "A Rocky Mountain Adventures mystery."
  ISBN 978-0-7387-2162-0
  1. White-water canoeing—Fiction. 2. Colorado—Fiction. I. Title.
  PS3607.R677D43   2011
  813'.6—dc22   2010042591

Midnight Ink
Llewellyn Worldwide Ltd.
2143 Wooddale Drive
Woodbury, MN 55125-2989
www.midnightinkbooks.com

Printed in the United States of America

DEDICATION

To my parents, David and Barbara Howell, whose firm love and fine example instilled in me the belief that I could be and do whatever I set my mind to.

ACKNOWLEDGMENTS

First I must thank my literary agent, Sandra Bond, who worked like a bull dog to find a publisher for this new series in a down economy when many other mystery series were being terminated. Also, thanks to Terri Bischoff, acquisition editor at Midnight Ink, for believing that an action-oriented whitewater series would appeal to mystery readers. Thanks to all the staff at Midnight Ink who contributed to this book, especially Connie Hill, senior editor. And thanks to my critique group, Maria Faulconer, Bill Mason, Barb Nickless, MB Partlow, and Bob Spiller, for pointing out where I had more work to do. Thanks to my family for believing in me.

I owe profuse thanks to many experts who gave of their time and advice to make this story as authentic as possible. My friend, Cynthia Hunt, shared stories from her years of river guiding. Darren Olson, owner of Whitewater Encounters, let me tour his business, answered questions, and gave me information on regulations, licensing, and river equipment vendors. Sean Shepard, River Section Supervisor of the Arkansas Headwaters Recreation Area (AHRA), and Stew Pappenfort, Senior Park Ranger of the AHRA, educated me about the career field of river rangering and explained rescue and tree-clearing techniques. Stew graciously allowed me to observe a day of his river ranger training course and to chat with the trainees. Keith Pinkston, Lead Investigator of the Chaffee County Sheriff's Department, educated me on how their procedures differ from those I learned in the El Paso County Sheriff's Citizen's Academy and explained how they work with river rangers in investigating deaths in the river. Texas pharmacist Luci Zahray contributed vital information from her area of expertise.

Any errors in fact or procedure are due to my exaggeration or misunderstanding of these experts' patient instruction.

The upper Arkansas River in Colorado is the most commercially rafted river in the United States, and having taken numerous trips down various sections, I can attest to the excitement and beauty of this unique whitewater wonder. The towns along the river, including Buena Vista and Salida, are chock-full of rafting outfitters and "river rats," that cowboyish breed of men and women who are addicted to the thrill of riding the bucking bronc called the Arkansas. They work as rafting guides, seasonal river rangers, or whatever jobs they can find—however low-paying— that keep them on the river. I tasted the thrill of running whitewater rivers in open-boat canoes along the foothills of the Appalachian mountains in the 1980s. Communing again with lovers of the sport was a true pleasure. Though the equipment has changed, the attitudes have not. I hope to continue researching and writing about river rat culture—and getting splashed by pure, free-running whitewater.

ONE

If a man is destined to drown,
he will drown even in a spoonful of water.
—YIDDISH PROVERB

"GONZO'S NOT GOING TO make it." Steve Hadley peered upriver, squinting as whitewater spray sparkled in the brilliant June sunlight. His voice held a sharp edge of concern.

"What?" Mandy Tanner dropped her half-eaten PBJ sandwich into the waterproof ammo box on a large boulder beside her. She leapt to her feet. "He never blows Number Four, even with a boatload of clueless tourists."

Gonzo Gordon was one of the best whitewater rafting guides on the Upper Arkansas River in central Colorado. He was manning the lead boat in this three-raft pod making its way downriver. He knew the Numbers section like an old milk cow knows the path to the barn. But now his raft teetered almost sideways to the rushing current at the top of the class V rapid's last big drop. Mandy's

1

fingers clenched as if she was the one straining with all her might on a paddle to fight the current—but in reality, nothing she could do would stop the impending disaster.

The forward side of the raft dove down the precipice, under the boiling foam. Passengers spilled out, legs and paddles flying. Even Gonzo pitched into the water.

Mandy craned her neck for a better view from her vantage point on the river bank, searching for heads as they popped, gasping, out of the waves. *Holy cow!*

The now lightweight raft, amazingly still upright, launched itself out of the tumbling waves. One wide-eyed woman remained inside, hugging the thwart on which she had been sitting, shoulders hunched in quiet desperation.

Steve sprinted toward a large rock that poked out from the shore into the surging river. "I'll jump in the raft and pull in bodies," he yelled over his shoulder. "Launch your cat and pick up anyone who washes downstream."

The roar of the churning water rang in Mandy's ears. While running to her cataraft tied up in an eddy nearby, she clipped shut the buckles of her personal floatation device and slapped the right front panel. Yep, her safety knife for cutting entangling ropes was still Velcro-ed to the PFD, and yep, her fanny pack with emergency medical supplies bounced on her rear.

My equipment is ready, but am I?

She unloosed the cataraft's bowline, which was tethered to a tree, and jumped into the oaring seat clamped onto a metal frame suspended between the two bright blue inflatable pontoons. With a strong pull on the oars, she spun out of the quietly circulating eddy current into the main current in time to see Steve take a flying leap off the rock.

He landed in the middle of Gonzo's raft, rocking the startled passenger, who stared at him in awestruck hero worship. Steve hopped to the other side of the raft, where a swimmer had managed to grab hold. With one giant heave, Steve gripped the shoulders of the man's PFD and hauled him in.

Mandy shoved forward on her oars. The current gripped the cataraft and propelled it downstream. She made a correction to avoid a pillow rock on the right, then dug deep with the oars to pull past Gonzo's raft.

Steve back paddled, trying to slow the raft, to give Gonzo a chance to catch up. Knowing Steve would soon have Gonzo's raft under control, Mandy focused her gaze downstream. Two heads bobbed in the water as the river swept them along a wide, left curve and out of sight.

Mandy knew she would need a full head of steam to catch up to those two swimmers. And they were in for a rough ride. The river section before Number Five was a rock garden full of unnamed class III and IV waves and holes that pinballed swimmers from one lethal rock to the next.

She recognized the surge of adrenaline she always felt—and relished—when she entered whitewater, and she was excited to finally put her training to the test. Still, she prayed as her cat bounced through the waves. *Please don't let me screw up. Please don't let me screw up.*

This was her second week on patrol as a brand-new seasonal river ranger, still under the supervision of Steve, the head river ranger. Sure, she had run all the whitewater sections of the Upper

Arkansas for years as a rafting guide—Pine Creek, the Numbers, Wildhorse Canyon, Brown's Canyon, Bighorn Sheep Canyon, and Royal Gorge. And she'd pulled lots of swimmers out of the water as a guide. But now guides like Gonzo relied on her to rescue their customers who'd been snatched out of their grasp by the river.

Slowly, Mandy gained on the second swimmer, a young woman. The man in front of her must have fallen out of the raft first or been swept up by the main current sooner. Though Mandy couldn't see his face, the man seemed strangely calm, unmoving. In contrast, the woman's arms and legs flailed in the seething whitewater. She bounced off a rock and got smacked in the face with backwash from a hole.

Mandy blew her whistle to catch the woman's attention then pulled the cat up alongside her. "Grab on!"

Sputtering, the woman slung an arm over the nearest pontoon. A lank strand of wet hair stuck to one cheek and an angry scrape oozed blood on the other.

Mandy leaned forward to grab the back of the woman's PFD. She tugged the woman up onto the pontoon, so she lay straddled across it, face toward Mandy and backside pointing downstream.

"Hold on to the frame!" Giving herself a mental congratulatory high-five, Mandy picked up her oars again.

According to her training, she should now ferry the woman to shore. But there wasn't time if Mandy was going to pick up the man before he entered the Number Five rapid, a class V monster, a killer. She just couldn't leave him to fend for himself.

Heart thudding, Mandy made two strong strokes on the oars and threw in an extra stroke on one side to compensate for her passenger's weight. She took her gaze off the male swimmer to make a quick check of the woman who lay panting on the pontoon.

"You okay?" Mandy yelled.

The woman nodded, too out-of-breath to respond verbally. Despite her shivering, her white-knuckled grip on the cat's frame seemed secure, and she had managed to wrap her legs around the pontoon.

Nearing the man, Mandy blew on her whistle, but he didn't respond. She blew again. Still no response. His head seemed to bob more than the force of the current would create. His limbs hung listlessly in the water. In that unconscious state, he wouldn't be able to grab onto the boat, and bumping him into an eddy in the fast-moving water was impossible.

"Looks like he's unconscious," Mandy shouted to the woman. "I'm going to need your help pulling him in."

The woman shot her a wild-eyed "What, are you kidding?" look, but Mandy chose to ignore it. The ominous roar of Number Five downstream was way more important.

Powering her oar strokes with her back, Mandy yelled out explanations. "I'll come up alongside him then pull him onto the other pontoon. I need you to grab whatever you can on him and help pull him up."

They bounced through a narrow chute between two huge rocks, then hit a relatively unobstructed section of river. It was now or never.

Mandy nudged her unoccupied pontoon next to the man. "Now!"

She reached down to grab him, but the swirling current spun the cat sideways. The pontoon hit the man, whacking his shoulder into a half-submerged boulder.

That's gotta hurt. Mandy spun the oars in opposite directions to orient the cat and reapproached him. "Okay, again!"

She grabbed the shoulder straps of his PFD and hauled back, bracing a knee against the inside of the pontoon. His chest hit the pontoon, then he started slipping. *No, no, no. Can't lose him.*

Just when Mandy thought her back would break, the young woman reached across the gap between the two pontoons. She grabbed one of the man's arms and pulled. That added enough extra force to get his body up and draped over the pontoon.

"Hold on to him!" Mandy shouted.

She plopped back into the oaring seat and yanked on one oar to counteract another spin the current had put on the cat. Her stroke pointed the front of the cat, weighted down with her two passengers, downstream. Keeping that orientation, with the man's legs acting as an anchor on one side, would take constant corrections with the oars. But Mandy was determined to get both of these folks safely to shore.

"Hang on to the raft!" she yelled at the woman. "Even if you have to let go of him."

The young woman gritted her teeth and nodded. Hugging one pontoon with her legs, she hung precariously between the two pontoons. One hand gripped the frame and the other still held the man's arm.

The deadly current tugged at the sluggish, off-balanced cataraft, pulling it toward the roiling waters of Number Five, an angry maw with sharp, rocky teeth that ate boats and swimmers alive. Mandy strained against the oars, battling the river for control.

What the hell do I do now?

The Chaffee County Road 371 bridge that signaled the start of the rapid loomed a few yards downstream. And there were no eddies large enough to hold the cat before the bridge.

Mandy's mind searched for an out. Just past the bridge, the river swung right. That, combined with a few large rocks on the left side, had created a small gravel beach on the shore. Next to the beach was an eddy large enough to hold the cat. But if she missed that eddy, the cat would be in the exact wrong position to run Number Five. The boat would flip. She'd risk three lives.

But there was no other option.

She braced her feet against the frame and pulled on the oars, again and again, trying to slow the cat's speed and set up a cross-stream ferry. The steep, rocky river banks slipped past as the cat moved relentlessly downstream.

More adrenalin surged through Mandy, fueling her strokes. She refused to let the river get the best of her. Ignoring the burning pains in her arms, she focused on keeping the cat at the proper angle.

Finally the force of the rushing water started pushing the cat toward shore. She pulled on the oars one, two, three more times. Still not there.

Number Five's horizon line loomed just yards away. A huge tongue of water plunged hungrily over the edge.

The young woman stared at the precipice then at Mandy, her eyes wide saucers of fear and doubt.

Unable to speak, Mandy grunted in sympathy at her and pulled again and again, aiming for the eddy line. If she could get the pontoon holding the man's body past the line, his legs in the upstream current of the eddy would help swing the cat around. She let out a groan on one more stroke, knowing this was her last.

Finally, the cat slipped across the eddy line into the quiet water behind the rocks. Mandy gave another feeble stroke, but it was enough. With the man acting as a makeshift anchor, the other pontoon slid out of the treacherous current.

She caught her breath, then yelled at the woman. "Stay there until I pull the raft onto the beach." If the woman put a leg out into the main current, she would be a goner.

Mandy slid into the thigh-deep water next to the cat. She gasped as the ice-cold water seeped into her wetsuit. Scrabbling up the gravel bank, she tugged the pontoon on which the man lay out of the water.

"Okay," she said to the woman. "Slide off this side of your pontoon and hold on to the other one until you're on the beach."

The young woman eased off her pontoon and stumbled onto the beach. Once there, she pulled on the cataraft also.

"Thanks," Mandy said, grateful both that the woman had the energy to help and was okay—unlike her other rescuee.

After they had beached the cat, Mandy tied the bowline to a tree. Then she checked on the man. He lay across the pontoon, unmoving, his face gray.

Not good. Definitely not good.

Wanting nothing more than to collapse on the gravel, Mandy knew she couldn't. She slipped her hands under the man's armpits and dragged him on his back onto the beach. He was tall, middle-aged, and had a fair-sized beer gut on him. He must have weighed well over two hundred pounds, which didn't compare well to Mandy's one-twenty-five. Her arm and leg muscles quivered with exhaustion.

Once on the beach, she fell to her knees beside him. She put her ear to his mouth and nose and watched his chest. A faint wisp of air tickled her ear, then another, as his chest rose and fell shallowly. Thanking God, she felt for a pulse. It was weak, fluttery.

Mandy pulled out her radio. She looked at the woman who knelt nearby, hands on her knees, catching her breath. "Will you watch him, let me know if he gets worse in any way, while I call for an ambulance?"

She nodded and scooted next to the man.

"Thanks again." Mandy keyed the mike. Between labored gasps, she relayed her location to the dispatcher.

"Hey." The young woman tugged on Mandy's arm. "I think he's stopped breathing."

Mandy shoved the radio at the woman. "Tell the dispatcher."

She put her fingers against the man's neck. No pulse. She listened for breathing. None. She gave him two full breaths mouth-to-mouth then rechecked. Still nothing. She unzipped his PFD and ripped it open. Counted to thirty as she did chest compressions.

What is up with this guy? Why is he going south on me so fast?

She blew two more breaths, then started compressions again. She repeated the cycle over and over and over again, until she fell into a zombie-like trance. Nothing mattered, not her pains, not her exhaustion, not the tears of frustration sliding down her cheeks, not the young woman's worried muttering.

Just two breaths, thirty compressions, repeat.

A vehicle rumbled across the bridge. Another raft bumped hers.

Two breaths, thirty compressions, repeat.

Feet clattered down the rocks to the beach. Someone splashed onto the gravel from the river, knelt next to her and put arms around her. "Stop, Mandy."

It was Steve. He pulled her to her feet. When she swayed, he picked her up and carried her to another spot on the beach. "The EMTs will take over. You can rest now."

Lying back on the warm stones, Mandy lifted her face to the bright Colorado sun. She started to shiver and closed her eyes.

"Will he live?"

———

An hour later, Mandy sat hunched on a rock above the beach, a cup of untouched cocoa cooling in her hands. Someone had thrown a space blanket over her shoulders, and the shivering had stopped. An EMT had checked her over and declared her "shocky," but not too bad off.

Certainly not as bad off as the man she had tried to rescue, whose body was now being zipped into a bag by the county coroner and her assistant.

Mandy's gut twisted as memories of the wrenching grief she felt when her parents died washed over her. A drunk driver had plowed into their car in Colorado Springs two months before her senior year of high school. This man's family would have to go through all the same heartbreaking emotions.

Gonzo plopped his awkward, lanky frame down on a rock beside her.

The two of them silently watched the coroner, her assistant, and two sheriff's deputies carry the body up to the roadbed.

Gonzo swept aside a chunk of bushy dark blond Rastafarian dreadlocks the wind had blown into his somber, sunburned face. "Bummer."

Mandy nodded. *Bummer indeed.*

He shot a worried gaze her way. "Hey, it's not your fault."

He picked up a pebble and halfheartedly tossed it aside. "If anything, it's my fault."

"No, Gonzo. He was alive when he left your care. He died under mine."

A shadow fell over her. She looked up and saw Steve Hadley, his well-muscled frame backlit by the sun.

He must have seen the devastation she felt in her face, because his expression softened. He knelt and put his hand on her knee. "Mandy, a death is hard for any of us. It was an accident, pure and simple. You could do no more than follow your training. If that wasn't enough, then it was meant to be."

Mandy worried her lip. Did she? Did she follow her training? Should she have done something different? Something better? Her throat constricted. Rather than expose her emotion by croaking out a response, she just nodded again.

"Hey man," Gonzo said to Steve. "Thanks for handling the wife. After Dougie walked his passengers downstream to the road, and the wife saw the EMTs working on her husband and screamed, Dougie looked at me like, hey buddy, you're in charge of this trip, so this is your scene. But I had no frigging idea what to do."

"Who does?" Steve said. "You just deal with it the best you can."

"I'd rather have a Boy Scout blowing chunks right on my Tevas than have to comfort some lady who's gone all hysterical. At least I knew his son, Jeff, some. Though I couldn't do much more than say I was really sorry, dude."

Mandy gulped down the knot in her throat. "Yeah, thanks, Steve. I probably should have said something to her. I know that's the worst part of the job, when someone—" She couldn't say *dies*, not yet. And the thought of trying to console that poor woman while Mandy struggled with her own resurrected grief had frightened her to the core.

"You were too worn out to be coherent. And I've had to comfort relatives before." Steve's brow furrowed in a troubled scowl. "But no matter how many times you do it, it never gets easier. I'm glad that sheriff's deputy volunteered to drive them back to your uncle's place to get their vehicle."

Steve studied Mandy. "You still look exhausted. Why don't you take tomorrow off? You were scheduled for only a half day anyway."

"Thanks. Sleeping in sounds wonderful."

"I'm bushed, too, after that swim," Gonzo added. "And now I've got equipment to scavenge. Who knows where all the paddles ended up? Your uncle will owe a few beers to guides who pick them up downstream. *I* could sure use a beer right now. That was some wicked whitewater out there today."

Mandy shot him a look, then decided not to say anything. If babbling was his way to cope, let him babble.

A swarthy middle-aged man in a Chaffee County Sheriff's Department uniform stepped up next to Steve and held out his hand to Mandy. "Victor Quintana, Sheriff's Detective."

Mandy shook his hand. "Mandy Tanner, river ranger."

"I understand your uncle owns the rafting company Gonzo Gordon works for."

"Right. I used to work for him myself, before I applied to be a seasonal ranger."

Quintana stroked his black mustache, a bushy complement to his short-cropped black hair. "You up to talking about this?"

Not really. "Sure, I guess."

Steve signaled Gonzo with his chin that they should move on.

After they left, Quintana took a seat on Gonzo's rock. "Why don't you tell me what happened after you saw the raft flip?"

Quintana took copious notes while Mandy told her story, then asked, "Did you see his head hit anything?"

Mandy thought back, remembering when the boat had shoved the man into a rock. "No, but …"

"But what?"

"Well, I feel a little guilty admitting this, but I hit him with the boat. It slammed his shoulder into a rock. Might have knocked his head, too."

Quintana scribbled on his pad.

"But he was already unconscious then," Mandy hastened to add.

"It's still good to note any injuries we know about—for the autopsy. What about before you reached him, when he might have still been conscious?"

"He seemed awfully still the whole time he was in the water. But I didn't watch him constantly, like when I was pulling the woman in."

"Hannah Fowler."

"I never got her name." Mandy looked around for the young woman, but didn't see her. "And I wanted to thank her again for her help."

"You'll probably get a chance later. She's local. Nate Fowler's daughter, home from college. You heard his radio commercials?"

"Is he the realtor who promises to find you a home in thirty days or less?"

"That's the one."

Mandy wasn't sure she wanted to know the answer to her next question, but she felt compelled to ask. "Who was the victim?"

"Tom King, developer of King Ranch Estates. At least his family won't suffer financially."

"I didn't see any blood or marks on him. Did he have a head injury under his helmet?"

"Nothing we could see, but we're trying to determine why he was unconscious when you pulled him out of the water."

"I wondered, too," Mandy said, plucking nervously at the frayed friendship bracelet around her ankle. "I thought maybe hypothermia. That water's still awful cold this early in June—mostly snowmelt."

"Cold enough to cause a heart attack in someone susceptible, too."

Mandy nodded. In training, she had learned that the most common type of death on the river was heart attack. Second was drowning—usually a fisherman or private boater not wearing a PFD. Third was entrapment, when a swimmer got caught underwater by a fallen tree or undercut rock.

"The man's skin was grayish when I pulled him out, and he had a weak pulse."

Quintana wrote this down then sat quietly for a moment, as if trying to think of something else to ask. Finally, he slapped his notepad shut and stood.

"The autopsy should give us some definitive answers, but that seems to be what we're looking at." He hesitated and looked Mandy over. "Not much a rescuer can do for a massive heart attack victim."

"Yeah, but I still had to try."

"Of course, but his death wasn't your fault." Quintana walked off.

Why does everyone keep saying it's not my fault?

TWO

It is with rivers as it is with people: the greatest are not always the most agreeable nor the best to live with.
—*LITTLE RIVERS*, HENRY VAN DYKE

MANDY WOKE LATE FRIDAY morning with a mouth that felt like she had been munching on cotton balls. Covers were bunched around her legs. She had fought the sheets all night, dreaming she was fighting the river for possession of Tom King's body.

And the river won.

A cold nose nudged her elbow. She rolled over and looked into the pleading eyes of Lucky, her golden retriever. The dog's whole back end wagged along with his tail.

Mandy smiled, reached out, and scratched his head. "I could've used some of your luck yesterday, boy."

The dog poked his wet nose in her face and whined.

"Oh, you think because the alarm didn't go off that this is a running day, huh?"

As if he understood the question, Lucky trotted to the bedroom door and looked over his shoulder at her.

"All right, all right, I'm getting up." Mandy pushed up on her hands, then collapsed and groaned. Every muscle in her body ached. She rolled to the edge of the bed and swung her legs over the side to lever herself into a sitting position. Her stiff back protested.

"I'm only twenty-seven. I shouldn't be hurting like this."

She stumbled into the bathroom and washed down three aspirin with a tall glass of water. After using the toilet, she pulled her shoulder-length blond hair up into her signature ponytail. She never had the patience to do anything else with it.

She slipped a hooded sweatshirt over the large T-shirt and flannel pants she slept in and chafed her arms to warm them. At 7,000 feet altitude, mornings in Salida were chilly even in June, but Mandy kept the heat turned off in the summer to save on the utility bills. At least she never had to worry about paying for air conditioning.

But she did have the water bill to contend with. The damn toilet was ghost-flushing again. Jiggling the handle had no effect, so she removed the tank lid. The chain was twisted. She reached in and straightened it out. *Does some ghost swoop in at night and twist it just to yank my chain?*

After washing her hands again, Mandy padded in her fuzzy pink bunny slippers to her tiny kitchen. She opened the back door to let Lucky do his business in the fenced-in yard. The orange and yellow marigolds she'd planted along both sides of the tiny concrete patio nodded their sprightly heads in the slight breeze, looking agreeably healthy. The tiny lawn needed mowing, however, and quite a few piles of dog poop lay scattered about. More chores to add to her To Do list.

Rubbing her sore arms, she turned the knob on the gas stove to heat water for instant coffee, but nothing happened. Wrinkling her nose at the rotten eggs smell of the gas, Mandy fished kitchen matches out of the cupboard, lit one and held it next to the burner. The fire started with a whoosh, making her step back.

Maybe the toilet ghost had a friend who kept blowing out the pilot light.

She put the kettle on, stuck a slice of whole wheat bread in the toaster, and sat down to wait at the folding card table that served as her dining table. The small cottage she rented consisted of two tiny bedrooms, one of which served as a storage room for her boating and skiing gear, one bathroom, a living room, and the puke-green linoleum-floored kitchen. Built in the 1960s, the cottage was definitely showing its age.

The problem was that the landlord lived a two-hour drive away in Colorado Springs, never answered his phone, and never responded to her voice messages about problems. And Mandy had neither the skill nor the time to fix all the little things that go wrong in an old place.

The cottage was her place, though, all hers. She didn't have to share it with anyone or listen to anyone tell her what to do. And she'd added her own touches that stamped her identity on the house, like the marigolds, the few furniture pieces she'd saved from her parents' house and augmented with garage sale finds, and her grandmother's embroidered alphabet sampler that hung on the wall over the toaster. She savored every flaky wall, nicked floorboard, and pockmarked screen.

She never regretted moving out of her uncle's home a few years back and into this little world of her own. It had been past the time when she needed to be on her own, but she had stayed out of sentiment. Her uncle had done so much for her, and she didn't want to seem ungrateful. And, she had to admit, it had been hard to leave after relying on him for so long. Lucky was the catalyst. Uncle Bill was allergic to dog hair, and Mandy couldn't abandon the sloppy puppy she had bought for five dollars from a kid in front of the Safeway. Lucky was the last puppy in the wagon. It was getting late in the day, and Mandy knew what the heavy-duty trash bag and the brick lying in the bottom of the wagon were for.

Her reminiscence was interrupted by someone rapping on her front door.

Mandy opened it, and her heart gave a little trill. "Rob."

Dressed in faded jeans and a Dixie Chicks T-shirt, Rob Juarez stood with his hands splayed against the small porch's walls on either side of him. He showed his pearly whites in a big smile and leaned his well-muscled frame toward her. His body owned every square inch of the porch. "May I come in?"

"I'm not dressed."

He looked her up and down. "Everything but your hands and head is covered. How is that not dressed?"

Mandy laughed and rolled her eyes. "You know what I mean. I'm a mess. I just got up."

But she stepped aside and ushered him in. She wanted to see him, very much so, and after all, they'd been dating for the last three months.

"You look great to me, especially given what you went through yesterday." Concern wrinkled Rob's bronzed brow. He ran a hand through his wavy black hair, making the standing waves tattooed on his bicep dance. "I heard about King. You okay?"

"Not really."

He closed the door. "Will a hug help?"

"Oh, yeah. I've been wondering when you were going to get around to that."

When he gathered her in his arms, Mandy inhaled his familiar scent of soap, leather, and the grassy outdoors. Her head fit perfectly against his shoulder, with the five-inch difference in their heights.

She clung to him, so his warmth seeped into her bones, and let her aching body relax. "This helps, more than you can imagine."

He rubbed her back, running his thumbs down either side of her spine. "I heard you managed to steer a cat with two people on board. That's amazing. I bet you're sore today."

"Um-hum. Keep on doing what you're doing." *This man's definitely a keeper.* Rob usually seemed to know when Mandy needed some TLC and was generous in supplying it.

"Anything for my little *querida.*" He massaged her shoulders and kissed the top of her head. Then he sniffed. "Is something burning?"

"Oh, no, the toast!"

Mandy ran back into the kitchen and popped the toaster. The bread was black and crispy. She tossed it in the sink. "Damn toaster doesn't pop half the time."

"Want me to see if I can fix it?" Rob asked as he sank into a chair at the table. "I've got my toolbox in the truck."

Mandy put in another piece of bread. "No, I'll just watch it this time. You've got to get to work, right?"

"I finished the morning shuttles, so I have some time. It won't be a good day, though, with word of King's death throwing a damper on things—for everyone. It's not like he's going to be missed much. He rubbed a lot of folks the wrong way, slapping up shoddy houses and raking in the dough with no concern for the environment, his subcontractors, or his buyers. But, any death on the river is bad for business."

Mandy continued to stare at the toaster, but she nodded in understanding. Rob managed another small whitewater rafting company, one of over fifty in the Upper Arkansas River valley, tucked between the Sawatch Range to the west and the Mosquito Range to the east. The boating outfitters had a strange symbiotic relationship with each other. Sure, they competed for customers, but they also loaned each other equipment and guides. And they worked together on issues such as training and ethics through the Arkansas River Outfitter Association.

When her toast was brown, Mandy popped it out manually and brought it and a huge, economy jar of peanut butter to the table. Given her pensive mood, she normally would have been fingering mouthfuls straight out of the jar by now, but Rob didn't know that dirty little secret yet.

She picked up the jar of instant coffee. "Want coffee?"

Rob wrinkled his nose. "You know I hate that stuff. Someday I'm going to buy you a coffeemaker so you can brew the real thing."

"Don't bother." Mandy spooned coffee granules into her cup and poured in hot water. "The way things go around here, it'll break, too."

She sat, slathered peanut butter on her toast, and took a bite. She savored the comforting smooth stickiness. "How much do you think the news will hurt business?"

"It'll scare off some customers—especially your uncle's."

"And they'll blame his company for the death."

"The man *was* in your uncle's raft."

"Shit."

Mandy threw down her toast. Now her uncle's business would be hurt, and him, too. If only she'd been able to save Tom King. She leaned her chin on her hands and stared into her coffee cup, running the rescue attempt through her mind.

Rob reached over and traced his fingertip along her cheek. "You want me to hang out with you for a while?" Mandy knew he meant just to offer comfort and company, but the prospect of more was lingering in his hopeful gaze.

The proposition was enticing, and she considered it for a moment. Then she shook her head. "I'll be okay. And we've both got things to do."

Lucky whined at the back door, so she got up to let the dog in. As soon as Lucky spotted Rob, he flounced over to his new friend.

Rob leaned over to tousle Lucky's floppy ears while the dog gave him a hearty welcome crotch sniff. "While I'm here, I should take a look at the toaster for you. And is that toilet still giving you problems?"

Slight annoyance tugged the edges of Mandy's smile down into a frown. "I've lived in this place for three years now. I can take care of it myself. I only need the time. And speaking of time, you need to get to work, and Lucky's looking for me to take him for a run."

Rob rose and held up his hands in mock surrender. "All right. I can tell when I'm not wanted."

Mandy blew out a breath. "You know it's not that. I want you plenty." She ran a hand along Rob's tattooed bicep and savored the little thrill she felt whenever she touched his warm, bronzed skin. "I just want to fix my own stuff—and recover in my own way."

Rob shot her a skeptical look. "Okay, but I plan to check on you later."

Mandy led him to the door. "I'm not someone who needs to be checked on, Rob."

"But I'm the kind of guy who likes to do it. See you later, *mi querida.*" Rob gave her a playful chuck under the chin and walked out, whistling down the path.

I'm not the kind of gal who likes it, though. Mandy watched him climb into his battered black Ford pickup. *But man, oh man, does that man fill out a pair of jeans.*

———

An hour later, Mandy climbed into her Subaru all-wheel drive wagon, its blue color muted by road dust and mud spatters. Lucky whined at her, with his nose stuck through the chain-link fence. He was obviously disappointed in their halfhearted jog around two blocks of small ranch-style homes and cottages similar to her own. But that was all Mandy could manage before stumbling into the shower to pelt her sore muscles with water as hot as she could stand.

When the nine-year-old car started right up, Mandy yelled "All right!" and high-fived the steering wheel. With a working shower and transportation, why worry about a cranky toilet and toaster? She threw the car into gear and drove out of her gravel driveway.

On the way to her uncle's place, she replayed her conversation with Rob. How could people blame Uncle Bill's company for Tom King's death? They must know whitewater rafting is an inherently dangerous activity, especially in the most difficult class IV and V rapids.

Duh, girl. She had been there when customers asked for guarantees that they wouldn't fall out of a raft. Then they would snooze through the safety talk and complain that wearing a helmet, mandatory on a Numbers or Royal Gorge run, would ruin their hair.

Customers would refuse to blame the beautiful but deadly river, because that would mean accepting the risks they themselves took on. So they would cast the blame on Uncle Bill, his equipment, the training or the management he gave his guides, whatever. Unless…

Unless King had a heart attack. Then the death wouldn't be the fault of the Arkansas River or Uncle Bill.

Or me.

Mandy turned the car around and headed for the Chaffee County building on Crestone Avenue. It was almost noon. Maybe Quintana would have the autopsy results by now. He should be willing to share them with her, given the close working relationship between the Arkansas Headwaters Recreation Area (AHRA) rangers and the Chaffee County Sheriff's Office deputies. They trained together, lunched at the same hangouts, and jointly investigated crimes that occurred within the park boundaries. Heck,

Tom King's accident was her case until she turned it over to Quintana. She would need whatever new information he had come up with for her own incident report.

She parked outside the old blond-brick office building that sat next to a brand-new jail and entered the lobby. Travel posters on the walls proclaimed the merits of Chaffee County, with the most 14,000-foot mountains in the United States, and the small communities nestled along the Arkansas River valley—Buena Vista, Nathrop, Salida, Poncha Springs. Her favorite poster showed a crown of jagged peaks ranged against a brilliant blue sky with the white waves of the Arkansas River slapping against dampened rocks below. Somehow the artist had captured both the playfulness and exhilarating power of the moving water.

Mandy hiked up the wide, worn stairs to the third floor, where the sheriff's detectives' offices were situated. She hadn't ever been to Quintana's office, so she had to snoop a little before she found the frosted glass door with his nameplate beside it. She knocked on the glass.

"Come in."

Quintana stood up from his desk when she entered. "Hello. I didn't expect to see you today. I heard Steve tell you to take the day off. Thought you'd be resting up."

Mandy shook his hand then took the seat he offered. "I did sleep in a little. I'm kind of sore, too, but curiosity got me moving."

Quintana's desk was crammed full with a computer and stacks of case files. A bookshelf overflowed with law enforcement textbooks, statutes, bound documentation, and more files. Every bit of wall space seemed to be covered by some plaque or photo of Quintana shaking someone's hand or posing with a group. In one photo, she recognized the mayor with his arm draped companionably over Quintana's shoulders. In another, Quintana stood next to someone who looked like Elvis—in his later, pudgy years.

She pointed at the photo. "Who's that?"

Settling back into his chair, Quintana smiled. "My older brother. He's an Elvis impersonator on the weekends. Does shows at retirement and nursing homes. Pretty successful at it, too."

"Cool. I'll have to catch one of his shows sometime. Rocking out to some Elvis tunes would be fun."

"Is my photo collection what you're curious about?"

"It's a great collection, but no. I'm wondering if you've got any autopsy results yet, if you know what caused King's death."

Quintana pulled a couple of handwritten pages out of the top file folder on his desk. "Your timing's good. We sent King's body to the Pueblo coroner's office yesterday. Since the forensic pathologist had no other cases waiting, he did the autopsy this morning."

"Has he finished the report?"

"Not yet, but he called me with some preliminary results, and I made these notes. He doesn't have a firm cause of death yet, but he ruled out some possibilities."

"Like what?"

"Like drowning." Quintana looked up at her. "Not enough water in the lungs. And like a head wound. King's skull was intact, and the brain was in good shape."

"What about hypothermia or heart attack?"

"Hypothermia's a no. And he said King had arteriosclerosis, but he didn't find a clot in a coronary artery."

Mandy sank back in her chair. "Oh, so no heart attack?"

"Not necessarily. The coroner said you often don't find direct evidence of heart failure."

"Really?" Mandy sat up straighter.

Quintana smoothed his mustache. "Clots can flush out or dissolve, and heart tissue damage that causes death looks very similar to the damage that occurs postmortem. As he explained to me, it's more a case of ruling out everything else. If there's no other cause, you blame it on heart failure."

"When will he know for sure?"

"After the toxicology and blood test results come in, in a day or two."

"Toxicology?"

"It's standard. Could show evidence of alcohol or drugs. And the blood test could reveal diabetes or some other disease, though King's wife said his last physical two years ago was clear." Quintana put down his notes. "Want to tell me why you're so anxious to know?"

Mandy blew out a frustrated breath. "I'm afraid King's death will hurt Uncle Bill's business. I hoped I could deliver news to him today that it was caused by a heart attack. Then he could tell that to any anxious customers who might blame him."

"Or you."

Mandy shot Quintana a look, but the man's expression wasn't accusatory. Instead, she read … compassion?

Her hands went cold and her mouth dried up, but she had to face this. "Or me."

Quintana folded his arms, an awkward movement with all the equipment on his uniform belt. "This is your first year as a river ranger, right? And probably your first death."

Mandy nodded.

"I bet you're having the same reaction patrol officers have when they encounter their first death. And many have it with every one. It's a wicked combination of emotions. The strongest one is guilt—wondering if you could have prevented the situation or turned it in a different direction somehow."

Blood rushed to Mandy's cheeks, and she smoothed her hands on her jeans to regain her composure. "You nailed it."

Quintana leaned forward. "Maybe knowing everyone goes through this, that it's part of being a public safety officer, will help."

Mandy met his gaze, and for the first time that day, felt a little calmer. "Maybe it does."

"I'll let you know as soon as I've got the final report." Quintana leaned back in his chair and frowned. "You're not the only one who's anxious. The coroner can't release the body until he's drawn a conclusion, and King's widow has already called me to ask when they can schedule a funeral."

"I can't imagine what she's going through. It must be awful."

Quintana pursed his lips as if debating whether to say something then shook his head. "She sounded more angry than sad. Said she was calling her lawyer."

"I don't understand. Was she wondering about the will?"

"No. Maybe you should warn your uncle. She said she was going to sue somebody."

THREE

*River guiding is a cowboy sort of job. Guides have inherited
the legacy of ruggedness and self-reliance once attributed
to mountain men and pioneers.*

—*WHAT THE RIVER SAYS*, JEFF WALLACH

QUESTIONS WHIRLED IN MANDY's head while she drove to her uncle's combination home-and-business a few miles north of town.
What did King's widow hope to gain by suing Uncle Bill? Everyone
signs a liability release agreement when they go whitewater rafting
with a commercial outfitter. If King signed one, too, how could his
widow win the case?

She parked under the ancient cottonwood tree shading the
small gravel car park beside the two-story wood-frame house. She
got out and made a quick scan of the equipment in the back lot.
The bus was still there, with two eight-passenger rafts tied to the
top, instead of stowed in the storage shed where they belonged.

But the thirteen-passenger van with its attached raft trailer was gone. So, a three- or four-raft trip had been planned and prepared for, but only one or two rafts had gone out, allowing all the customers and their guides to fit in the van.

Not good.

Mandy opened the front door that led into a customer check-in entryway, with company logo T-shirts and hats, sunglasses, and sunglass cords hanging on the wall for sale. She looked over the countertop, where those liability forms got signed, into her uncle's small office on the other side. He sat at the cluttered desk, a phone pressed to his ear.

He didn't look happy.

"But sir, I can't give full refunds for last-minute cancellations. That's clearly spelled out in our policies on the website and on the confirmation letter I sent you. I've already scheduled guides to work your trip."

Bill Tanner swiveled his barrel-shaped torso in his chair, saw Mandy, pointed at the phone and rolled his eyes. He rubbed his lined forehead with sausage-shaped fingers, then picked up his reading glasses to check his computer screen.

She hiked herself up on the countertop to wait.

As her uncle listened on the phone, his frown deepened. "No matter which outfitter you use, whitewater rafting is an inherently risky activity. If you check with the rangers at the Arkansas Headwaters Recreation Area office, you'll see our safety record is good—as good as any other outfitter's."

He paused, tapping a pencil on his desk. "Yes, even with the recent death. We still don't know the cause. It could very well have been a heart attack."

He listened some more and sighed. "This isn't Disneyland. We can't make guarantees because we don't control the river. We just ride it." Another pause. "Yes, sir. I'm sorry, too. But with only one day's notice, the best I can do is a fifty-percent refund. There's sunk costs I can't recoup. You'll be missing out on a great run."

After a few more nods and um-hums and sips from the can of root beer on his desk, he finally hung up. He took off his reading glasses and rubbed the bridge of his nose. "That's the fourth cancellation today."

"I saw the bus didn't go out," Mandy said. "You get some no-shows this afternoon?"

"Yeah. Then they had the nerve to call and ask for a refund. When I refused, they said they'd complain to the Headwaters office. Fat lot of good that'll do them, but I've lost them as customers. They'll never raft with me again."

"Rob came by this morning and warned me this might happen. At first, I didn't believe him, but..."

"Happens all the time. Folks can be skittish." Uncle Bill pushed himself out of his chair with a grunt. "But enough of my problems, baby."

He gave her a hug. Then he stood back and looked her over. "I guess Robbie boy came by to check on you. I should have done that myself, but as you can see, I've been busy with the phone. How are you?"

Mandy slid off the counter into the office. "Sore, tired, but I'll be okay."

"Ah hah. You're finding out that being a ranger isn't all fun and glory. It can't have been easy to deal with a death your second week on patrol."

"Sure it isn't easy, but everyone bringing it up again isn't making it any easier. Look, I'm fine. I'm more worried about what this is doing to your business."

"That's not your worry. You don't work here anymore, remember?"

So, he's still bugged about that. The thought stirred up old memories. Bill Tanner was a widower with no children of his own when Mandy's parents had died. Since Mandy was living with and working for her uncle, as she had the previous summer, it was natural for her to stay on and transfer to Salida High School when classes started. She wasn't eighteen yet, and her brother David couldn't care for her. Heading into his junior year of college, he had his own education and grief to worry about. He had been relieved to be able to focus on finishing his accounting degree and starting his career.

Then, it was natural for Mandy to become a full-fledged rafting guide after she graduated. She fell into a pattern of working spring through fall for her uncle and serving on the Monarch Mountain ski patrol during the winters. Whenever she could, she took a course or two at Colorado Mountain College in Buena Vista until she earned an associate's degree in outdoor education.

Her uncle had assumed she would take over his business someday. But a few years back, she started itching to prove herself, to tackle some challenge that Uncle Bill didn't already know everything about. That's what led to her moving into her own place, and this year, applying for the seasonal river ranger position.

And, it's what led to their first serious argument.

Mandy put a hand on her uncle's shoulder. "We've been over this before. Just because I'm not here every day doesn't mean I don't still care about the business—and you. You know that, you ole grouchy bear."

He stared at his feet and scuffed the floor with one bedroom slipper. "I know. But you've got to know I still want you here. Who am I going to leave this business to, if not you, baby girl?"

Mandy noted the slippers. His gout must be bothering him again. She would have to find some way to quiz him about his diet without getting on his nerves.

"I'm not a baby girl anymore. And you're not retiring anytime soon that I know of. Are you?"

Fear stabbed Mandy's gut as she peered at her uncle. He was in his late fifties, overweight and with high blood pressure. Was he hinting something else was wrong?

"No, I'll be manning this desk and driving the shuttle vehicles for quite a few years yet. Got to wait around for you to change your mind."

She hugged him. "You're more stubborn than a black bear trying to get at a hummingbird feeder, you know that?"

Uncle Bill grinned, showing off a straight row of gleaming teeth, a Tanner trait. "Where do you think you get it from?"

Mandy slid into the extra chair in his office. "Tell me about yesterday's trip. Was it all locals?"

Uncle Bill dropped into his chair while holding one foot out, then gingerly lowered it to the floor. "Yeah. Lenny Preble set it up."

"The environmentalist?"

"He said he wanted to show some developers and local politicians why it was so important to reserve recreation water rights on the Arkansas. He used funds from his nonprofit organization to pay for the trip, plus asked me for a discount."

"Did you give it to him?"

"He was throwing business my way, a three-raft trip, so he and one other staffer rode free. And it was for a good cause. Anyway, he invited Tom King and Nate Fowler, a couple of city councilmen, and any spouses and grown children who wanted to come along, since we don't take minors down the Numbers."

"I picked up Nate Fowler's daughter," Mandy said. "I want to get her contact information from you and thank her for helping me with King. She kept her cool and didn't get all hysterical on me. But why invite King and Fowler? What was so special about those two?"

"They're in a bidding war over some combined forest and pasture land down south that has prime agricultural water rights tied to it. They both want to develop the land into high-priced country estates. Lenny said he'd like to convince whoever winds up buying the land to donate some of those water rights for recreation use." Uncle Bill took a few gulps of root beer.

Another thing he should be giving up—those six or seven sugary sodas he drinks every day. The man's sweet tooth was worse than the average black bear's by far. "And why the councilmen?"

"Most of the councilmen know darn well how important recreation on the Arkansas is to Salida. We're not back in the eighteen hundreds when hard industries like the railroad and gold mining kept the town pump primed. Nowadays, the economy is driven by tourism. Without the river and the tourists dripping money that it attracts, there'd be damn few city taxes to pay the salaries of those councilmen."

"You're preaching to the choir here, Uncle Bill."

"I know you know all this. But Frank Saunders isn't on board, so to speak. That's why Lenny invited him. And he asked two others who are river supporters to come, hoping they would help his case, lean on the developers and Saunders some."

"Okay, why the Numbers? Why not take these folks on a tamer run?"

"Most of them have already run the tamer sections lots of times. Hell, I bet you could blindfold them all in Brown's Canyon, and they could tell you what rapid's coming up next. Plus, you know it's the upper river runs like the Numbers that change the most when water levels drop."

"It was running high yesterday." *Over two thousand cubic feet per second.* "If the CFS had been any higher, I probably wouldn't have made it to shore before Number Five. How did Lenny plan to get his point across about low flows?"

"He wanted to contrast high and low water runs through the Numbers and point out spots where low water made passage difficult. And he had photos taken during the 2002 drought to show them after the trip wound up. One of a fish kill was downright gross. Never got around to showing them, of course." Morosely, Uncle Bill shook his head.

Hoping to cheer him up some, Mandy said, "I stopped by the Chaffee County Sheriff's office today to ask about the autopsy results on Tom King. The pathologist can't say what the cause of death is yet, but it sounded to me like he's leaning toward heart attack. That could be helpful for you."

"How so?"

"If it's not drowning or head injury or some other river-caused death, then your company can't be blamed."

"But if the shock of the cold water caused the heart attack, we could be. Because if the man didn't fall in the river, he might still be alive. Can the pathologist figure out whether the heart attack occurred before or after King hit the water?"

Mandy nibbled her lip. "I don't know. I'll have to ask Detective Quintana."

The front door opened and Gonzo walked in, his wet river sandals slapping on the wood floor. "Hey, Mandy. Slumming today? Can't get enough of this place?"

"Or of you." Mandy shot him a wide smile and a wink, though her heart wasn't really into their usual repartee.

Gonzo thrust his hip out, threw his head back and fluffed his tangled dreadlocks, as if posing for the cover of *Vogue*—or more likely, *Mad Magazine*. "Too sexy for you, I know." For him, too, the wordplay seemed forced.

"Hey, sexy beast," Uncle Bill shouted. "What'd I tell you about coming in here with dripping wet shoes?"

"Sorry man, but a customer needs change." Gonzo handed a twenty over the counter. "I think he's going to give me a sorry-ass five- or ten-dollar tip for taking his whole family down Brown's. None of 'em could paddle worth a darn, they didn't laugh at my river snake joke, and I bet they don't turn their wetsuits right-side out for me either. Why is it that the customers who are the hardest to work with tip the least?"

Mandy passed him the small bills her uncle had dug out of his desk. "At least he *is* giving you a tip. Thank the river gods. He could be stiffing you."

"Then he'd suffer from bad Gonzo karma." He waggled his fingers as if casting a spell, then leaned on the counter to get a good look at Mandy. "Speaking of bad karma, how're you doing today?"

"Could be better, a *lot* better, but I'll live." *Unlike King.* Mandy shuddered, then she noticed how bleary-eyed Gonzo looked. He must have drunk some of those beers last night that he was talking about.

He stuffed the money in his pocket. "Any word on how King died?"

"Nothing definite yet."

Uncle Bill sat forward in his chair. "Maybe you can help us out, Gonzo."

When both Gonzo and Mandy stared at him, Uncle Bill said, "We were talking about the possibility of a heart attack and whether it could have happened prior to King hitting the water or after. You notice anything about him in the raft?"

Gonzo stared at the ceiling for a moment. "Come to think of it, his strokes got weaker before we hit Number Four. They were pretty strong for the first half of the trip. Then all of a sudden I had to compensate, which probably led to the raft going sideways on me."

"Anything else?" Mandy asked. "Like wooziness, profuse sweating?"

"Sweating, yeah. It was warm out, but King wiped his head a lot. He reached for his drink bottle right before we had to line up for Four. I yelled at him to wait. Come to think of it, the look he gave me when I said that was kinda weird."

Mandy came over to the counter, excitement making her edgy. "Weird how?"

"Like he was having a hard time processing what I said to him."

Mandy turned to her uncle. "Sounds like maybe he was already having a heart attack before the raft spilled. That's good news."

Gonzo raised his brows. "Good news how?"

"If that's the case, then no one can blame Uncle Bill, me, or you for his death." Mandy turned to her uncle. "Quintana wanted me to pass on a warning that Mrs. King is talking to her lawyer and said she was going to sue someone."

Uncle Bill raised his hands and looked skyward, as if saying, "Why me?"

Gonzo let out a low, slow whistle. "Man, I hope that don't happen. But, if it's like you're saying, King was already dying when he left the raft, then that should get Steve Hadley off my back, too."

"Steve?" Mandy peered at Gonzo. "Why's he on your back?"

"Oh, he said it was standard practice after a fatal accident, but I've never been asked by a ranger to do it before. Only by outfitters for job-screening."

"Do what?"

"Piss in a jar." Gonzo turned and stomped out.

———

After checking that her uncle had liability release forms in his file signed by all the passengers on Lenny Preble's trip, Mandy went out back. She helped Gonzo and his fellow rafting guide, Kendra, unload and partially deflate the rafts while trading taunts and river rat jokes to lighten the load. Then they rinsed the customer's wetsuits and booties in disinfectant, and hung them up to dry. Normally her uncle would have done these chores, but the gout flare-up had him limping in pain.

While Mandy swept out the women's restroom, Kendra brought in rolls of toilet paper and paper towels. The guide's black skin glistened with sweat and suntan oil. "Hey, Gonzo and I are meeting some of the gang at Vic's tonight to get 'victimized.' Want to join us?"

At first, Mandy felt inclined to refuse. But then she thought hanging out with her rafting guide friends at the Victoria Tavern might help her stop rehashing the events of the day before, even get some sleep. "I'll have to feed and exercise Lucky first."

"That's cool. We aren't planning to meet up there until after eight anyway. I've got to wash this Arkansas River mud off first and see what bills have arrived that I can't pay." She cocked a finger at Mandy before walking out. "Catch you at eight."

Mandy locked the restrooms, checked the changing rooms for anything the customers had forgotten, and handed the keys over to her uncle. "How long has your foot been bothering you?"

"Couple of days."

"Have you been watching your diet, laying off the beer and sodas?"

Uncle Bill put down the root beer he had been sipping. "You're not my mama."

"No, I'm not." Mandy smiled and crossed her arms. "Only your niece—a niece who doesn't like to see you hurting."

He sighed. "Okay, okay. Go on and drink a beer at the Vic for me. I'll just sit here and sip on green tea." He wrinkled his nose in disgust.

The incongruous image of her uncle sipping from a dainty china cup while demurely holding out his pinkie kept Mandy smiling most of the ride home. She fed Lucky and tossed a tennis ball to him in the back yard until the ball was sodden with dog drool, then went inside to clean up and eat before going to the Vic.

———

When Mandy walked up to the historic two-story red brick building with its distinctive green awnings, she could feel her spirits lifting before she even opened the heavy scroll-worked door. Later, the door would be propped open to let in fresh air and let out the throbbing beat of whatever roaming Colorado rock band was booked to play that night. The well-oiled original wood floor from 1900 creaked under her feet as she pushed past chattering groups on her way to the bar to find her friend, Cynthia.

The Vic's stamped tin ceiling, built to deflect sound away from the hotel rooms above, magnified it in the main barroom, so Mandy had to shout, "Cynthia! Cynthia!"

Cynthia Abbott, her brunette hair pulled back in her trademark French braid, looked up from pouring beer out of two taps into pilsner glasses. Her purple tank top showed off a peek of cleavage and the tattoo on her upper arm—of a hummingbird drinking nectar out of a flower.

"Hey, best buddy! The usual?"

Mandy flashed a thumbs-up and leaned her elbows on the enormously long, polished wood bar to wait. She caught her reflection in the stained glass panorama behind the bar—an exotic display with multicolored parrots and toucans peeking out from lush jungle foliage. Not quite your typical Rocky Mountains panorama. Mandy never tired of looking at the glass, dreaming of one day being able to afford a tropical beach vacation. She scanned the room, but didn't spot Kendra and Gonzo.

Cynthia slammed a sweating bottle of Fat Tire Ale on the bar next to Mandy's elbow, making her start. "Okay, here's a good one. Why does a blonde have T.G.I.F. written on her shoes?"

Today was Friday, but why thank God for the fact on your shoes? Mandy shrugged. "I give up."

"Toes go in first!" Cynthia snickered then glanced over her shoulder and straightened. "Give me a sec to fill some more orders, then we can chat." She hustled off before Mandy could respond.

Still chuckling, Mandy took a long, cold draught of beer, letting the soothing liquid slide down her throat and ease the tightness in her chest. Cynthia poured half a dozen tequila shots and served them with a bowl of lime wedges and a salt shaker to a rowdy group of young men. From their excited chatter, Mandy concluded they were celebrating a day of jousting with the river and crowing and preening like a bunch of roosters over their battle victories. She scanned their clothing for college logos.

"Okay, where'd that crowd come from?" Cynthia asked as she put a foot up on a crate behind the counter.

Mandy squinted at the group, who had just let out a cheer. "Colorado State."

"Darn." Cynthia slapped the bar. "How'd you know?"

"The hat on the tall guy in the back. You can't see it, because it's backward, but there's a ram above the brim."

"I checked their shirts, and when I didn't see any from the university, I thought I'd catch you. They already told me where they hailed from when I checked their IDs. You won this round."

"You mean this one in my hand?" Mandy winked, held up her beer, said, "To friends, especially best buddies," and took a sip. Identifying the origins of out-of-towners in the bar was a game

Mandy enjoyed playing with Cynthia, especially since Mandy often won. Cynthia could easily confirm their guesses by chatting up the customers or having one of the waitresses do it.

"Speaking of best buds, how's that friendship bracelet I made you holding up?" Cynthia stood on tip-toe to look over the bar.

Mandy put her foot up on the barstool next to her, showing Cynthia the frayed hand-woven strap around her ankle, before she dropped her foot back down to the floor. "Probably has a few more weeks left before it falls off."

"I'd better get started on another one."

"How's yours doing?"

Cynthia glanced at her ankle. "You're off the hook. Since I'm not a river rat like you are, mine don't wear out as fast. I think I've made you twice as many as you've made me." Then Cynthia slapped the counter again, making Mandy dribble the beer she'd just raised to her lips down her chin. "Hey, I heard about your rescue yesterday. Toughie, huh?"

"I really wouldn't call it a rescue." Mandy put down the beer, which suddenly tasted stale.

"You saved Nate Fowler's daughter, and you pulled Tom King out of the river, too."

"Yeah, but—"

"Mandy. What's cooking?" Gonzo put a hand on her shoulder. "Couple pitchers of Bud, please," he said to Cynthia.

Kendra leaned out from under Gonzo's other arm. "Dougie's staked out a pool table for us in the back room. Want to shoot a few games with us?"

"Wouldn't miss it."

When Cynthia returned with the pitchers, Mandy said her goodbyes.

"Sink the eight ball for me." Cynthia took Gonzo's money. "Catch you all later."

Sometimes, like now, Mandy wondered if Cynthia regretted having to work behind the bar, because she never got to hang out with her friends for long. She and Kendra picked up the glasses and followed Gonzo as he led the way, reverently protecting the two pitchers from stray elbows.

They commandeered a small table under the incongruous shark mounted on the wall and pulled up a few chairs. Mandy paired with Dougie in a few spirited games of team eight-ball against Gonzo and Kendra until their friend and fellow guide, Ajax, arrived with some other guides. Letting them have a turn, the four sat down. Gonzo poured the last dregs of the two pitchers into their glasses.

When Dougie went to fetch two more pitchers, Kendra leaned across the table to make herself heard above the band, which had started their first set. "I want to hear how you missed going over Number Five with two passengers on your cat. That must have been a tight spot."

"I really don't want to talk about it." Mandy tapped her feet to the music. Her head had a soft buzz going, but not enough to drown out her guilty thoughts.

"Oh, c'mon. It's got to make a good story."

Waiting for his pool shot, another guide shouted to Mandy. "I hear you were a real rescue ranger yesterday. Too bad you lost one."

Yeah, too bad. Mandy stood. "I'm going to the ladies' room."

As she walked away, she overheard Kendra say to Gonzo, "Boy, I didn't realize she'd be so prickly about it."

Mandy spent as much time as she could in the restroom, combing her hair and reapplying lip gloss, until a young woman with muscular shoulders shoved open the door. "You Mandy Tanner?"

Not another guide wanting to hear the story. Mandy thought she would get away from her nightmares by coming to the Vic, but they were stalking her there. She ducked her head, said, "Yeah, sorry, got to go," and walked out.

She insinuated herself into the next pool game and kept busy making shots and tossing out ribald comments on the other players' shots—anything to deflect the topic of conversation from her attempted rescue. By midnight, she was having trouble standing up straight and her game had deteriorated. She plopped down on a chair across from Gonzo.

He held out the pitcher, but Mandy shook her head. "You've been slugging down beer all night, and you still out-shot us all. How do you do it?"

"You drink enough beer every night, your body gets used to it."

"You drink the nights before you guide, too?"

"Usually."

"Doesn't it affect your timing on the river?"

Gonzo took another gulp. "Not so as I'd notice."

"How many beers did you have night before last?"

He shrugged. "I don't know. Maybe most of a six-pack. What's it to you?"

Mandy drummed her fingers on the table as she reviewed Gonzo's raft tipping over. "I was surprised you didn't make it through

Number Four yesterday. Usually you breeze right through it. I've never seen you flip in that rapid, even if a paddler's strokes are off, like you said King's were."

Narrowing his eyes and frowning, Gonzo stared at her. "What're you implying?"

If she hadn't been drunk, she never would have said what she said next. "Maybe if you weren't hung over, your raft wouldn't have flipped."

Gonzo stood up too fast and knocked his chair over, sending it clattering to the floor. "Oh no. You're not pinning King's death on me because you can't take the guilt. You took full responsibility yesterday. What happened to you today?"

Mandy stood and stepped in close. "You said it was your fault yesterday, and I had to talk you out of it. What happened to you?"

"You convinced me. King's death wasn't *my* doing." He walked away, letting the implication that it was Mandy's fault hang in the air.

Mandy looked around. The pool players had stopped their game. They hastily turned their backs on her, clearing their throats and asking each other whose turn it was.

She slumped back in the chair, poured the last of the beer in the pitcher into her glass and slugged it down. As she wiped a sleeve across her mouth, she noticed Cynthia watching and covered her eyes.

Cynthia sat down across from Mandy. "You don't look so good."

Mandy's stomach gave a flop, and she burped up some beer gas. "I don't feel so good either."

"You got a ride home?"

Mandy sank her chin down on her hand and shook her head. The walls shimmied in her vision, and she held her head still to combat the dizziness. "Gonzo and Kendra can't drive me home. They're as bad off as I am, though they're probably more used to being 'victimized.' And Gonzo's pissed at me anyway."

"Wait here." Cynthia stood. "I'll bring you some water and see what I can do."

After Cynthia returned with a big glass clinking with ice cubes, Mandy leaned against the wall and sipped the water. The room spun lazy circles around her, and the rock rhythms of the band's last set pounded a mammoth headache into her brain.

A muscular pair of jeans-clad legs stepped into her field of vision. "Hey, ranger gal."

It was Rob.

"Cynthia called. I'm taking you home."

Feeling too awful to fight about being rescued and secretly glad to hand over control to someone else, Mandy staggered to her feet. "Okay, Robbie boy."

He looped an arm around her waist and, with a nod to Cynthia, steered Mandy toward the door. "Maybe I should have hung around this morning."

Mandy kept her mouth shut, not willing to admit she might have been wrong. Plus, just putting one foot in front of the other took her full concentration.

She dozed in Rob's truck on the way home, and woke up as he laid her on her bed. She felt her shoes being eased off, and a blanket being pulled over her, then a soft kiss on her forehead.

"Sleep well, *mi querida*."

She mumbled something, she didn't know what, and listened to the front door close behind Rob. The river was already reaching for her when her eyes rolled back in her head.

FOUR

There is nothing—absolutely nothing—half so much worth
doing as simply messing about in boats... or with boats...
In or out of 'em, it doesn't matter.
—*THE WIND IN THE WILLOWS*, KENNETH GRAHAME

THE SOUND OF A car pulling into her driveway roused Mandy from her disturbed slumber. She reached the front window in time to see Rob climb out of her Subaru and into the driver's seat of his truck after the driver, probably one of his guides, slid over to the passenger side. They drove off in a cloud of dust, which is what her throat felt like.

Mandy leaned her head against the cool glass. Rob sure knew how to worm his way into a woman's heart. Deeply grateful that he had brought her home last night and her car home this morning, she couldn't help feeling a smidgen of resentment that he assumed she needed taking care of.

C'mon, he's doing you a favor. Thank him and move on.

She checked her watch—thirty minutes to get into work. If not for Rob bringing her car, she would have been late. Mandy gave Lucky a thorough head-scratching and let him outside then downed four aspirin, two for her muscle aches and two for her throbbing head. After feeding the dog, she donned her off-the-water ranger uniform consisting of black jeans and a black shirt with the AHRA logo. Then she grabbed a yogurt and ran outside to the Subaru. She scrabbled around under the floor mat until she found the keys and took off.

When she arrived at the Arkansas Headwaters Recreation Area headquarters building, she went in search of coffee, drank half a cup standing in front of the pot, then refilled her cup. Before she could reach the four-desk cubbyhole she shared with half of the eight river rangers, Steve cornered her.

"Let's go into my office."

Mandy followed her boss into his private cubicle. Blond and blue-eyed, he had broken a lot of hearts in Salida when he married nine years ago. But as evidenced by the collection of family photos on his desk, he doted on his two young boys, and his devotion to his wife never wavered. That didn't mean he didn't care about his staff, though.

Once they were seated, Steve said, "How do you feel?"

"Lousy."

"Hey, you pulled two people out of the river."

"But one died."

"And Hannah Fowler's thanking the river gods that you were there."

"I guess." Mandy took a gulp of her coffee.

Steve cocked his head. "So you knew exactly what to do, total confidence, and made no mistakes, right?"

Mandy jerked her head up and saw the wry half-smile on his face. "Hell, no."

"'Course not. You had to think on the fly in the middle of danger, chaos, and huge uncertainties. Now that you've had a chance to sleep on it, do you think you should have done anything differently?"

Mandy reviewed the rescue in her mind. "I wish I hadn't hit Tom King with the boat. And trying to steer the cat with two people on the pods was almost impossible. I guess I should have tried to get them up on the oaring seat frame." She scratched her head. "But I don't see how I could have done that with Tom King unconscious. What would you have done?"

Steve pursed his lips as if hesitant to continue. "I would have stopped with Hannah Fowler. Would have helped her onto the frame, then ferried her to shore."

"And left Tom King to ride out Number Five, alone and unconscious?"

Steve gave a solemn nod. "You made contact with Hannah, so her safety was your first responsibility. Tom King's wasn't yet. You thought you could save both of them, but I don't think I would have been so confident."

Mandy slumped in her chair. "So I screwed up."

"No, you pulled it off." Steve steepled his fingers under his chin. "But if you hadn't, and she got hurt, we might be having a different conversation. You made a judgment call, based on what you thought you could do. And it worked. I can't fault you for that. I'm only saying my call would have been different. Neither approach is right or wrong, Mandy, and our manuals can't possibly cover every situation that can arise on the river. That's the lesson. You trust your gut and go with it."

Mandy bit her lip and nodded. Problem was, she and her gut hadn't been sure she could pull it off. "Tell me, how did you feel after your first death on the river?"

"Lousy." A troubled, faraway look came into Steve's eyes. "The first time someone died on me wasn't while I was a ranger. It happened while I was still guiding. I pulled an older guy out of the river after our raft flipped, and he couldn't get a breath. Sure, cold water can shock someone, but this was weird. He was gasping like a fish out of water."

"Was he having a heart attack?"

Steve shook his head. "The guy hadn't listed any medical problems on his release form, but I pressured his wife as he lay sputtering in her lap. I said there must be something medically wrong with him. She admitted he had emphysema, but he hadn't wanted to divulge it because he didn't want to be kicked off the trip. He'd left his oxygen tank in the car."

Pulled in by the tale, Mandy leaned forward. "What did you do?"

"We paddled like heck to the next takeout, and I called 9-1-1. By the time the ambulance arrived, two of us were doing CPR, but the old guy didn't make it."

"Bummer."

"Yep, but there was nothing I could have done differently, just like you." Steve shook his shoulders, as if shaking off the bad memory, and resumed a businesslike tone. "You need to start writing your incident report today, before your memory gets fuzzy. And you need to review the outfitter boat accident report your uncle dropped off yesterday. If he left anything out, I want you to include the missing information in your report. We'll be briefing the park managers at the end of the day, and I want both of us to be as prepared as possible."

Like most of the rangers, who chose the occupation for the opportunity to work in the great outdoors, Mandy hated reports. And she could bet she would be pinned behind a desk all day working on them. She downed the rest of the coffee in her cup. "Anything else?"

"Yeah. King's widow filed a complaint against your uncle."

"I'm not surprised. I guess filing a lawsuit wasn't enough."

"She mentioned that in the complaint. Sorry to hear about it. Look, I'll address the complaint myself, but I want you to look it over for any factual errors." Steve held up a hand. "Now don't go ballistic when you read it. You know I'll investigate it fairly."

"Is that why you took a urine sample from Gonzo?"

Steve nodded. "Partly. Gonzo's got a rep for packing the booze away, but I'd try to get one from any rafting guide who had a customer death. I'm kind of surprised Gonzo did it, frankly, because most of the outfitters' legal counsels advise the guides not to honor our requests."

Mandy rubbed her forehead, which had started aching again. "Good God."

Peering at her, Steve said, "You don't look so hot. Should you have taken another day off?"

"No, this I did to myself. Got victimized at the Vic last night." She glanced at the bottom of her empty coffee cup. "If I could mainline a pot of this stuff into my vein, that might help."

"Relaxing with friends last night was probably a good thing—stress reliever. Though I know the hangovers afterward are no fun." With a wink, he turned toward his desk.

Mandy refilled her cup and returned to her own desk. *Trouble was, last night didn't relieve any stress. It only added to it.*

She opened her blueberry yogurt and started scanning the report form that her uncle had filled out. He had done a thorough job interviewing Gonzo and Dougie and checking the river depth gauges for water levels. She read in the accident description that two paddles had been lost. Yet another expense her uncle could do without right now, but maybe they would be retrieved by another outfitter's guides downstream and exchanged for the customary can of beer.

When she reached the section describing what had happened to the victim, she decided to call Quintana. After he answered, she said, "I'm working on the boat accident report today. Do you have any more information from Tom King's autopsy?"

"Not yet."

"I have some information for you. I talked to Gonzo yesterday, and he said Tom King had been acting woozy right before the spill." She listed the symptoms Gonzo had given her.

"I'll relay this information to the pathologist."

"Given Gonzo's report, do you think the pathologist could figure out if Tom King was having a heart attack before he hit the water?" Mandy crossed her fingers.

"I'll ask. Why's that important?"

"If it's true, it might mean the King family has no case against Uncle Bill."

"How'd he take the news that Mrs. King is thinking of suing him?"

"How do you think? He's already pinching pennies so hard his fingers hurt. Paying a lawyer to deal with the lawsuit is the last thing he needs."

"I feel for him, but I wouldn't hold out hope for a definite cause of death from the pathologist. Unless there's a bullet hole through the heart, he tends to make the ruling pretty general. The best thing for your uncle might be for the insurance company to settle."

"Then his premiums will go up." Discouragement and frustration made Mandy's voice sharp. "He can barely afford them now."

After that unsatisfactory conversation, she finished reviewing the boat accident report and started on her own report, not ready yet to look at the complaint form. Two hours later, after numerous escape trips to refill her coffee cup and empty her bladder, she had a reasonable rough draft. She e-mailed it to Steve and headed outdoors for a lunch break.

Feeling buzzy and lightheaded from the caffeine, she walked across the street to Bongo Billy's to order a turkey avocado sandwich from the counter. It was an expensive indulgence, but she hadn't had time to make her customary PBJ. To avoid returning to the office and second-guessing herself, she took her sandwich down to the town boat-launch ramp and ate it while perched on the rock wall overlooking the river.

A light breeze rustled the leaves of the cottonwoods lining the banks, and the midday sun warmed Mandy's back, warming her heart, too. A kingfisher perched on a limb overhanging the river until it spotted movement below. It dove in the water and came out with a small fish in its bill for lunch. Three kayakers were executing cartwheels and enders in the manmade rapid upriver from the boat launch. Probably practicing for the kayak rodeo event in the upcoming FIBArk Festival, Mandy thought, mentally translating the acronym: First in Boating on the Ark(ansas).

Soon, the kayaks gave way to a family float trip bobbing through the Salida Whitewater Park. Giggling kids and smiling parents filled four big oar rafts. The adults upped the excitement by yelling "Hold on tight!" and "Here it comes!"

Some of the passengers slapped ineffectively at the water with their paddles. The guides sitting on raised platforms and pulling and pushing on their long oars did all of the actual steering. One guide told his passengers not to paddle at all as they went through the boat ramp rapid, presumably so no one would interfere with his strokes.

Another guide Mandy knew by sight grinned at her as he bounced up and down in his seat, adding some extra thrills for his passengers. Mandy smiled and waved back. Since his group consisted of young girls and women, all screaming with delight, she decided it must be a Brownie Girl Scout troop or mother-daughter outing.

After the four-raft pod sailed through, the kayakers returned to their antics. Reluctantly, Mandy got up to return to work. Watching folks have fun on the river had improved her mood, but only slightly. She wished she could join them, rather than have to deal with the aftereffects of the accident.

Back at her annoying desk, she finally felt up to looking at the complaint Paula King had filed. The woman made outrageous charges that Gonzo must have been drunk or high. Uncle

Bill knowingly hired unreliable guides and didn't train them adequately. The river was running too high for a Numbers run—not! As Mandy read on, the turkey and avocado roiled in her stomach.

Fed up, she stomped into Steve's office. "That woman burns me up. I've never read so many blatant, outrageous lies. I'm surprised she didn't claim Uncle Bill snuck into the river and moved the rocks in the middle of the night to make the rapid tougher!"

Steve leaned back in his chair. "I seem to remember some advice about not going ballistic."

"How could I not go ballistic over that pile of…you know what?" Mandy sank into his visitor's chair.

"Now that you've read it once, the best thing to do is to ignore it until you calm down." Steve turned to his computer screen. "I reviewed the draft of your report and sent comments back to you. There are a few more pieces of information the park managers will want to know. Why don't you call your uncle? By the time you revise your report, it'll be time for the meeting. Leave the complaint for the end of the day."

"I don't know if I'll be able to look at the complaint calmly even then."

Steve smiled. "At least your heart rate will be down." He waved her out of his office.

Back in her office, Mandy called Uncle Bill and filled in the holes in her report.

After they were done, he said, "You sitting down?"

"Uh-oh. This sounds bad. What's up?"

"Mrs. King's lawyer served me with papers today. From what I can tell with all this legal gobbledy-gook, not only is she suing me for gross negligence, but she wants to close my business."

"What!?" Mandy shot to her feet. "How could she close your business? I wish I could go over there and tell her what a bitch she's being."

"Hold on. Rein in that prancing horse of yours. Remember, she's a brand-new widow. You going over there would be a very bad idea."

"I know that! That doesn't keep me from wanting to wring her neck, though." Mandy blew out a breath and sat down again. "What're you going to do?"

"I'll have to hire a lawyer of my own."

"That'll be expensive."

"Yep, but hopefully we can keep this thing out of the courts."

"How? You aren't going to settle, are you? You haven't done anything wrong."

"No, but paying her off to keep quiet may be the cheapest option in the long run. I'm still losing customers, and publicity about this suit would only make things worse—a lot worse."

Mandy rubbed her head. The throbbing behind her brows had returned. "How many customers?"

"Enough to cut a day off all the guides' schedules, even Gonzo, my best trip leader. I told him I can't give him a full week's work for a while, but he bounced back pretty quickly."

"How?"

"Your friend Rob called, said more people than usual had been calling him to book trips, and he needs more guides. He offered to hire Gonzo for whatever days he's available."

"So Rob's picking up your customers."

"Maybe."

"I'm calling him."

"Mandy, don't." But she was already hanging up.

When Rob answered, he asked, "How's your head feeling after last night?"

"Right now, it's throbbing, but not because of the Vic. I'm as mad as a weasel in mid-war dance."

Rob laughed. "I'd love to see your version of that dance. What're you mad about?"

"Tom King's widow is suing Uncle Bill."

"I heard that on the river rumor circuit. Anything I can do to help?"

"Yeah, stop stealing his customers."

"I'm not stealing your uncle's customers."

"What do you call it then, when he gets cancellations and people call you instead?"

"Mandy, most callers don't say why they're calling. They don't tell me they've just cancelled a trip with your uncle's company."

"What about the ones who do? You could tell them they've got their facts wrong and they should go back to my uncle's company."

"I could, but I don't because then we would both lose their business. People who've cancelled on your uncle have already made up their minds. I can't change that. All I'd do is piss them off enough that they'd call someone else. How would that help Bill?"

"How is booking his customers yourself helping him?"

"For one thing, I'm giving work to his guides, so they don't leave him." Rob paused. "Look, I can understand why this whole situation's upsetting you. But there's nothing you can do to fix it, so you might as well relax. It's Saturday evening. Let's go see a movie or something, then we can talk about this. I'll even buy you one of those toffee-coffee shakes you like at the ice cream store."

"Oh, no. You're not bribing me with treats."

"That's not what I—"

"I'm too upset to go out with you tonight. Besides, I've got to work tomorrow, and I'm sure you're busy managing all those extra customers you've booked." Too late, she realized she had spit out the last sentence with too much venom.

"That's not fair, Mandy," Rob shot back, "and you know it. Stop being such an idiot."

Idiot! She opened her mouth to reply, but the line was dead. Rob had hung up.

———

At a quarter to five, Cynthia poked her head into Mandy's office. "Hi. Thought I'd stop in on my way to work. Ready for the latest blonde joke?"

Mandy felt drained after the meeting with the park managers, but she rolled her eyes, the expected response to Cynthia's friendly jabs at Mandy's natural hair color. "Go ahead."

"A blind guy on a barstool shouts to the bartender, 'Wanna hear a blonde joke?' The guy next to him says, 'Before you tell that joke, you should know something. Our bartender is blonde, the bouncer is blonde. I'm a six-foot-tall, two-hundred-pound black belt. The guy next to me weighs two thirty, and he's a rugby player. The fellow to your right is six-five, pushing three hundred, and he's a wrestler. Each of us is blonde. Think about it, mister. Do you still want to tell the joke?'"

Cynthia paused for effect. "The blind guy says, 'Nah, not if I'm gonna have to explain it five times.'"

Mandy gave out a little snort, but couldn't bring herself to actually laugh.

After a long look at Mandy's face, Cynthia propped a butt cheek on the corner of Mandy's desk. "Okay, spill it. I heard about Paula King's lawsuit. Is that what's bugging you?"

That opened the floodgates. Mandy launched into a twenty-minute rant about stupid paperwork, stupid rafting customers blaming her uncle for King's death, and *stupid* Rob for stealing her uncle's customers.

Cynthia folded her arms. "C'mon, Mandy. Rob's not stealing your uncle's customers."

"It sure looks that way to me." Mandy folded her own arms across her chest.

"Why would he do that to your uncle? Rob's obviously got the hots for you. Why would he mess that up?"

"Money. Why else?"

Cynthia cocked her head. "Is something else going on between you and Rob?"

"Oh, no, you aren't turning this into some relationship thing. It's business. Underhanded, sneaky business, but just business."

Though the unresolved issue of Rob wanting to take care of her still grated on Mandy's nerves, she wasn't going to let Cynthia sidetrack her from what really mattered. "Trouble is, Rob's not thinking about how much this hurts Uncle Bill, what with the complaint and lawsuit from King's widow to deal with."

Cynthia's brow wrinkled. "You know, her suing him doesn't make sense to me."

"Why?"

"Last I heard, Paula and Tom King were estranged. She shouldn't be all that upset and wounded over his death. In fact, she might even think he got what he deserved. He's been having an affair with Evie Olson."

Mandy remembered the passenger list for the rafting trip King was on. "Daughter of Hank Olson, the city councilman?"

"One and the same. You've seen her around town. It's hard to miss the gauzy skirts, clanking bracelets, and all that long crinkly brown hair."

Mandy nodded. "Yeah, a throwback to the flower children of the sixties. She's too young for that stuff, must be in her thirties, right?"

With a smirk, Cynthia said, "She's well-preserved. Celebrated her thirty-ninth birthday more than once at the bar. That reminds me of another blonde joke. What do blondes and cow pies have in common?"

Mandy gave a theatrical shrug.

"The older they get, the easier they are to pick up."

"Okay, enough with the jokes." Mandy flashed a smile at Cynthia, though, to show she wasn't really bothered. "Back to Evie. Both she and her father came on that rafting trip."

Cynthia raised an eyebrow. "That couldn't have been too comfortable for Paula King. I'm surprised she put up with having her husband's lover along, even if he wasn't living with her anymore."

"Tom King had moved out?"

"About a month ago. Right after Paula found out about Evie. One of their neighbors told me the scene was straight out of the movies. Paula's tossing his clothes out the second-story window, and he's running around picking them up and yelling at her to stop being an idiot."

"Like that's going to work." The memory of how mad she had been at Rob for calling her the same thing ate at Mandy's nerves.

"Yeah, next came his bowling ball, right through a window that she hadn't opened yet." Cynthia arced her hand through the air. "Glass flew everywhere. He was ducking and running for cover. When he yelled that she could have killed him, she hollered, 'You're a dead man.'"

FIVE

When Kansas and Colorado have a quarrel over the water
in the Arkansas River, they don't call out the National Guard
in each state and go to war over it. They bring a suit
in the Supreme Court of the United States and
abide by the decision. There isn't a reason in the world
why we cannot do that internationally."
—SPEECH, KANSAS CITY (APRIL, 1945), HARRY S TRUMAN

MANDY WAS STILL MULLING over the disconnect between the scene Cynthia described and Paula King's lawsuit when she went out on the river the next day with Steve Hadley. In contrast to her gloomy mood, the weather was clear and sunny, with only a few puff-ball clouds in the brilliant blue sky. She lathered the sunscreen on thick, even though no matter what she used, or how often, by the end of the season she ended up as brown as a chestnut mare.

They launched their catarafts at the Buena Vista town ramp and intended to take out at AHRA headquarters in Salida, about thirty miles downriver. By ten o'clock, they were tied up a few yards upstream of the Fisherman's Bridge put-in for the Brown's Canyon run and bobbing in the undulating water. The spot was the busiest on the river, especially on weekend days. This Sunday was no exception.

River Runners, one of the largest outfitters on the river, was launching four pods of four rafts each from their land on the west bank. The lead guide shouted out names from his clipboard, divvying up the tourists among the rafts.

At the public boat access site on the east side, other outfitters and private boaters guided rafts down the waist-high metal rails in the center of the wide concrete steps. Everyone was in high spirits, anticipating the most popular whitewater section of the river. The water sparkled, and so did the tourists, chattering with excitement and snapping photographs.

With all the happiness around her, Mandy's mood brightened. She rolled her shoulders to relax them and stretched out her legs to soak up some of the sun's warmth. In deference to the hot weather, she wore a sleeveless neoprene shortie wetsuit under her official ranger PFD with the AHRA logo.

Steve capped his water bottle after taking a swig. "Wonder what Pike would think of the Arkansas these days."

"Zebulon Pike?" Mandy asked. "I didn't know he made it out this far west."

"On a second expedition after he failed to reach the top of Pikes Peak, he and his crew explored the headwaters of the Arkansas. First white men to do so. He'd probably be shocked by the hustle and bustle now."

Mandy nodded and returned her attention to the teeming masses. She knew she and Steve were there more as a preventative measure, reminding the outfitters and private boaters to pay attention to both river-running etiquette and basic safety rules. The outfitters choreographed the timing of their launches fairly well, letting pods form up and float a ways downstream before launching the next group. And all their customers were required to wear PFDs.

The private boaters were the ones who needed the most minding.

She watched a father buckle his young daughter into her PFD. He hefted her into the middle of the family raft. Then he tied a Pelican bag, a large waterproof case that likely held their lunch and hopefully some emergency supplies as well, to the middle thwart.

When he glanced in her direction, Mandy gave him a thumbs-up. This guy knew what he was doing. While he and his wife launched their raft, Mandy let her troubled mind wander back to the conversation with Cynthia. She remembered that Steve had grown up in Salida. He was a few years younger than Evie, may have even gone to school with her.

"Steve, do you know Evie Olson?"

"Just to say hi to. We only overlapped in high school one year when she was a senior and I was a freshman. She ran in a different crowd than I did, too."

"What crowd?"

"The one that hung around the woods behind the school after the bell rang to smoke pot."

Mandy smiled. "And I suppose you never indulged."

"I'm pleading the fifth. But I can tell you, playing football and smoking weed don't mix. And now eradicating marijuana plots on park land is part of our mission. Why are you asking about Evie Olson?"

"Did you know she was having an affair with Tom King?"

Steve shook his head. "Not surprised, though. She's got a reputation for being kind of a drama queen, always on the lookout for the next prince to carry her off on his white horse—or in his luxury SUV. What's it to you?"

"I can't figure out why Paula King is incensed enough over her husband's death to sue Uncle Bill, given that she was estranged from Tom King."

"Must be pure greed. She's rolling in money already, but the richer you are, the more you want, I guess," Steve said while scanning the activity on the banks. "I know more about Tom King's business affairs than his personal ones. I'm on the Water Issues Board with Nate Fowler, and he and King were bidding on the same land."

"I heard about that. Uncle Bill said that's why Lenny Preble took them on the trip, to see if whoever winds up with the land could be convinced to donate some of its water rights for recreational use."

"Nate Fowler probably would. He and I have had some talks about the importance of river recreation to real estate development in the valley. He knows most people move into Chaffee County for one reason or another related to the river. And, he knows that right now, the RICD is low man on the totem pole."

"What's RICD?"

"The Recreational In-Channel Diversion right established for the Salida Water Park. It's only for 250 CFS, and—"

"That's nothing," Mandy knew the best flows for rafting the river were between 1500 and 2200 cubic feet per second. "250 CFS isn't even enough to support the trout population. What recreation does that support?"

"It doesn't matter what the amount is, because it's the most junior water right on the Arkansas now. When it comes time to dole out limited water in a drought situation, everyone else's rights will be satisfied first anyway."

"How would donating more water rights for recreation help?"

Steve tucked his oar handles under his thighs and leaned on his knees. "Water rights are ranked by issue date, with the oldest ones issued having the highest priority. Because the RICD was granted in 2006, it's the youngest, and thus the lowest ranked. Most agricultural water rights were granted in the late eighteen hundreds, when ranches and farms first got established in the valley."

"So if King or Fowler donated the agricultural rights for recreation, then they'd have higher priority, and during a drought, some water would have to remain in the river for boating and fishing."

"Right. Then the lawsuits would start flying, because farmers with dying crops and homeowners with dying lawns would argue their needs are more important than those of the boaters and fishermen."

And how can you quantify the need of people to reacquaint themselves with the natural world they live in, to feel the flow of life around them, and to reenergize with that flow like Mandy was doing now? "Did Tom King feel the same way as Nate Fowler about the issue?"

"I don't think so. I never talked to him directly about it, but Nate said Tom King's planned project included a golf course, which uses a heck of a lot of water."

As she was about to ask for more information about the Water Issues Board, Steve said, "Would you look at that?"

A skinny, middle-aged guy with a gray ponytail and wearing faded, sagging swim trunks loped down the concrete steps. He had an inner tube slung over his shoulder. No companions, no PFD, no water bottle, nothing. He stepped into the water then paused to observe a trio of river guides herd their gaggle of tourists into the appropriate rafts.

"You talk to him, Mandy." A smile twitched across Steve's lips. "See what you can do. I'll observe."

"Gee, thanks."

Mandy loosed her stern line and swung the cat out into the current. After a couple of deft strokes, she had positioned herself next to the man and hopped out into the shallow water. She heaved her cat up onto the bank then held out her hand to the tube rider.

"Hi there. My name's Mandy Tanner, Arkansas River ranger."

The man hesitated, then shook her hand, but didn't give his name.

"You waiting for some friends?" Mandy asked.

"Nope."

"So you intend to float down by yourself?"

"Yep."

The guy had been real communicative so far. "You know this section has class III and IV rapids, right?"

"Yep."

"Everyone on the river in the Arkansas Headwaters Recreation Area is required to wear a PFD. You got one?"

"Nope."

She glanced at Steve and got a blank look in response. PFDs were required, but most rangers preferred to convince private boaters to wear them than flex their muscles and issue citations.

Mandy waved a hand at the procession coming down the steps. "I'm sure one of these outfitters has an extra PFD you can use. Cost you only a few dollars for the day, I bet. It could save your life."

A scowl crossed the man's face. "Got no money. Left it in the car at Stone Bridge. I rode my bike here."

Great. Taking out at Stone Bridge meant the man intended to run Siedel's Suckhole, the meanest rapid in the canyon, one the outfitters avoided on their half-day trips. After seeing rafts mangled from getting caught in the rapid's recirculating hydraulic, she couldn't imagine what it would do to a guy in an inner tube.

"I see." Mandy rubbed her chin. "Can I talk you out of running Seidel's Suckhole? It's pretty hairy for someone in an inner tube to run."

"Nope. Gonna do it."

Mandy looked at her cat. She always carried two extra PFDs on her raft, her backup and one to use for rescues, in case a swimmer lost his. She tugged one out of the gear basket in the back of the cat and held out the PFD to him.

"How about borrowing this PFD from me? I'd feel a lot better about your chances for making it out of the river alive today if you did."

When the man just stared at her, she pushed it closer. "You can leave it for me beside the big, gray rock next to the takeout."

Reluctantly, the guy took the PFD and shrugged it on. "Okay." He stepped farther into the river.

"May I?" Mandy reached over and buckled the PFD. "Next time, please bring one of your own. And bring at least one friend, preferably two, to go tubing with you."

The guy gave a grim nod, then sank his butt into the tube and swirled out into the current. He paddled his arms and kicked his feet, as if trying to get as far away from her as quickly as he could.

When Mandy returned to her station next to Steve, she asked, "Well, how'd I do?"

"Pretty good. You were polite and nonconfrontational, got him to listen to some advice, which he *might* apply next time he rides the river. I doubt I could have done any better, given how uncommunicative he was."

Pride swelled Mandy's chest. Maybe, just maybe, she was getting the hang of this job. "I doubt I'll see that PFD again, though."

"Hey, at least you got him to take it," Steve said. "And here's hoping that if we do see it again, it's not on his dead body."

SIX

Do not insult the mother alligator
until after you have crossed the river.
—HAITIAN PROVERB

AFTER ANOTHER RESTLESS NIGHT, Mandy sat at her kitchen table sipping a cup of strong coffee. She hoped it would kick her fuzzy brain into gear, though she didn't have to go into work. Monday was one of her days off, since few boaters traveled down the river the first day of the work week. While flipping the pages of *The Mountain Mail*, Salida's local newspaper, she remembered yesterday afternoon and smiled.

Wonder of wonders, near the end of the day, she and Steve had found her PFD neatly stashed behind the gray rock at the Stone Bridge takeout, just as she had requested. That day, the man with the inner tube had been lucky.

Unlike Tom King.

She flipped another page and put the coffee cup down hard. Tom King's photo appeared in the obituaries section.

His memorial service was planned for ten o'clock that morning. She checked the clock on her kitchen stove. Eight thirty. Maybe going to the service would help her close the book on not being able to rescue Tom King, bury the guilt, banish the nightmares. Or at least turn a page.

A few minutes before ten, Mandy stood at the corner of 4th and D streets, the center of gravity for Salida's church population. Episcopal and Catholic churches stood one block away. Clustered at this intersection were the First Christian Church, the First Baptist Church, and directly across 4th street from her, the First United Methodist Church, where Tom King's service was due to begin.

Staring at the red brick edifice, she smoothed clammy hands down her black skirt and flattened the collar of a brown button-down shirt. She had found the shirt stuffed in the back of her closet and had hastily ironed it. The shirt and skirt didn't go together, but they were the two darkest and most conservative pieces of clothing she owned.

An older couple walked up the concrete steps of the church, the man leaning heavily on the rail. The woman turned to wait for him. She peered at Mandy, as if trying to discern who she was and if she was related to the deceased.

Mandy had a sudden urge to run and had to force her legs to stay still. She licked her lips. *C'mon girl, you have as much right to be here as anyone else.* She squared her shoulders then marched across the street and up the steps.

Once inside, she slid into a back pew. Almost instantly, she wished she had worn a sweater, because the antique building's thick walls and dark lighting kept the interior cool. The multi-colored sunlight that filtered through the stained glass windows on the east side cast little warmth, and the solid seat of the carved wooden pew chilled the backs of her thighs. She tucked her skirt tighter around her legs.

Paula King sat in the front pew, her tall back stiff, her blond hair perfectly coiffed. A young man in an ill-fitting suit brought her a cup of water and sat next to her. Mandy recognized the tall, lean frame of Paula's son, Jeff King, his wavy brown hair pulled into a neat ponytail. She flashed back to the scene of Paula screaming hysterically on the river bank and a stunned Jeff patting his mother on the back like an automaton.

Then another memory surfaced, one she thought she'd drowned long ago, of her parents' funeral service, in a cool, dark church like this one, though it was larger and situated in downtown Colorado Springs. Mourners had filled the pews, and Mandy had felt the collective weight of their sympathetic stares as she squirmed in the front pew.

The whole ceremony had been a relentless torture while she held in her tears, refusing to break down in public. She had counted backward from five hundred, made imprint designs in her palms with her fingernails, indexed the colors in the stained glass windows—anything but listen to people talk about how her parents had died so young, leaving her and her brother so alone. If not for the methodic massage of her uncle's hand on her shoulders, easing her tension and giving her overwrought senses something to focus on, she would have broken down and screamed out her grief.

Stifling a present-day, sympathetic squirm, Mandy shook off the memory and glanced around to see if her uncle might be in attendance at Tom King's service, too. If so, maybe she could creep up and sit next to him. He'd understand her need for his touch. She couldn't spot him, but she did see something that surprised her.

Rob sat a few rows ahead, his back to her and his hair curling over the collar of his only sport coat. His head was bowed and his lips moved. When he raised his head, he crossed himself, an instinctive movement from his Catholic upbringing. She'd attended a few Sunday services at the Catholic church with him, but she wasn't sure she could ever get used to all the genuflecting.

Why did he come to the funeral, and why didn't he tell her he was coming? What was his connection to the King family?

Looking farther, she spied Detective Quintana in the other back pew across the aisle from her. The man was systematically surveying the attendees and making notes in a small notepad. When he noticed Mandy, he gave a nod, then continued writing.

What was up with that?

A deep chord struck by the organist drew Mandy's thoughts back to the service. She scanned the program crumpled in her hand. It looked like the service would be mercifully short, with only a eulogy by King's son and a few testimonials by others. And there was no casket up front, thank God.

Mandy eased out a slow breath in response to the solemn music. She pulled out a pack of tissues and prepared to suffer. She used one tissue during the soloist's haunting melody. Two more were soaked when Jeff King's voice cracked with emotion toward the end of the eulogy, and he struggled to finish.

When Rob got up to speak, Mandy felt shocked, until he mentioned Tom King's contributions to the local chamber of commerce. Rob served on the board. His steady voice helped Mandy regain her composure enough so that she only needed one last tissue after the closing prayer. When the service ended, she quickly slid out of her pew and was one of the first to leave. She stood blinking on the sidewalk in the glaring sunlight while she fished in her purse for sunglasses.

Detective Quintana approached her. "Can you stop by my office in about half an hour? I have something to tell you."

"What?"

"I don't want to discuss it here."

Mandy assumed he must have new information about Tom King's death. "Okay, I'll see you there."

With a nod, Quintana walked off, stroking his mustache. Caught up in wondering what the detective had to tell her, Mandy didn't notice Rob approaching until he had rubbed a hand across her back.

"I'm surprised to see you here," he said.

Her body responded instinctively to his touch, and she leaned toward him until she remembered that she was supposed to be irritated with him. She stiffened and slid on her sunglasses. "I was surprised to see you, too, until you got up to speak. Why didn't you tell me you were coming?"

Rob let his hand fall to his side. "Because I didn't think you'd want to come, or even want to know the service was happening."

"Fooled you."

Rob tugged at his bolo tie—the one his grandfather had carved out of silver and fitted with a large, lumpy turquoise stone, the one Rob reserved for special occasions. "Mandy, about our phone conversation—"

Jeff King came up and laid a hand on his shoulder. "Thanks for that testimonial, Rob."

Turning, Rob shook his hand. "Glad to do it. Your father did a lot for the business community in this town, especially in beefing up the chamber of commerce."

"That was him." Jeff's mouth turned down in a frown. "All business, no play."

"Jeff, sweetheart?" Paula King called in her breathy Texas accent. She walked up then stopped when she noticed Mandy. Her voice turned steely hard. "What are you doing here?"

Mandy tensed. "I came to pay my respects to your husband, Mrs. King. I'm sorry for your lo—"

"Oh, cut the sugar-coating. Tom would still be alive if your uncle ran a respectable business and hired proper guides."

Mandy's face flushed as she jammed her fists on her hips. "Gonzo's one of the best river guides on the Arkansas."

"Who drinks like a lush." Paula King crossed her arms confidently across her ample breasts, which looked suspiciously perfect.

"Who said that?" Mandy glanced at Jeff, who sheepishly stared off into the space over her head. "Gonzo may drink in the evenings, but he runs the river stone sober." *That had better be true.* "Besides, his skill as a guide isn't even an issue. If your husband had a heart attack and fell in the river, that's no one's fault. No one could have saved him."

Paula thrust out her chin. "You'd like to believe that. Then you'd have a clear conscience, wouldn't you, honey pie?"

Mandy spluttered in disbelief, her mouth opening and closing. "What? What are you saying?"

"You didn't save my husband, did you? You either failed due to incompetence or—" Jeff's hand clamped down on his mother's arm, and she glared at him "—you were covering up for your uncle's mistakes."

Shaking her head, Mandy stumbled back until Rob caught her. "No, no, that's not true…"

The woman's vehemence was like a physical force pushing her, pushing her back into the abyss of her nightmares about her parents' deaths.

Rob and Jeff nodded to each other and pulled the two women further apart. Rob hustled Mandy around the corner of the church into the side parking lot.

There, Mandy regained her speech. "Can you believe that witch? I've a good mind to march back there and tell her to go straight to hell." She whirled toward the front of the church.

Rob stepped in front of her and put his hands firmly on her shoulders. "Mandy, look at me. Nothing will be gained by you going back there."

Literally shaking with fury, Mandy stamped her foot. "Did you hear what she said?"

"Yes. She must be in a lot of pain to lash out at you like that."

"What? Are you sticking up for that she-devil?"

"It's the day of her husband's funeral. Let her grieve in peace."

In disbelief, Mandy raised her arms and slammed them down at her side. Her purse slid off her arm and crashed to the sidewalk, spilling keys, comb, and lipstick out onto the asphalt. She bent down to scrape the contents inside. Rob knelt down to help, but by then, she had shoved everything, plus some gravel, back in her purse.

"Why does she have to take it out on me? And Uncle Bill?" Mandy stood and slung her purse over her shoulder. "What did we do to her? What gives her the right to be so evil?"

A family on their way to their car turned and glared at Mandy.

Rob rose and gave her arm a little shake. "This is not the time or place. Use some sense, Mandy. People are staring."

Ice crystals formed in Mandy's veins, their sharp points slicing into her heart. She spoke between clenched teeth. "So now I'm stupid again."

Rob put up his hands. "You know I don't mean that. And I didn't then."

"Then why do you keep saying it?"

"Let's go somewhere private where we can talk."

"I have nothing more to say to you right now. I have an appointment."

Mandy stalked across the street. A nest of demon emotions fought for control of her heart—anger, pride, sorrow, and one green-faced imp rubbing his hands gleefully in the corner of her mind because he knew he would conquer her sleep that night—guilt.

———

Mandy screeched her Subaru into a parking spot in front of the Chaffee County government building. She pounded her hands against the steering wheel until her palms burned red. Then she marched up and down the row of cars until her ears stopped steaming and her heart resumed a regular beat. When she thought she could speak coherently, she entered the building and strode up the stairs to Quintana's office.

He was on the phone when she knocked, but he opened the door and waved her into his guest chair.

As he hung up, a patrolman poked his head through the open door and handed a couple of sheets of paper to him. "Here's the guest list for the King memorial service, sir."

"Thanks." Quintana laid the papers on his desk.

"Why do you want to know who attended the memorial service?" Mandy asked. "And why were you there, taking so many notes?"

"For the same reason I need to talk to you. The Pueblo coroner's office finished their toxicology test and reached a conclusion on the cause of death for Tom King."

Mandy leaned forward. "Did he have a heart attack?"

"No."

She slumped back in the chair. "Damn. What did he die of then?"

"Poison."

That made her sit up straight. "P-poison?"

Quintana nodded. He fished a page out of the Tom King file on his desk, now twice the size it had been when Mandy last saw it. "Aconite, to be exact, and this particular aconite came from the Western monkshood plant. The purple-blue flowers are supposed to be very popular with bees."

"Does that grow along the river?"

"It does grow wild in this area, plus I'm told some people grow it in their flower gardens, if they don't have pets."

A thousand questions battled for access to Mandy's tongue, but the first one to fight its way out was, "So how did he get poisoned by it?"

"He ingested it."

"Why would he eat wildflowers?"

Quintana leaned forward and peered at Mandy. "We don't think he chose to eat it. The dosage was more than you get from a few flowers. We think someone slipped it to him in something he ate or drank."

"Ohmigod." Further implications crowded Mandy's brain. "Ohmigod. That means—"

Quintana nodded. "That means Tom King's death probably wasn't accidental. He was most likely murdered."

"Is there an antidote? I mean, if he'd been pulled out of the river earlier, could he have been saved?"

"There's no antidote, only treatments for the symptoms if the dose is small enough for the body to purge it in a few hours. But aconite is one of the strongest plant poisons. A dose of one-sixteenth of a grain can kill an adult. The toxicology report indicated at least twice that much was in Tom King's bloodstream. He was a doomed man before you even got to him."

A dizzying wave of relief washed over her, flooding her senses until her throat clogged and her eyes burned with unshed tears. She couldn't have saved him. She wasn't responsible for his death. She put her hand over her mouth and looked out the window to try to regain her composure.

When she looked back at Quintana, she saw that he understood—perfectly. "Thank you," she said in a hoarse voice. "Thank you for telling me."

He gave her knee a couple of quick pats and moved his tissue box closer to her. "This also means your uncle can't be faulted in Tom King's death. Paula King's negligence lawsuit now has no basis."

"What about the media? Will they be told? If the newspapers say it was murder, Uncle Bill's customers will stop blaming him and calling to cancel trips." Her ballooning excitement made Mandy jump out of her chair. "I need to tell him right away."

"Hold on." Quintana put a hand up. "We need to talk about this. You can tell your uncle that King was poisoned, but not what substance was used. We're doing the same in our press release."

"No problem."

"You can also tell him that in light of this new information, we'll need to re-interview him and all his staff who were involved with that trip."

Mandy plopped back down in her chair. "You don't think any of them killed Tom King, do you?"

"Right now everyone on that trip has to be treated as a suspect, plus anyone else King had contact with that morning. But our immediate need for information is on the timing of the appearance of King's symptoms. If we can map the progression of the poisoning, we may be able to come up with an educated guess as to when he ingested the aconite."

"How long does it take for aconite to kill someone?"

"The Pueblo coroner is consulting some poison experts, but his best guess is anywhere from thirty minutes to a few hours."

"Were the symptoms I saw—the unconsciousness, gray skin, and weak pulse—consistent with the poisoning?"

"The poison was attacking King's heart by the time you got to him, and he was going into ventricular fibrillation."

"And the weak paddling strokes, sweating, and thirst that Gonzo saw?"

Quintana consulted the toxicology report. "Muscular weakness and excessive sweating are listed as symptoms. And a tingling in the mouth when it's ingested that the subject can confuse with thirst."

"What about the wooziness?"

"The way Gonzo expressed it was that King was having a hard time processing what Gonzo said to him. That's consistent with the symptom of impaired hearing. The man could also have been confused by what was happening to his body."

Mandy imagined what her own confusion and terror would be if her body was falling apart on her and she had no idea why. She shuddered. "What a horrible experience to go through."

"Not a pleasant way to die, I imagine. But most ways aren't."

And who would want to do that to Tom King? "So your only interest, then, in talking to Uncle Bill and the guides is to get information on symptoms and who had access to Tom King?"

"No. As I said, right now everyone who got near King that morning is a suspect."

"But Uncle Bill and the guides would have no reason to kill him. They barely knew the man! You should be talking to his bitchy wife instead. She's got to be your prime suspect."

With a cock of his head, Quintana asked, "Why's that?"

"Because Tom King was cheating on her." Mandy related Cynthia's story of Paula tossing King's things out on the lawn.

Quintana smoothed his mustache again. "When you said bitchy, my impression is that you meant it a little more personally."

Mandy rolled her eyes. "We had an argument after the funeral." After giving Quintana the gist of it, she said, "I can't wait to tell that woman she's totally wrong."

"Oh, no. You're not going anywhere near her. Certainly not before I have a chance to question her. In fact—" Quintana steepled his fingers and peered at her. "I know this is your case, too. But given your personal involvement, and the obvious emotions that engenders, you should probably stay away from all the suspects—the King family and everyone else on that trip."

"I'm not staying away from Uncle Bill!"

"Of course not. But after telling him that Paula King's suit has no basis, I recommend you refrain from discussing the case with him or anyone else. I'll keep you informed, of course, about our progress."

Mandy wasn't sure she agreed with this. Having her hands tied left her feeling decidedly uneasy.

———

As soon as Mandy returned to her Subaru, she tried to call Uncle Bill on her cell phone but got no answer. He was probably out working in the equipment yard or returning from running a shuttle since it was after one o'clock, the time when afternoon trips departed. She decided to tell him the good news personally.

While driving to his place, her thoughts returned to Paula King. The woman certainly had enough venom in her to be a killer. Paula had a strong motive, too. She had to have been angry and wanting revenge for her husband's affair. Though if Mandy were Paula, she probably would have poisoned Evie Olson first. But could she have gone so far—to actually kill someone over a love affair?

Mandy tried to imagine how she would feel if Rob went out with someone else. *Awful.* But still, they weren't married like the

Kings, who must have loved each other at some point. Mandy and Rob had only been dating for three months, and though she cared for him deeply, deeply enough to scare her sometimes, they hadn't made any promises to each other—yet.

Mandy rubbed her arm, remembering Rob's hands on her arms after the funeral. She was already regretting her angry words and wanting his hands on her again—and his lips on her mouth. She decided to visit him after Uncle Bill, apologize, and find a quiet place to savor a few make-up kisses. Then, maybe she could convince Rob to pass on the news about how Tom King died to those new customers he had booked. That news could both assure them the river wasn't King's killer and that Uncle Bill's company had nothing to do with the death.

With that plan in mind, she whistled a jaunty tune while she parked under the cottonwood tree by her uncle's house. She got out and scanned the yard, calling his name. The only living creatures in the vicinity were two mule deer mamas and their spotted fawns munching on the grass. The four animals lifted their heads and twitched their large ears at Mandy, but when she proved not to be a threat, they resumed their grazing.

Not finding her uncle, Mandy went inside and looked over the check-in counter into Uncle Bill's office. He sat in his chair, slumped forward on his desk, with his head on his arms and facing away from her.

Mandy smiled. "Caught you napping!"

When he didn't awaken, she passed through the entryway door into the house, turned into his office and tapped his shoulder. "Uncle Bill?"

The hair on the back of her neck bristled. The office was quiet—too quiet. And Uncle Bill was too still.

Mandy stood paralyzed, trembling, staring at the back of her uncle's head like a pronghorn antelope staring at the headlights of an approaching Mack truck. She forced herself to take a step, then another, so her uncle's face came into view.

It looked gray, lifeless.

Mandy slammed back against the office wall and slid to the floor. The Mack truck ran over her heart.

"No, no, no, no …"

SEVEN

I do not know much about gods; but I think that the river is a strong brown god—sullen, untamed and intractable.
—*THE DRY SALVAGES*, T. S. ELIOT

MANDY LAY ON HER bed, curled into as small a ball as she could make. Lucky whimpered on the floor nearby. The poor beast undoubtedly sensed his mistress was upset, but wasn't sure what he'd done wrong. Next to Mandy, Cynthia sat stroking her hair, murmuring God knows what. Mandy couldn't hear her over the howling inside her head that screamed over and over again, "Uncle Bill is dead, Uncle Bill is dead."

Her body seethed with raw pain. Her eyes burned, tears had seared her throat, and her heart lay in splintered shards. First her parents died, now Uncle Bill. She felt totally alone, drowning in silent agony at the bottom of a pitch-black dungeon of despair with no idea how to claw her way out.

Somehow, she had managed to call 9-1-1 from her uncle's office. When the ambulance crew arrived and realized they could do nothing for her uncle, they directed their concern to Mandy, shivering in the corner. It took a while for her to focus enough for them to find out who they should contact to be with her. She had given them Rob's office number, but Rob was leading a day trip through the Royal Gorge and couldn't be reached. So, Cynthia was called.

Cynthia had rushed over and driven Mandy home. She was the one who had thought to call Mandy's brother, David, in Colorado Springs and urge him to come to Salida right away. She'd been with Mandy for hours since, rocking her while she sobbed, laying a cool washcloth over her swollen eyes, disposing of the sodden tissues, or just holding her hand while Mandy stared, unseeing, at the blank bedroom wall.

When the phone rang, Cynthia answered it and listened for a moment. "She's here, but I'm not sure she can talk yet."

Cynthia bent down to whisper in Mandy's ear. "It's the coroner's office. They know how your uncle died. Do you want to talk to them?"

Mandy squeezed her eyes and lips shut.

Cynthia put the headset to her ear. "Can you tell me, and I'll tell her?" She scribbled on a pad on the nightstand. "What kind of clot? How do you spell that? Um, hum, and how long ago did the heart attack happen?"

She glanced at Mandy. "If anyone had been with him, could he have been revived?" She paused. "Okay, thank you. I'll have Mandy call you if she needs more information."

She hung up the phone and rubbed Mandy's back. "They found a huge clot still stuck in his pulmonary artery. The heart damage was massive. It was his time, Mandy. They said no one, not you or anyone else, could have saved him."

"I could have forced him to eat better, to exercise, to get more sleep." And a probing, vicious little voice added, *and I could have continued working for him instead of becoming a river ranger. I would have shouldered some of the stress, would have been there when the heart attack happened. Selfish, selfish, selfish fool!*

A knock sounded at the door and Cynthia rose. She spoke with someone in hushed tones at the doorway.

Cynthia returned and laid a hand on Mandy's arm. "Your brother's here. I'll leave now to go to work, but I'll call you later. And I'll come by to check on you tomorrow."

With a few rustles, Cynthia left, and Mandy felt a heavier presence sit on the bed next to her. "Hey, Mandy. I'm sorry about Uncle Bill."

Mandy slowly opened her eyes. David's solemn face swam into view, an almost exact copy of their father's, with his blue eyes, almost-white blond hair, and a broad smear of freckles over both cheeks and his nose. In his pressed khaki pants, button-down Oxford shirt and loafers, David looked like the number-cruncher he was.

He gave her a halfhearted pat on the shoulder, then laced his fingers together in his lap. "How are you feeling?"

"Awful."

"Yeah, I guess that was a dumb question." He glanced around the room, as if trying to figure out what to say next.

The action brought memories of her parents' deaths flooding in, and David's extreme awkwardness in dealing with her overpowering grief—and his own. Here he was again, at a loss for words and unsure what to do with his hands, even though he was a grown man of thirty. Mandy watched him in almost morbid fascination, trying to guess what would come out of his mouth next.

His stomach rumbled. "I threw some clothes in a bag and drove out as fast as I could. Made no stops. Have you eaten anything since you found him?"

"My stomach's too upset to eat."

"Well, I haven't eaten since breakfast. How about if I make you some tea while I rustle up a sandwich for myself? You always have peanut butter and jelly on hand, right?"

Mandy wouldn't have guessed he'd bring up the subject of food. She nodded.

"Come with me into the kitchen." David put an arm around her shoulders and lifted her into a sitting position, then pulled her to her feet. "Cynthia said you've been on this bed for hours. Moving around some will be good for you."

Feeling dizzy after being made to stand so quickly, Mandy staggered against him and held on until the stars floated out of her vision. "Maybe you're right."

Her throat did feel raw. Some tea with honey might help. But nothing else. She couldn't stomach anything else, not even peanut butter.

David led her into the kitchen, set her in a chair, and filled the teakettle. The burner lit for him, no problem. He put the teakettle on to boil. Needing to focus on something, anything other than her dead uncle, Mandy watched while he opened cupboard doors, looking for a plate and sandwich fixings. His biceps were larger than when she had last seen him at Christmas.

"You've been working out."

He shot her a look then glanced at his arms. "Yeah. At Christmas time, I saw how muscular your arms had gotten. Couldn't let my little sis out arm-wrestle me."

He flashed a small smile, but when she didn't reciprocate, he opened another cupboard and pulled out tea bags. He made himself two PBJ sandwiches, fixed her tea and handed the mug to her, then sat down to eat.

Mandy curled her fingers around the hot mug and breathed in the steam to ease the swelling in her nose.

David made fast work of the sandwiches, taking businesslike bites, then got up, poured a glass of water and drank the whole thing down while standing at the sink. When he returned to the table, he said, "We need to talk."

Mandy sipped her tea, now cool enough to drink. "About what?"

"Uncle Bill's business for one. Funeral arrangements for two."

Mandy put down her cup. "I'm not ready for this." Tears burned her eyes again.

"I know this is hard, really hard, for you." David drew circles on the tabletop with his finger. "But we need to make some decisions. When Uncle Bill updated his will after you turned twenty-one, he sent me a copy. We're co-inheritors of his business. But I can tell you now, Mandy, I can't stay here and run his company. I can take a week or two off work, tops. Then I've got to get back to the Springs."

He sat back and gave her an appraising look. "And, you're a river ranger now. You don't have time to run the company. What do we do about the rafting business?"

Business would be the first thing David would think about. "How the hell should I know?"

"It's a problem we've got to solve, and I'm sorry, but the solution can't wait. What do we do about all the trips that are already booked?"

A sudden realization washed over Mandy. When she'd gone to Uncle Bill's early that afternoon, the van had been missing from the equipment yard, and a few cars had been parked in the side lot. She glanced at the clock. Almost five.

"I think a trip is coming back right now. And one or two trips are probably scheduled for tomorrow."

"Should we call those customers and cancel, or can the guides run those trips on their own without Uncle Bill?"

Mandy's head throbbed. She put her elbows on the table and dropped her chin on her hands. "I don't want to do this. Not now."

David reached across the table and took one of her hands. "We've got to make sure Uncle Bill's customers are taken care of. He would want that. And we've got to figure out what to do with his business."

When Mandy shot him a bleak look, he said, "Let's just start with today and tomorrow. Get through these two days, then we'll go from there. Where did Uncle Bill keep his customer contact information?"

"On his computer. I can show you—"

A knock sounded on the door, and it swung open, hitting the wall with a thud. "Mandy?" Rob's voice called from the living room. He strode into the kitchen. "As soon as I heard about Bill, I came right over."

He stopped short, eyes glued on Mandy's hand in David's. "Oh, I didn't realize you had company."

David looked Rob up and down then lifted an eyebrow at Mandy, as if to say, "Who's this guy who feels like he can waltz into your house without knocking?"

Mandy pulled her hand from David's grasp and stood. She plucked at her matted hair, knowing she looked awful. "Rob, this is—"

Then she saw the puddles forming under Rob's feet, still clad in sandy river sandals. Big drops plopped from his clingy swim trunks. Even though she wanted nothing more than to feel his arms around her, this last little mess snapped the thin veneer of sanity over her ragged emotions. Her grief lashed out.

"You're soaking wet and dripping all over my floor!" As soon as the awful words were out of her mouth, she regretted them. She covered her mouth with her hand.

Rob looked down. "Oh, sorry." He gestured toward the kitchen door. "I'll go out in the yard and chan—"

Then he glanced at David again. "No, I should just leave. I'll call you later, Mandy." He turned and squished his way back across the living room carpet and out the front door.

David studied the sodden footprints. "Odd guy. What's his name?"

With a groan, Mandy started toward the front door. "Rob Juarez, and I think he's got the wrong idea about who you are. Give me a minute."

She sped up her pace and yanked open the front door to yell, "Rob, wait!" as he was climbing back into his truck.

Rob's square jaw looked chiseled in stone. "I thought you might need some comforting, but it looks like you've already got some."

"Yeah, but—"

"I guess you were right about having nothing more to say to me. You work fast, Mandy."

He slammed his door shut.

Mandy yanked it open. "You idiot!"

"Oh, so I can't call you stupid, but you can call me an idiot?" Rob folded his arms across his chest.

Mandy had half a mind to walk off and let Rob stew in his own selfish, jealous juices until he found out for himself what an idiot he was. But she cared too much for this blustering, prideful, and totally endearing man to let him suffer. A smile was already tugging at the edges of her lips over the ridiculous situation. "That's my brother, David. I told you about him, remember?"

Rob groaned, slumped in his seat, slapped his forehead. He looked back at the house, where David stood in the front doorway, arms crossed. "You're right. I'm an idiot."

David came over. "So, are you going to introduce me to the idiot?"

Mandy waved her arms. "David, Rob. Rob, David. Rob and I started dating three months ago."

David reached into the truck to shake Rob's hand. "Off to a good start, I see."

Feeling totally drained, Mandy pushed open the back door of her uncle's house and stepped inside. After she had gotten David set up with her uncle's computer, she met the van as it drove into the backyard and pasted on a smile to greet customers when they disembarked. Then she helped Gonzo and Kendra unload two rafts and wash the customers' wetsuits.

Noticing her stiff posture and quivering lip, they asked her what was wrong. She kept putting them off with "later" until the last set of customers climbed into their car and drove away. Then in a burst of tears, she told them about Uncle Bill.

Kendra followed her into the house, sniffling and wiping her nose with the back of her hand. "How can you stand to be here, Mandy, after finding him, you know?"

Spying her brother sitting in her uncle's chair at his computer, Mandy halted as if she had slammed into a wall. "I *can't* stand to be here. I can't. But I can't abandon the business either."

Mandy turned to Kendra and Gonzo and took a deep breath. "Are any runs scheduled for tomorrow?"

Gonzo shuffled his feet, gulped, and nodded. He took a moment to draw himself up to his full height, obviously holding in tears. "The Brown's Canyon afternoon run was cancelled. But we've got a full-day run down Bighorn Sheep Canyon in the morning with seven customers. Dougie and I are down for it."

"Do you think you could still do it?"

"We need someone to run shuttle. Normally Bill..." Unable to finish, he scrubbed a hand across his mouth and looked away.

"Oh God, Gonzo." Kendra ran a comforting hand down his arm, then looked at Mandy. "I'll do it."

"But it's your day off."

"I'll do it," Kendra said fiercely, "and I won't take any pay for it."

Fresh tears sprang to Mandy's eyes. She managed to push out a thick "Thanks."

Then she fell apart again. Kendra wrapped her arms around her, and Gonzo patted her back. The three of them stood in a little knot in the hall, whimpering in raw pain, until David came out with a box of tissues.

After a round of blows and wipes, they were able to make plans for the next day. David volunteered to handle the payments and paperwork. With heads bowed in grief, Gonzo and Kendra left.

David tried to lead Mandy into Uncle Bill's office, but she resisted. "I can't go in there. Not yet."

He sat her down on the living room sofa. "Wait here. I'll print off some stuff and bring it out to explain to you."

He returned with a few sheets of paper, mostly spreadsheet printouts, and laid them on the coffee table. "While you were out back, I went over the accounts. I need more time to understand everything, but from what I can see so far, Uncle Bill's company was on a slow, but sure, one-way trip to bankruptcy."

"See here, and here?" He pointed to totals on the spreadsheets. "His expenses have been greater than income for months now."

Mandy fell back against the cushions. "Damn. He never told me things had gotten that bad."

"Probably didn't want you to worry."

And she was too wrapped up in her river ranger training to wonder why he was belt-tightening, like patching the oldest raft instead of ordering a new one.

"He could have continued like this for another rafting season maybe, but the recent cancellations really hurt him. I doubt he would have made it through the end of this season. And he knew it."

David handed her a bookings list printed out that morning with some notes in her uncle's scrawled handwriting. The last line read 'Not enough,' and was underlined.

The desperation her uncle must have felt washed over Mandy. "What do we do, David? How can we save his business?"

With sad eyes, David appraised her then said softly, "Do we really want to save it?"

"What do you mean?" Mandy looked around the darkening house, dusk shadows lengthening across the floor. It was now an empty shell without the jovial presence of her protective uncle. "He poured his life into the company. It was his legacy to us. He wanted me to run it after he ..."

"Died?"

"No, retired! We can't let his life's work die with him, David. We've got to try."

"I already told you, Mandy. I can't stay here. And you've got your new career to think about. You can't run this business and patrol the river at the same time."

"I'll quit."

David took her hand. "No, you won't. You weren't willing to give up being a river ranger for Uncle Bill before. Why do it now when he's not here to care?"

Tears of frustration and guilt clogged Mandy's throat. "Because I care."

David pulled her into his arms. "I know, and I'm sure he knows. But you shouldn't give up your new career for a hopeless cause that has almost no chance of succeeding. Maybe we could sell—"

Mandy's groan of protest was muffled against David's shoulder. She stiffened and tried to push him away.

"Okay, too soon to talk about that. How about this idea?" He pulled back and looked at her. "Find someone to manage it through the rest of the summer. Then when things slow down, you and I can revisit the situation. Take the time to look at it logically."

"When I'm not so emotional, you mean."

"Well, yeah."

Mandy sat silently, staring out the back window at the equipment yard, looking forlorn and dilapidated in the encroaching gloom of twilight. She didn't want to accept any of this, Uncle Bill's death, the death of his business, the death of her dream of becoming a river ranger, the death of everything bright and sunny in her life.

David gave her a few minutes, then asked tentatively, "You know anyone who might be able to help us manage?"

"I guess we could ask the other outfitters." The memory of her argument with Rob over stealing her uncle's customers made her sigh. "Maybe Rob knows someone."

"I'll talk to him. And I'll come in here tomorrow to get a complete picture of the business, unless you want my help planning the memorial service."

"Oh, God. I can't face that yet."

"We probably should hold it this weekend."

"This weekend?" *Why isn't that going to work?* "Oh no, we can't. FIBArk is this weekend. The Chamber of Commerce kickoff is Wednesday night. All of Uncle Bill's friends and associates are involved with the activities." *As am I.*

"The First in Boating festival? What's so important about that? Why can't these people take a break from it to attend a memorial service?"

"Because the river is their livelihood. And FIBArk pulls in way more rafting customers than any other weekend. It's been the most important event in this town since the first race was run in 1949. Every guide and outfitter will be working their tails off when they're not competing in races or volunteering. No way would Uncle Bill want us to interfere with the festival."

"His friends aren't going to be in a very festive mood."

"They'll put on a brave face for the tourists. And putting on a good show for the tourists is what matters. Uncle Bill knew that. I know that, and so do his friends."

"Okay, we'll plan the service for next week sometime." David glanced at his watch. "It's getting late, though. Let's talk about it tomorrow. Are you going to stay home or come in here with me in the morning?"

"I'm supposed to work."

"I'm sure you can call in sick."

Mandy suddenly itched to get out of this gloomy house, away from the morbid memory of finding Uncle Bill slumped dead over his desk mere feet away. She couldn't face coming back and spending the next day here. Nor could she face being alone at home. She had to get out, get away, get on the river.

"I probably could, but I need to go to work. If I sit around here or at home, I'll just cry all day. I couldn't stand that." *And Uncle Bill wouldn't want me to. He understood my need to be on the water. The river thrummed in his blood, too.*

David stood. "Okay, let's go."

Mandy began gathering up the papers David had printed. When she picked up the bookings sheet, a realization hit her and the sheet fluttered to the floor. "Whoever killed Tom King is responsible for Uncle Bill's death, too."

"What?"

"Don't you see, David? The bad publicity from King's death caused those cancellations, and worrying about them caused Uncle Bill's heart attack. If Tom King hadn't been murdered, Uncle Bill would still be alive today."

David's return gaze was sad, solemn, knowing—too knowing. Knowing that she was searching for someone to blame other than herself.

"Uncle Bill wasn't exactly in the prime of health, Mandy. No one can say for certain that this situation caused his death."

"No, not for certain, and maybe I'm not totally rational right now, but my gut says that if Tom King hadn't died, Uncle Bill wouldn't have either. Not yet. Sure, his health wasn't great, but he was an old bull, fighting until the end." Mandy leapt up from the sofa and started to pace. "And I won't rest until his killer is made to pay."

———

After David had ordered a pepperoni pizza and forced Mandy to eat a slice, she handed him a stack of bedding and towels. "You sure my sofa's going to be all right?"

He eyed it, pushed down on the cushions, and gave a casual shrug. "I slept on worse during my college years. Am I intruding on anything by staying here?"

"Like with Rob? We're sort of on the outs now, anyway. We had a dumb argument, and I said some things I shouldn't have, so we've got some patching up to do first."

David laid the pile of linens on the coffee table and unfolded a blanket. "You be sure to let me know when things are patched up between you two and three's a crowd. And if you have trouble sleeping tonight and need to talk to someone, promise you'll wake me."

"Promise." She stuffed a pillow into a pillowcase and handed it to David. She hated the reason he had come to visit, but decided it would be nice to spend some time getting reacquainted with her brother, even if they had some definite differences in opinions.

The phone rang, and David said, "I'll take my turn in the bathroom now in case that's Rob."

When Mandy picked up the phone, though, Cynthia answered and almost immediately asked, "You want me to come over tonight after work?"

"No, I'll be okay with David here."

"How're you holding up?"

"I've reached the numb stage, and I'm exhausted, and David and I have a new worry—keeping Uncle Bill's business from going under."

"Maybe now that Tom King's death has been ruled a murder, Paula King will drop her lawsuit against your uncle's company. That might help."

"Maybe, but finding his killer would help even more. I want to do everything I can to help Detective Quintana solve the case, especially since the killer caused Uncle Bill's death, too."

"Oh, the heart attack? From the stress of the cancellations? I see what you mean. In that case, I've got some information for you."

"What's that?"

"Evie Olson came into the bar tonight with a couple of her aging hippy friends. Since they sat at the bar, tossing back chocolate martinis like they were Yoo Hoos, I overheard most of the conversation. When the others asked how she felt about Tom King's death, she said the bastard deserved it."

"I thought she was seeing him."

"So did I. But she told this tale of woe to her friends about how Tom had decided to break up with her and go back to his wife to try again. She sounded angry, but she was also pretty broken up about it and his death. It wasn't all her natural theatrics either. She actually started to cry."

"Had Tom already gone back to Paula before the rafting trip?"

"I don't know."

If he hadn't, Paula may have still thought he was seeing Evie. Could either woman have been jealous or angry enough to have poisoned Tom? "I wonder how we can find out."

"Evie and one of her friends made plans to go to the Final Touch Day Spa late Wednesday morning to get gussied up for the FIBArk kickoff. Evie said she needed some pampering after all the trauma she's been through. She asked her friend to come along so she'd have someone to talk to. Someone to kvetch to, more like it."

"You think you should go there and eavesdrop?"

"I think you should go. If anyone's had trauma and needs pampering, it's you. I'll spring for a manicure."

Mandy looked at her utilitarian nails, cut blunt for work on the river. "I haven't had a manicure in years."

"Then it's about time. Are you still planning to attend the kick-off?"

"Rob asked me to go with him, and I haven't told him I can't. And I guess I'm the official representative for Uncle Bill's business now. I'll have to go." The last few words came out sounding strangled.

Cynthia's voice softened. "Oh, Mandy, what are you going to do about the business?"

What am I going to do about my life, period? "I don't know. After tomorrow, I haven't the faintest idea what I'm going to do."

EIGHT

Mother, may I go out to swim?
Yes, my darling daughter:
Hang your clothes on a hickory limb
And don't go near the water.
—RHYME

WHEN MANDY WALKED INTO the Arkansas Headwaters Recreation Area ranger headquarters the next morning, Steve Hadley's eyes opened wide. "I didn't expect to see you here. You sure you want to work today?"

"I need to work. And I need to be out on the river. And—" Her voice caught, and she started again. "Please, Steve."

His brow furrowed with concern, Steve laid a hand on her shoulder, long enough to offer comfort but not long enough to set her off crying again.

"I've got just the thing. Hard labor. We've received some calls from guides about a strainer in Bighorn Sheep Canyon blocking one side of the entrance into Three Forks rapid. It's a big old cottonwood with lots of branches, and it'll take awhile to clear it. You haven't had any hands-on experience with the chain saw yet, so this will be good for you."

And good for her in other ways. Hopefully the work would exhaust her so she could sleep, instead of tossing and turning like last night. "That's perfect. I won't have to talk to many people. I think I would choke up if someone mentioned Uncle Bill."

Mandy helped Steve load two chain saws and other equipment into the catarafts and muscle the rafts onto a trailer behind one of the ranger trucks. She followed in a second truck, going east on Highway 50, until they reached the Texas Creek put-in. There, they unloaded the rafts, then drove to the busy Parkdale takeout a dozen miles downstream to leave a truck and returned to their starting point.

A short distance downstream, they eddied out above the tree on the side of the river opposite the railroad tracks. They tied up the rafts and hiked to where the toppled cottonwood had lodged among the rocks. Torn from the riverbank, the root ball lay exposed, and the thick trunk angled over the water downstream. Branches stuck out all over—in the water, above the trunk, and to the sides.

Mandy tagged along while Steve walked the bank and studied the situation. She didn't like the looks of the chest-deep water rushing through the branches at all. If one of them fell off the trunk and got tangled up in the underwater branches, a certain drowning death awaited. No wonder the guides had called in the hazard.

"Here's the plan." Steve folded his arms across his chest. "There's no way we'll be able to pull the tree to shore so we can work on land. So we'll work over the water one at a time. Whoever's on shore will hold a rope attached to the quick release harness on the sawyer's PFD."

"There's a rat's nest of branches out there. How can we use a chain saw safely?"

"We'll cut off smaller branches first with the big clippers to give us some working room. Too bad we don't have a little twelve-inch chain saw to make the job go faster. I've got a couple of them high on my equipment request list, but replacing the busted cataraft was higher."

Mandy eyed the two twenty-inch chain saws they had brought with them. "And a twelve-inch one would be a lot lighter than these monsters."

"Yeah, there weren't too many female river rangers when we bought these years ago. If your arms get tired, let me know, and I'll spell you. We'll use these suckers to cut off the large limbs and section the trunk."

"What do we do with the pieces?"

"The small branches can float downstream. We'll rope up the large limbs and trunk sections before we cut them off. We'll haul them onto the bank where we can saw them into firewood-sized chunks. Then we can toss them into the river because they'll be small enough that they won't impede navigation or cause log jams."

Trying to show some enthusiasm for the time-consuming process, Mandy rubbed her hands together. "Let's get started."

Over an hour later, she straddled a large lower limb of the cottonwood, which gently undulated in the current. Her feet hung in the cold water, but the hot sun caused sweat to bead up on her forehead and slide down to sting her eyes behind the safety glasses. Steve had monkey-walked efficiently up and down the trunk, but after slipping a few times, she had opted to sit and slide along on her butt.

How was she ever going to stand up with the chain saw?

"After you clear those side branches, come back to shore," Steve yelled over the roar of the river. "We'll eat lunch, then start chainsawing."

Mandy nodded to show she had heard him and clenched her teeth while pushing the handles of the heavy-duty clippers together. She strained to close the five-inch curved blades until, with a snap, a branch fell into the water and swirled away. She positioned the clippers on the next branch and gripped the handles again with her gloved hands.

The heavy gloves were too big and already rubbing blisters into her fingers, but she welcomed the pain. Better the physical burn than the deep ache over losing Uncle Bill. She could bandage the blisters, but not her heart.

She clipped off a few more branches, then slid backward until she reached the main trunk and felt secure enough to stand and walk back along its length to the shore. After stripping off the gloves, goggles, and safety rope, she took a grateful swig of the water bottle that Steve held out to her.

As she bit into her PBJ sandwich, rustling and crunching upstream caught her attention. Two people were slowly walking down the bank, each holding a bulging trash bag. Two more patrolled the opposite bank, also with trash bags. Occasionally one would stoop to pick up something and put it into a bag.

When they neared, Steve yelled out, "Hey, Lenny!"

Mandy studied the thin, stooped-over man who straightened to his full, tall height and waved before bending down to pick up another object. "That's Lenny Preble, the environmentalist who arranged the trip Tom King was on, right?"

"The same."

"What're he and his friends doing?"

"Lenny organizes periodic trash pick-ups along different sections of the river. He's good about it. Stays off private land and lets us know when and where his teams will be. They all wear PFDs and work gloves, travel in pairs, and carry radios to call out if they run into a problem."

When Lenny and his shorter partner approached, Mandy could see they both wore jeans and work boots, even though it was a summer day, presumably to protect their legs from being scratched by brambles and other riparian shrubs. The men wore sensible sun hats and matching forest green T-shirts emblazoned with a circular logo encompassing a cottonwood tree, not unlike the one she'd been cutting, overhanging a river.

Steve stepped forward to shake Lenny's gloved hand. "You picked a good day, Lenny. Sunny, but not too hot."

Lenny swept back a lank of long dark hair that had fallen across his eyes. His frown emphasized the sharp angles of his face.

"Someday, when these God-damned tourists realize the Arkansas River is not their personal refuse can, we won't have to do this."

He shot a sheepish glance at Mandy. "Sorry about the language. The callousness of some people irritates the he … heck out of me."

"That's okay," Mandy replied. "Frankly, I agree with you." She held out her hand. "I don't think we've been formally introduced, though I've seen you around town. I'm Mandy Tanner."

In the process of reaching out his own hand, Lenny stopped, then recovered and grasped hers firmly. "I heard about your uncle. Good man, Bill Tanner. Cared about the river."

Past tense. Mandy mumbled her thanks.

"My friend here is Kurt Maxxon." Lenny clapped a hand on the shorter man's shoulder. "Kurt is a retired race driver who now cares for the environment."

With an abashed grin, Kurt shook hands with Mandy and Steve. "Trying to make up for some of the damage done by all that oil I burned in my youth."

Lenny introduced his other two companions across the river, who waved and continued on with their work. "We're all members of 'Citizens for the Arkansas,' my nonprofit." He pointed at the logo on his shirt.

"Sorry, I've got to take a leak, so I'm going to find some privacy." Kurt walked toward a grove of cottonwoods downstream.

Before she could give in to her grief, Mandy dove on this opportunity to find out more about the people on the fatal rafting trip, one of whom could have killed Tom King. "So you organized the trip that Tom King was on when he died. How'd the trip come about? Why'd you pick Uncle Bill's company to run it?"

Lenny shifted his gaze around, as if looking for an escape route.

The realization struck Mandy that he probably felt uncomfortable talking to the grieving niece of a man who just died. A lot of people would probably react this way around her in the days to come. *Unlike Cynthia and Steve, thank God.*

After an awkward pause, Lenny said, "Your uncle cared as much as I did about securing high-priority recreation water rights on the Arkansas. I asked him for a donation a while back. He said he was strapped, but he'd do whatever he could to help out. When I decided that Councilman Saunders and the two developers needed to see firsthand the environmental damage that low flows cause, I called your uncle."

"I wouldn't think you'd be on the same side as the river runners," Steve said.

"Ideally, this river should be left alone," Lenny replied, "to recover from the damage humans have inflicted on it. But the high muckety-mucks in your office aren't about to yank outfitter licenses. I've talked to them until I've gone purple in the face, but no luck. So, I've had to resort to Plan B."

He waved a hand at the bulging bag he had set on the ground. "I hate the trash the tourists leave all over the place, but that's minor compared to fisheries disruption from low flows and pollution from agricultural runoff. I decided recreational use of the river is the least of a whole host of evils. I'm focusing now on trying to convert some of the old agricultural rights to recreation."

"Were you making any progress with Tom King and Nate Fowler?" Mandy asked.

"More with Fowler than with King. King insisted that he needed a golf course in his development plans, which is downright dumb.

Everyone knows the river, not smacking little white balls, is why people come to Chaffee County."

"So you hoped Fowler would win the bid for the land down south."

Lenny nodded. "The lesser of two evils. Didn't look like his chances were good, though. I can't tell you who, but a source told me the city council was more favorable toward Tom King's plan. Had more homes, thus more tax dollars. It all comes down to money, doesn't it?"

"I guess so." *And with Tom King out of the picture, Nate Fowler's lone remaining bid could sail right through the council. How convenient for Nate.* "Did you notice anyone acting suspicious toward Tom King on the trip?"

Lenny narrowed his eyes at her. "You working with the cops?"

Mandy shook her head. "Not really. The case got turned over to them once the rescue operation was done. I'm just curious. Now, about my question?"

"The only weird thing was the ugly looks Paula King and Evie Olson kept shooting at each other. You'd think the man would be smart enough to keep his wife and his mistress apart. I was surprised when Evie's father asked if she could come along, but I couldn't say no at that point. At least I kept the two women from getting in the same raft. Got downright awkward, you know?"

Kurt came tromping back up the bank. "There's a big pile of garbage down past those trees. Looks like someone's picnic leavings."

"Damn tourists." Lenny picked up his trash bag. "Sorry. Seems I can't say the word 'tourists' without the adjective they deserve.

Good day to you." He tipped his sun hat and left with his friend in tow.

"He's pretty serious about taking care of the river, isn't he?" Mandy asked Steve.

"Yep. His nonprofit seems to eat up all his time. I've never seen him with a woman or even just out drinking a beer." Steve dropped his sandwich bag and apple core in his waterproof case and buckled it shut. "Ready to do some chain-sawing?"

After they donned protective chaps, Steve showed Mandy how to undercut limbs from below before finishing the cut from above, so they would break off cleanly. "Keep the trunk between your legs and the saw blade. And make sure that when the limbs fall off, you aren't standing in the way."

"This sounds dangerous."

"The biggest danger is kickback, when the chain catches on something and kicks the blade back toward you. Don't ever cut with the nose of the blade, only the middle." Steve paused and peered at her. "Think you can handle it?"

Mandy wasn't about to admit her fear of the noisy machine. If this was something river rangers had to do, she would do it. "I'll watch you first, then I'll give it a try."

The process was slower in the afternoon, with three ropes involved. One was tied to the chain saw and a tree on shore, so they could retrieve the saw if it fell in the water. A second ran from Steve's PFD to Mandy. A third was tied around each larger limb before Steve sawed through it, so the two of them could tug the limb to shore afterward.

By the time they took a rest break, Mandy felt confident she knew what to do, though she was less confident she could actually do it. But with butterflies fluttering in her stomach, she said, "My turn."

Steve gave her a thumbs-up and attached a rope to her PFD.

Mandy walked out along the cottonwood trunk to a large limb, tied on a rope then returned for the chain saw, started it up, and carried it, idling, with her. She braced her feet, positioned the center of the blade under the limb and glanced at Steve for confirmation.

He flashed an okay sign.

The chain whined and ground into the wood, spitting sawdust out the back. When she'd cut through about an inch, she extracted the blade and started from the top. The saw broke through the limb with a loud crack, and the sudden release of pressure against the blade threw her off balance. She stumbled and scampered sideways. *Hell, if I can't get this balance thing, I'll fall in the river for sure.*

She shut off the machine, clipped it with a carabiner to a nearby branch, then hauled on the rope tied to the cut limb to help Steve pull it to shore. After she untied the rope, she asked Steve, "You never seem to have any problem keeping your balance out there. Any hints?"

"Practice wading in the river," Steve said with a grin. "That'll tune up your core muscles for all kinds of balance situations. And bend your knees a little before starting a cut. If you feel yourself falling, throw the chain saw in the river. The water will shut off the engine, and we can retrieve it with the rope. We won't be able to use it again today, but that's why we brought two. I'd rather clean and repair the saw than patch up your leg."

"Me, too." Mandy surveyed the mutilated tree. "Well, one down, about a dozen to go." She took the end of the rope and walked out again to the next limb.

After Mandy had cut a few more limbs, a flotilla of bright yellow inflatable kayaks, called duckies, bobbed and weaved through the riffles on the other side of the river, their riders madly paddling with varying degrees of control.

One of the guides yelled out to her covey, "Stay far away from that tree!" then to Mandy, "Thanks, ranger!"

Mandy gave her a wave and fired up the chain saw again. As she touched the blade to wood, something bumped the cottonwood trunk. She lost her balance and tossed the machine aside. It splashed into the water. She fell to her knees, hard, and looped her free arm around the limb she'd been about to saw to stop herself from plunging headfirst into the river. The rope on her PFD went taut as Steve tensed to haul her in if she fell.

Once the sharp pains zinging up from her knees subsided, and she knew she wasn't going to take a dive into the swirling water, she turned her head to see what bumped the tree.

A wide-eyed teenage boy with an orange Mohawk gaped at her. He sat in his duckie, gripping the end of the trunk. "So-sorry. Are you hurt?"

"What the hell were you thinking?" Mandy yelled, all her training about being polite to river users overwhelmed by her pain and anger.

"Get away from there!" his guide yelled.

"Let go of the tree!" Steve hollered.

"I-I just wanted to see what you—"

"Oh, shut up." She was about to say more, but the chagrin on the boy's face cooled her anger enough for her to remember she was a professional. She counted to three and took a deep breath.

"Listen to me carefully," Mandy said with a deliberately fierce tone. "If the water sweeps you under this tree, you could be trapped and drown. Push off *now* and paddle like hell toward the other side of the river."

"But—"

"Now!"

The boy pushed off and, with head down, windmilled his paddle madly to propel his boat over to the rest of his group. As soon as he was out of danger, his guide started chewing him out.

Mandy sat up and checked her pants legs. One was torn, and blood oozed out where the bark had scraped her skin. *Great, another sewing job.*

"You hurt?" Steve called.

"Just a scrape." Shakily, she clambered to her feet.

"Sorry about that," the guide yelled. "I'll keep a close eye on this kid for the rest of the trip."

"Tell him he's lucky he didn't kill two people," Steve shouted back. "Himself and a river ranger."

The boy's face flamed red. He focused his gaze resolutely straight ahead, so he couldn't see all the derisive stares directed at him. His hunched back showed he felt them, though.

Mandy hobbled to shore and sat down next to her first aid kit while Steve hauled in the drenched chain saw. "I don't think the kid will do anything that stupid again."

"No, you can count on that imbecile causing trouble again real soon." Steve dug in the kit and pulled out alcohol wipes. "Stupidity and teenage hormones are as volatile a combination as lightning and scrub oak."

The alcohol burned her scraped skin, and Mandy sucked in a breath. Worried that she had let her emotions get away from her, she asked, "You think I was too hard on him?"

"No. In fact, I'm surprised you didn't really let him have it, especially after … everything."

"Uncle Bill, you mean."

"Yeah." Steve handed her a couple of gauze pads and ripped off a length of first aid tape. After they finished doctoring her knee, he repacked the first aid kit. "Why don't I finish up the job?"

"I can do it."

Steve grabbed the second chain saw, attached a rope to his PFD quick release harness, and handed the other end to Mandy. "I know you can."

NINE

After a trip with particularly badly behaved kids,
one guide rushes to the drugstore to buy more condoms.
—*WHAT THE RIVER SAYS*, JEFF WALLACH

It took another couple of hours to saw the remaining limbs off, section the trunk and limbs into two-foot lengths, and split the large sections with a chisel and maul on shore. Since Steve had commandeered the one working chain saw, then the maul, Mandy took on the job of throwing hunks of wood into the river.

By the time they finished, every muscle of her body was crying, "Enough!" She had bandaged the blisters on her hands during their last break, but they still stung. She smelled pretty ripe, too, but she welcomed the physical exhaustion, hoping it would help her sleep that night.

While they paddled downriver to the Parkdale takeout, Mandy reviewed her conversation with Lenny Preble about Nate Fowler.

The developer had a viable profit motive to kill Tom King, his rival for the land south of Salida, but King's mistress, Evie Olson, and his wife, Paula King, also had motives of a more personal nature. If what Cynthia had found out about Evie was true, she was the woman scorned. But after Mandy's run-in with Paula at the memorial service, she could easily visualize that woman having enough venom in her to kill someone, especially a philandering husband.

Hopefully, she would be able to get a better idea about Evie Olson the next day at the day spa, but how could she scope out Nate Fowler? The FIBArk kickoff! He would probably be there. Mandy now had yet another reason to attend.

As she dragged her cataraft onto shore, the sounds of honking horns and shouts drifted down to the river.

Steve heaved a great sigh. "Let's go. Must be another parking lot altercation." He trudged uphill, his shoulders drooping.

Following, Mandy rubbed her own sore shoulders. *The poor guy must be as bushed as me—or even more so, given that he did the majority of the wood splitting.*

When they reached the parking lot, she saw her uncle's van, with the boat trailer attached, positioned nose-to-nose with a large pickup truck, which was blocking the parking lot exit. A trio of middle-aged men stood beside the truck, their raft half-in and half-out of the truck bed. Gonzo stood nose-to-nose with the middle one, a sunburned heavyweight with clenched hands.

The man's hefty beer belly hung over a baggy pair of psychedelic swim trunks. His words were slurred and spittle flew from his lips as he shouted at Gonzo to "move your God-damned vehicle."

Gonzo swiped a fleck of spit from his cheek. "Move your own God-damned vehicle! You've been blocking the exit for twenty minutes. I've got people here who have to leave *now*."

The man folded his arms across his hairy chest. "I've got as much right to be here as you do."

"Oh yeah, asshole," Gonzo shot back. "I don't see a vehicle permit on your dash. You got one? You paid your two-dollar daily pass fee?"

The man's face flushed even redder. He took a swing at Gonzo, who easily stepped out of the way. The man's fist swished through air and pulled him off balance. Staggering, he spluttered and swore again.

"I'll take the drunk," Steve said to Mandy. "You take Gonzo."

He stepped up to the man, put a hand under his elbow to steady him and steered him a few feet away from Gonzo. "Sir, let me introduce myself. I'm Steve Hadley, chief river ranger. Now, how can I help solve this problem?"

As Mandy took Gonzo's arm and dragged him away, Gonzo glared at her. "Why's Steve kissing up to that asshole? He should be ticketing him."

"He probably will, as soon as he gets the guy calmed down enough so he doesn't want to kill you anymore. Why'd you egg him on? You know better than that. What kind of impression do you think you're making on the customers?"

Gonzo glanced over at his group of rafters, whose faces held a mixture of shock, disgust, impatience, and anger. He swung back to Mandy, a retort on his lips.

But she had her own ready. "How's this help Uncle Bill's business, Gonzo?"

His chest swelled with bluster instantly deflated. "I'm sorry, Mandy. That fat slob made me so mad I couldn't think straight. I promised these folks we'd be back at the office by five thirty, and it's past five already. I don't know what to say to them."

Mandy blew out a breath. "I'll talk to them. Maybe the ranger outfit will help. And I'll help you load the rafts."

"I don't know how to thank you."

"Yes you do. Act like an adult and stop getting into fights with drunks." Mandy strode off to talk to the customers before she could make the mistake of adding, "like yourself."

She introduced herself, explained the situation, and told them that as soon as her supervisor got the other man to move his truck, Gonzo would be able to drive his vehicle to the boat ramp so they could load the rafts. She asked the group to follow her down to shore so they could preload paddles and PFDs into the rafts to speed up the process. With a mixture of diplomacy, assurances that they would be on their way soon, and jokes about wildlife on the river, she soon had the group back in a holiday mood and working together to pack up.

Twenty minutes later, she was waving goodbye to the customers as they loaded the van. She had an idea and turned to Gonzo. "As soon as I unload our equipment at the ranger station, I'll head out to Uncle Bill's. I want to talk to you there, so wait for me."

"Okay," he mumbled and rounded the front of the van to climb in.

As he drove away, Steve joined her.

"Did you ticket the drunk?" Mandy asked.

"I collected the money for his vehicle and pass fees and asked the most sober-looking of his buddies to drive the truck out. Long day, huh?"

"And it's not over yet."

———

Mandy pulled into her uncle's parking lot and stepped out of the car. All the rafters had gone, and their wetsuits were hanging out back to dry in the long rays of the setting sun. Gonzo and her brother sat in lawn chairs on the back porch, quietly talking and drinking beer.

Mandy slumped into a vacant chair, then shifted her weight to keep from sinking through the hole left by one torn strand of webbing. David wordlessly handed her a can of beer. Mandy took a long, cool drink to soothe her parched throat.

David poked his nose her way and gave a good sniff. "You don't smell too good."

"Thanks for the compliment, bro. I've been chopping up a tree all day. What have you been doing?"

"The cops came here this afternoon," David said.

"What did they want?"

"Don't know. They wouldn't tell me. But they had a search warrant and carted away all the trash from the bin out back."

Mandy thought about this. "King was poisoned." She turned to Gonzo. "Did you or any of the other guides bring food or drinks on the trip and give him any?"

"Like I'm going to give away food," Gonzo said. "You think manna rained down on my campsite or something?"

Mandy stared at him, hard.

Gonzo held up a hand. "I didn't bring anything, and I don't remember Dougie or Kendra or Ajax bringing any food either. Hey, we mooch off the customers whenever we can."

"Maybe someone else did," David said.

Mandy nodded and took another sip of beer. She leaned her head back and closed her eyes, trying to soak up a little warmth from the setting sun to ease her aching muscles. A fly buzzed around the opening to her beer can, but she could care less and didn't have the energy to brush it away.

"Okay, I can't stand it anymore," Gonzo said. "You can commence chewing me out again over the parking lot fight."

Mandy opened one eye to give him a baleful look.

Gonzo gave a theatrical shudder. "She's putting the evil eye on me."

"That's not why I wanted to talk to you. I want to know about Jeff King."

"Any relation to Tom King, the man you tried to save?" David asked.

"His son." *And another participant on that doomed rafting trip.*

David frowned. "What business is it of yours what his son is up to?"

Mandy didn't want to admit to her brother and Gonzo that she was ignoring Detective Quintana's request to stay out of the investigation. "Humor me. Gonzo?"

"I know Jeff from hanging out at the Salida boat ramp. He's a kayaking nut. Most summer evenings, he's there, taking his turn in the play queue. His father wanted him to get a business degree and go into real estate with him, but Jeff would have none of that. He's too busy having fun on the water. He dropped out of college after his freshman year."

"What's he doing now?" Mandy asked. "Is he a trustifarian, living off his father's money?"

"He wishes." Gonzo took a swig of beer. "Tom King cut Jeff off, said he could fund his own damn kayaking obsession."

"So what's Jeff do for money?"

"Guides kayak trips, enters events trying to win prize money, mooches off his friends. In the summer, he camps out on forest land. He signed up for the Pine Creek Boater X race, hoping to take home the Wave Sport kayak that's going to the winner. Says he's tired of patching up his old boat."

"Is he making enough to get by?"

"Not really. He's maxed out on his credit card, owes money to just about everyone in town, and all his friends, including me, are getting tired of him sponging off us. He's getting kind of desperate nowadays."

"And how did he feel about his old man cutting him off?"

"How else? Hates his guts."

Gonzo crumpled up his empty beer can, tossed it in the trash, and stood. "If you're not going to chew me out, am I free to go now?"

———

"You gonna tell me what that was all about?" David asked after Gonzo left. "Is this related to what you said last night about making the killer pay?"

"Don't worry," Mandy said. "I'm not out on any personal vendetta. I'm just trying to dig up leads that the Chaffee County Sheriff detectives can follow." *And that I can, too.*

The sun had slipped behind Mount Ouray, and the temperature dropped. Mandy rubbed her arms. "Tell me what you found out about Uncle Bill's business."

David stood. "Let's go inside where it's warm first. I'll heat up some stew. Uncle Bill left half a case of Dinty Moore in the kitchen. He seemed to live on that and Power Bars."

Mandy followed David inside. As she watched him open a couple of cans and dump them into a pot, she felt another twinge of guilt. "I kept telling him he should stop eating that stuff. It's full of saturated fat. Why didn't I throw those cans out and buy him some heart-healthy food?"

"Don't beat yourself up, sis. He wouldn't have eaten what you bought and would've restocked what he liked. You aren't responsible for what he ate." David turned on the stove burner. "Okay, here's today's bad news. When Gonzo pulled out the rafts for his trip today, one had a split seam between a side pontoon and the floor."

"Did he say whether he could repair it?"

David shook his head. "The material was shredded on one side, and Gonzo showed me where two other seams were gapping. He said the boat was dangerous. Shouldn't be out on the water."

Mandy sighed. "So it needs to be replaced."

"And that's expensive." David stirred the stew. "But there's no need to order a new one. We don't have enough customers scheduled in the next couple of weeks to run all the rafts anyway."

"More bad news." Mandy rested her chin on her hands. "Any good news?"

"Paula King dropped her lawsuit."

"Too late. The damage's already been done."

"I talked to your friend, Rob Juarez, about whether he could recommend someone to manage the business through the summer. He's quite the go-getter, you know. He used to put in long hours working construction at the same time as guiding in the summer and driving ski buses in the winter. He lived cheap and saved up a down payment on a business loan so he could buy his rafting business from the original owner. And to top it all off, he took business classes at the community college at night."

While he talked, David brought the stew pot to the table and scrounged up bowls and spoons, studying her all the while as if gauging how to break even more bad news to her.

Mandy had never asked Rob how he'd been able to buy his company, and felt a little piqued at herself that her brother had found out before she had. "Sounds like you two got pretty chummy."

"You know me. Love to talk business." David filled two bowls and passed one to her.

Impatient, Mandy asked, "And did Rob recommend a manager?"

"He said he might have a buyer for us, if we're interested in selling."

"I'm not interested in selling."

David blew on a spoonful of stew. then chewed on it slowly. "This stuff's not bad. Not good, either, but not bad."

"Did you hear me?"

"Yes, I did. And this guy Rob seems to have you pegged pretty well. He said you'd say that, and that I should talk to you before we went any further with the idea."

Mandy pushed her bowl away. After a few bites, she suddenly couldn't stomach the stew anymore. Suspicion was leaving a foul taste in her mouth. Suspicion that David and Rob had talked about more than this ridiculous idea of selling the business. Like how to handle her. And she didn't want to be handled.

"Well, I don't want to talk about it."

"We don't have to talk about it tonight.," David said. "I can see you're bushed, but we'll need to talk soon. In the meantime, we've got to start planning Uncle Bill's memorial service."

Mandy's eyes teared up.

David covered her hand with his and gave a gentle squeeze. "I know this won't be easy, but I'm sure you want his life honored in the right way."

He pushed a lined pad of paper and a pen toward her. He had written across the top, "Memorial Program."

———

Mandy spent Wednesday morning sweating and grunting at a self-defense class in the parking lot of the ranger station. Only the full-time head rangers were certified to carry weapons. The seasonal land and river rangers had to rely on the self-preservation techniques taught in the annual class when their diplomacy skills and status as law enforcement officers weren't enough to calm down agitated tourists.

During her lunch break, Mandy rushed over to the Final Touch Day Spa for her manicure appointment. The unassuming red brick building sat behind the Super Bowl Lanes facing Highway 50. On the window by the front door was a drawing of a woman's graceful hand holding a flower. When Mandy walked in the door, a wind chime tinkled in the breeze, announcing her presence. A white jarred candle glowing on the reception desk scented the room with vanilla, though it didn't completely mask the underlying chemical odors of hair coloring and nail polish.

Mandy signed in and refused the receptionist's offer of coffee or chamomile tea. She sat on the edge of a waiting chair and scanned the labels on an arrangement of colorful hair and skin care products and aromatherapy jars on the shelves across from her. *What is clear glossing gel used for? And what the heck is ylang ylang?* Just as she was about to grab a jar and take a sniff, a manicurist with spiky black hair and heels to match sashayed out and called her name.

The manicurist led her past the large pedicure chairs with their foot tubs to one of the three manicure stations in an airy, open room lit by plate glass windows facing west toward the highway and Methodist Mountain. Mandy mentally compared the young woman's chic black capri pants and green silk lingerie top to her own smudged and wrinkled shorts and T-shirt. Trying to smooth her T-shirt, Mandy wished she had changed clothes before coming to the spa, but it was too late now.

She spotted Evie Olson seated at the left station, wearing a yellow and pink print flowing skirt and a sleeveless pink top. Her wooden bracelets and necklace clattered as she tossed a hank of her unruly hair over her shoulder and leaned over to say something to her friend on her right. A woman brought them Styrofoam cups of tea, which they grasped gingerly with outspread fingers, their nails bright with drying polish.

The manicurist steered Mandy to a chair at the station behind Evie's friend and settled onto a stool across the white tabletop from Mandy. "You getting dolled up for a special event or treating yourself?"

Great opening. "I'm going to the FIBArk kickoff tonight."

"Oh, just like these two." The manicurist nodded toward Evie and her friend, who turned their heads.

Mandy leaned out to look around the manicurist at the two women. "Since we'll be at the same party, maybe I should introduce myself. I'm Amanda."

"I'm Shirley Logan," the friend said, "and this is my friend, Evie Olson."

"Nice to meet you both."

"What color polish do you want?" the manicurist asked.

"I have no idea." Mandy turned to Shirley. "Any suggestions?"

Evie examined the color of her own orange-pink nail polish at arm's length and seemed to approve. "What're you wearing?"

Mandy only had one dress in her closet, a little black number that Uncle Bill had paid for when she 'walked' for her associate's degree at Colorado Mountain College in Buena Vista. Before her eyes could start watering, she pushed the memory to the back of her mind.

"A short black dress," she answered.

A discussion ensued between Evie, Shirley and the manicurist about which was the best color for the combination of the black dress, Mandy's blond hair, and her green eyes. Intimidated, Mandy just listened.

"What color are your accessories?" Shirley asked.

"Ac-cessories?" Mandy stammered. She hadn't given a thought to anything but the dress.

"You know, shoes, purse, jewelry. Are you wearing something in your hair?"

This getting gussied-up is too damn hard. "I have a pair of black pumps and a black purse, but I hadn't thought about jewelry or anything else." She remembered her graduation gift from her brother. "Oh, I do have a gold chain necklace and hoop earrings to match."

"Gold and black," Evie said. "And are you going with a special someone?"

Mandy blushed and nodded.

"Okay, you should choose red, cherry red, and buy a lipstick to match."

The manicurist pulled out a bottle of polish and a tube of lipstick in a bright red color to show Mandy.

Mandy had never put such a bright color on her lips before. Usually, she just wore lip balm, to prevent chapping when she was out on the river. She only owned one tube of lipstick, a pale, pink color for when she hung out at Victoria Tavern. But she wanted to get on Evie's good side, so she nodded.

The manicurist reached for Mandy's hands and tsked over how short her nails were.

"If they were any longer, I'd break them off at work." Mandy was about to say what she did for work, but decided she shouldn't reveal that to Evie yet. "Just do the best you can."

While the manicurist filed Mandy's stubby nails, Mandy decided that since Evie had broached the subject of dates, her next question shouldn't be too suspiciously forward. "You two going to the kickoff with anyone?"

"My boring husband," Shirley answered. "Who will probably find a couple of equally boring husbands to talk football with. I swear if I hear another word about the Denver Broncos, I'm going to stampede out the door myself."

"I don't have anyone to go with now," Evie said with a sniff.

Shirley tsked. "Don't say that. You're coming with Mike and me. If he goes off to talk sports, we'll prowl the room and scout up some new prospects for you. You're too attractive to be without a man for long."

Mandy leaned forward. "Did you just break up with someone?"

Shirley put her empty tea cup down. "The guy she was dating just passed away, poor thing." She pointed her chin at Evie.

"Oh, I guess condolences are in order," Mandy said. "I'm sorry for your loss."

Evie harrumphed. "I'd already lost him before he died. The bastard broke up with me a few days before, went back to his wife." She put her empty cup on the side table next to her.

Feigning ignorance, Mandy asked. "So he was separated?"

Evie pursed her lips in disgust. "Yeah, the turncoat said he was divorcing his wife, but he moved back in with her three days before he died. I'll never forgive him for lying to me." Evie's voice went soft and sentimental. "Even though he's dead now."

Is she faking? "Wow, you sure got a raw deal out of that relationship."

"I agree, what a bummer." The manicurist shook her head and started applying the first coat of polish to Mandy's nails.

Mandy almost winced at the bright red color.

"Bummer indeed," Shirley said. "So who're you going with, Amanda?"

Focusing on the implication that Paula likely no longer had a motive to kill her husband since she had accepted him back into her house, Mandy replied without thinking, "Rob Juarez."

"Rob Juarez?" Evie's eyes narrowed in suspicion. "I know him. Are you Mandy Tanner?"

Caught, Mandy could do nothing but nod.

Shirley stared wide-eyed at Mandy. "You're the one who pulled Tom King out of the Arkansas."

"Yes, I'm afraid so."

Shirley glanced at Evie, her mouth pursed in a small "oh."

"And you come in here all sweet and innocent and pretend you don't know I was seeing him." Evie's tone was laced with hostility. "That was a dirty trick to pull."

Even the manicurist was frowning at Mandy now.

Mandy had to lie and lie good. She took a deep breath. "I'm sorry I didn't let you know right away who I was and that I knew who you were," she said to Evie. "I didn't think it would come up. And I do have a legitimate reason to be here. I really am going to the kickoff tonight and my nails looked terrible."

"That's for sure," the manicurist said.

"But you egged me on with your questions. Why are you so curious about Tom King's love life?"

Mandy feigned a casual shrug. "I feel a connection of some sort with him, I guess. Wish I could have saved him."

"How could you if he was poisoned?" Shirley asked.

"I didn't know that when I pulled him out of the river, and we still don't know who poisoned him."

The manicurist gasped and looked pointedly at Evie.

Evie stood and draped a large upholstery purse over her shoulder. "C'mon, Shirley. I don't like this snoopy ranger's questions." She glared down her nose at Mandy. "It's like she thinks I killed him."

———

Before going in the ranger station, Mandy used a tissue to wipe off all traces of the garish red lipstick the manicurist had liberally applied to her lips. She hid her nails in her fists while she went to her cubicle to check for messages. Rob had called while she was out.

She returned his call, knowing he would be running a shuttle soon for an afternoon trip, if he wasn't on the road already. When he answered, she could hear road noise and people talking in the background.

"I can't talk long, Mandy. I'll be in a dead zone soon. But I called to check if you still wanted to go to the kickoff tonight, what with your uncle and all. I'll understand if you back out, you know, and—"

"Yes, I'm still going." Rob was rambling, uncomfortable talking to her because of where they had left things, but Mandy wasn't going to bail him out—yet. Not when he wasn't in kissing range. "I'll be ready at five."

"I'm glad. I'll see you then." Static broke up what he said next. "—the canyon—losing signal." The line went dead.

Steve appeared in her doorway. "Time for class to resume. Whoa, what's with the nails?"

Two seasonal rangers appeared behind him. One shielded his eyes. "I'll need shades to protect my eyes from those flashers."

The other one grinned. "Red paint isn't going to give you any kind of advantage. You're still going to end up on the mat all afternoon."

"Oh, shut up." Mandy stalked outside to the sounds of snickers behind her. She assumed a belligerent stance on the far side of the mats lining the parking lot and shot her best combat glare at the other rangers assembled there. "First one who says something about my nails gets a fist in the gut."

TEN

*Ships are but boards, sailors but men: there be land-rats
and water-rats, land-thieves and water-thieves.*
—*THE MERCHANT OF VENICE*, ACT I, SCENE III,
WILLIAM SHAKESPEARE

MANDY STOOD IN THE shower with the water turned up as hot
as she could tolerate. She could wash off the sweat from the self-
defense class, but not the humiliation. She'd lost focus during the
class, rehashing Evie's news, plans for her uncle's service, and what
she might say to Rob to make up with him. So, she had been tossed
to the mat all afternoon. Fighting back tears of frustration, she had
gritted her teeth harder and harder through the afternoon until
her head was pounding.

During a break, she had gone inside her office and searched
in her desk drawer for aspirin. Finding none, she slumped in her
chair with her eyes closed and rubbed her head. Steve found her

there and offered her some of his own aspirin. Then he sat down and gave her a pep talk, saying it was understandable she was having a bad day. After all, her uncle had just died.

Mandy wasn't sure how much she could believe Steve's assurances that she was turning into a good river ranger, one he could count on. She sure felt inadequate now.

She stepped out of the shower and grabbed her towel. Two of her fancy-painted nails had broken, and polish was chipped off most of the rest. She would have taken off the polish, but she didn't have any remover in the house. And she couldn't send David out to get some. He had already left to grab a bite to eat in town before meeting her and Rob at the kickoff. He claimed he needed more sustenance than the itty-bitty snacks served at such events.

She was zipping her dress when the doorbell rang, sending Lucky racing out of the bedroom to bark and slobber at the door. Mandy slipped on her shoes and followed the dog. She opened the door and sucked in her breath.

Rob stood on the stoop with his wavy hair slicked back, his face clean shaven, and wearing a clean white dress shirt, a blue tie, and a shy smile. He looked good enough to eat, and she was hungry.

He opened the screen door and put out a hand to prevent Lucky from jumping on his dress pants. "Wow, Mandy, you doll up nice."

"I could say the same about you." She reached out a tentative hand to caress the crisp cotton fabric covering his chest. "Nice shirt."

He gently kneed the dog aside, stepped up to Mandy and ran his fingertips down the back of her dress. They burned a trail of fire through the fabric. "I missed you, *mi querida*. I hate you being mad at me. Can we kiss and make up?"

Her legs turning to pudding, Mandy said, "We've got some talking to do first."

"Kiss first. Then we talk." He bent his head.

She leaned into him and gave him a long, lingering kiss. She forgot all about why she had been mad at him, what he'd done wrong, because right now he was doing everything right. His hands roamed up and down her back, stoking the fire they had started.

When he lifted his head, she breathed in his musky cologne and put her arms around him to pull him to her again. She gave herself, and her lips, up to him. They kissed hungrily, with mouths open and tongues lashing, until they were both panting with desire. She felt him harden against her.

"Forget about the kickoff." His voice rasped with hoarseness. "I'll dance with you right here and now."

Lucky took that moment to snort in doggy-disgust and pad off to the kitchen. He started barking and clawing at the back door.

That was enough to break the spell for Mandy and clear her head. "Lucky, stop!"

The barking just got more frantic.

Rob grinned down at her. "Your dog obeys real well."

"Oh, hush. He must sense something's wrong out there. I'd better check." Reluctantly, she slid out of Rob's arms.

With a groan of frustration, he followed her into the kitchen.

Mandy tugged on Lucky's collar to pull the dog away from the back door and keep him from adding more scratches to its already marred surface. "What're you going on about?"

Rob sniffed the breeze coming in from the cracked-open window over the sink. "A skunk."

Mandy caught a whiff of the pungent animal. "No way am I letting you outside to get sprayed," she said to Lucky. "Please close the window, Rob."

He cranked it shut, but the smell was still strong. "Must be right outside. I'll chase it off." Rob put a hand on the doorknob, and Lucky strained against his collar.

"No, don't," Mandy shouted over Lucky's barks while she struggled with the dog. "What if it sprays you?"

But Rob was already outside. Lucky tugged Mandy to the open doorway. The stench was even worse outside. Rob went around the corner of the house toward the kitchen window, clapping his hands.

A dark shape with a white stripe down its back bounded across the yard.

Lucky leapt in the air, jerking Mandy off her feet. She landed on her knees, but managed to keep a hand on the dog's collar.

Rob rounded the corner. "Problem gone." When he saw her, he rushed to her aid, taking hold of Lucky's collar and lifting Mandy to her feet.

She checked her legs. Her hose were ripped, and the scab had come off the old scrape on her knee and was oozing blood. "Great. Now I have to change my stockings." She strode back inside.

Rob dragged Lucky inside and closed the door. "Can I watch?"

Mandy laughed, then glanced at the oven clock. "Sorry. We need to go, Rob. We're almost a half hour late already. Could you get Lucky settled down while I change?"

He dropped his hold on the dog and put his arms around her. "Can't we pick up where we left off?"

"We've both got businesses to represent at this function. You know we need to be there. And showing up late is no way to give a good impression."

He rested his chin on top of her head and took a deep breath, then pulled away and looked at her. "You're right, of course, but I'm taking a rain check that I plan to redeem as soon as I bring you back home."

"It'll be my pleasure." Mandy gave him a saucy wink before she headed back into the bedroom.

While she yanked off her torn hose and cleaned and bandaged her knee, Rob locked her back door and rummaged in the dog biscuit bag. Lucky's tail thumped loudly against the linoleum floor until his jaws snapped shut on what must have been a tossed biscuit.

Mandy tugged on a new pair of hose, yanked down her skirt, and slipped on her shoes. While she transferred items from her fanny pack to her black purse, Rob came back and leaned against the doorjamb, his appreciative gaze still making her pulse race.

He cleared his throat. "I want to apologize for what an idiot I was Monday, mistaking your brother for ... you know."

Mandy smiled at him. "A rival?"

"Yeah. Can't help wanting you all to myself, *mi querida*."

A flush of pleasure that she meant so much to him was soon followed by a tinge of annoyance at the tone of his comment, like she was a possession that no one was allowed to borrow. But she buried the annoyance quickly. She didn't want anything to spoil this evening.

Rob folded his arms across his chest. "He called me yesterday, though, and we talked for a good long while. He seems like an okay guy."

"He'd better be. He's my brother." Mandy shouldered her purse. "What did you two talk about?"

"You, of course." He held out his hand. "C'mon, you're the one who doesn't want to be late."

She grabbed her jacket and followed him out the door. They crunched across the driveway, Mandy teetering on her heels in the uneven gravel, to Rob's truck. While he drove to the Salida Steamplant, the old electrical power plant that had been converted into a performing arts center, her anxiety rose. Being this late, they'd never find a close parking spot, and walking from a far one would make them even later. She'd have to plunge right into networking.

"Who should I make sure I talk to?" she asked Rob.

He started naming all the owner-representatives of the different rafting outfitter businesses. While she listened, a small voice in the back of her head kept saying she and Rob had unfinished business of their own to settle.

Rob cruised slowly on Sackett Street past the tall red brick building squatting on the banks of the Arkansas River in downtown Salida. They both hunted for a parking spot on either side of the road. Everything was taken, including all the spots in the ranger station lot across the street.

Mandy finally located a spot three blocks west and Rob parked the truck. Trotting as fast as she could to the Steamplant, she stumbled in the unfamiliar high heels.

Rob caught her, tucked her arm in his, and pulled her close. "Slow down. Being another couple of minutes late won't make a difference. You don't want to rip another pair of stockings."

"And this is the last unripped pair I have."

Rob slowed their pace. "A lot of people are going to want to say something to you about Bill. He was well liked, and folks are going to miss him. Can you handle that?"

Mandy hadn't realized she would need to spend the evening talking about her dead uncle. "I—I don't know. I hope so."

"I'll try to stay close, and your brother will be here, too, right?"

"Yeah. But he's no better at this stuff than I am." They had reached the wooden steps up to the front door, and Mandy hesitated.

With his hand on the doorknob, Rob waited.

She took a deep breath. "Okay, let's go."

Rob opened the door. The loud buzz of conversations filled the lobby, along with a crush of people. Everyone else seemed to have arrived ages ago.

Mandy spotted glasses in many hands. She decided a drink would be a good idea, give her some courage. "Let's find the bar," she shouted over the noise to Rob.

He nodded, looked around the room, and steered her toward a corner bar on the left. A chime sounded three times, signaling that people should take their seats. Suddenly Mandy and Rob were trying to swim upstream against the current of people flowing into the theater.

Rob stopped and turned to Mandy. "Can you wait? If we don't go in now, we won't get seats."

"I guess I can wait." Mandy followed him into the theater and down the aisle until he located a couple of seats.

After she sat, an older woman on her left patted her hand and leaned toward her. "Sorry to hear about your uncle, honey."

Suddenly choked up, Mandy nodded and mumbled her thanks.

Rob gave her other hand a squeeze. "Courage," he whispered.

Thankfully, the emcee called for attention, and the lights dimmed. For the next hour, the FIBArk race competitors were introduced, the Board and Commodore of the event were honored, and a long list of volunteers were thanked. Finally, when Mandy thought her hands would fall off from clapping so often, the program ended. People streamed into the party room next to the theater to dance, drink, eat, and most importantly, since this was a Chamber of Commerce event, to network.

Mandy's stomach rumbled, and she still needed that drink. She grabbed a plateful of cheese, crackers, and veggies, and stood in a corner munching while Rob swam through the crowd toward the bar.

She spotted Detective Quintana nearby and approached him. "Hello, Detective."

"Hello, Mandy. Call me Vic. I'm off duty."

Instead of his Chaffee County Sheriff's uniform, he was dressed in jeans and a Western shirt. "So you are."

"Hey, let me offer my condolences. I was real sorry to hear about your uncle. He was a good man."

Mandy looked at her plate. "Yeah, thanks." She inched a piece of cheese onto a cracker, but decided against eating it. She would have to get rid of that lump in her throat first. "Any news on the King case?"

Quintana peered at her. "Still obsessing about that?"

Mandy blushed. "Not obsessing. Just interested."

"Uh-huh." Quintana looked around,then drew her away from the crowd, against the wall. "We found out that Lenny Preble brought a case of sports drink bottles and a few dozen donuts to the launch area and passed them out to the trip participants."

"Is that why you came by my uncle's place?"

Quintana nodded. "We collected all the trash from the trip and scoured the vans and rafts. We found the poison in one of the bottles."

"You think Lenny did it?"

"Not necessarily. One of the witnesses saw him cutting the heavy-duty shrink wrap off the case at the launch point, so he couldn't have doctored one of the bottles ahead of time. While the gear was being organized and loaded into the rafts, bottles were being passed around, tossed, and handed off. Anyone could have slipped the poison into King's bottle before handing it to him."

"I guess the big question is who had access to the poison."

"Right. And there's a profile that goes with poisoning. It's usually a woman's method of murder, because they don't like to get their hands dirty, so to speak."

"Now you're sounding sexist." Mandy smiled to show she was teasing.

"I know, so I'm not letting that influence me. Besides, anyone who's an avid gardener could have figured out how to make the powder. And there's the possibility that the poison in the bottle was a plant."

"A plant? What do you mean?"

"Someone could have given King the poison before the trip even began, then doctored a bottle to throw suspicion on the trip participants."

"Someone like his wife or son, who both had reasons to hate him?"

Quintana raised a brow. "I thought you were going to stay out of the investigation."

"People have told me things, like my friends, Cynthia and Gonzo. I discovered a few things about the trip participants that you should know." Then Mandy slipped in a little white lie. "And I ran into Evie at the Final Touch Day Spa when I got my nails done today at lunchtime."

Quintana glanced at her hands. "They didn't do a very good job."

"That was my fault. I chipped them at work this afternoon."

"So what did you find out from Evie?"

"First, let me tell you about my conversation with Lenny Preble in Bighorn Sheep Canyon yesterday." Mandy summarized what Lenny had said about the bidding war between Tom King and Nate Fowler and the angry looks Evie Olson and Paula King had been giving each other. That led naturally into her conversation with Evie and her friend Shirley Logan at the day spa.

Quintana stroked his mustache. "We've been investigating King's affair with Evie—probably why she was so touchy with you. But she acted aloof about King with us, as if she couldn't care less about him moving back in with his wife. You know, *que sera sera*. Interesting that she told you she couldn't forgive him, even though he was dead. Anything else?"

"Yes. Gonzo told me about King's son hating his father for cutting him off." She relayed how deep the young man's money problems were.

"Very interesting. When we interviewed Jeff King and his mother at their home, they both gave the impression that he was living there."

"Maybe he is, now that his father's gone," Mandy replied. "Maybe his mother doesn't feel the same way about Jeff's kayaking lifestyle but had to follow her husband's lead when he was alive."

"This information is useful, Mandy, but remember what I said. Leave the investigation to me. I'll follow up on Evie Olson and Jeff King, and I've got an interview with Nate Fowler tomorrow." Quintana scanned the room. "He's here tonight with his family. You wanted to meet his daughter, Hannah, right?"

"Yes, I need to thank her."

"I see them over there. I'll introduce you to her."

As they approached a family that included a middle-aged man and woman and a younger brunette, the brunette spied Mandy, squealed, and tugged on the man's arm. "There she is! The river ranger."

Mandy recognized the young woman as the one she had rescued, though she looked considerably different in a slinky maroon dress and heavily made-up eyes. Hannah Fowler gave little excited hops while Detective Quintana made introductions.

When he concluded, she almost leapt on Mandy to give her a crushing hug. "Oh, thank you, thank you, thank you for saving me."

Mandy pulled back. "I was going to thank you."

"Whatever for?"

"For holding on to Tom King and helping me get him out of the water. I couldn't have done it without you."

"I just did what you told me to do. Bummer that he died anyway, though. I might have, too, if not for you."

Nate Fowler stuck out his hand. "My wife and I also owe you our thanks, for bringing our daughter to shore, safe and sound."

Too embarrassed to say anything coherent, Mandy shook his hand and that of his wife. The two were both elegant and attractive, in their late forties. Nate had a patrician nose and a full head of wavy gray hair and wore a heavy gold watch and college class ring on his right hand. His handshake was confident and firm, but not crushing, like those of males who had something to prove.

A petite Hispanic woman matching Quintana in age came up to him and pulled on his arm. "Vic, I have someone you need to meet."

Detective Quintana waved goodbye, leaving Mandy to fend for herself with the Fowlers. She looked around for Rob, but couldn't spot him. She really needed a drink. Then she realized Nate Fowler had said something to her, but she had to ask him to repeat it.

"I was asking if you were related to Bill Tanner," he said.

"Yes," Mandy replied. "He is, was, my uncle."

"The whole community's going to really miss him. Were you two close?"

"He became my legal guardian after my parents died. Taught me everything I know about running rivers, and about running my life. So, yes, I'll miss him like hell." Mandy couldn't say any more, and popped a carrot in her mouth. She realized that was a mistake when she actually had to chew it.

Nate's wife gently touched Mandy's arm. "You have our deepest sympathies, dear."

"Did you inherit Bill's business?" Nate asked.

Mandy nodded. "That's one reason I'm here, so soon after…well, I thought I should be here to represent his business. There are a lot of people he had dealings with whom I've never met. Mister Fowler, maybe you can help me."

"Please. Call me Nate."

"My boss, Steve Hadley, told me that you serve on the Water Issues Board with him. I probably need to meet the others."

"I'd be happy to introduce you to the ones who are here." He turned to his wife and daughter. "Can we leave you two?"

"I'm sure we'll find some way to amuse ourselves," his wife replied.

"I'm glad one of us can help you, Mandy, in some small way," Hannah added. "I owe you so much for pulling me out of the river."

Nate took Mandy's arm and led her to a group of older men, who turned out to be fishing and hunting outfitters and guides. Two served on the board, and almost all of them had known her uncle. After accepting their condolences, Mandy let Nate steer her to a group of realtors and developers. He introduced her to them all, including one woman who served on the Water Issues Board with Nate.

That woman, a stern-faced fast-talker in an austere navy blue suit, asked, "Have you wrapped up that deal on the old Wilson estate yet, Nate?"

He scowled. "No."

"I thought with yours being the only bid left, it'd be smooth sailing." While peering at him, she stirred the olive in her martini then sucked it off the toothpick.

"Some of the councilmen preferred King's bid because it would bring in more tax money. I almost think they're waiting for someone else to step in with a similar plan." Nate took a sip of his Scotch and grimaced. "But that's not going to happen. In the three months since King and I bid on that property, no one else has shown any interest."

"What about someone picking up King's ball and running with it?"

"I've already talked to Paula King. She's not going forward with his plan, nor is anyone else she knows. This foot-dragging by the council is starting to piss me off. King's death seems to have actually slowed down the process."

Mandy decided to speak up. "Lenny Preble told me about this land deal. It includes old water rights, correct?"

Nate nodded.

"Lenny said he supported your bid over Tom King's," she continued, "because you plan to donate some of those rights for recreational use, while King was going to use them to develop a golf course."

"Right," he said. "Lenny's goal for that disastrous rafting trip was to either swing a couple of councilmen to my bid or to convince Tom he should reserve some rights for recreation if he won. I favored the first outcome, of course."

"Wasn't it uncomfortable for you two to be on the same trip, being rivals and all?"

The realtor woman gave a sarcastic snort, then folded her arms and looked at Nate, as if saying *I want to hear this.*

"Tom and I ran in the same circles, saw each other all the time. Going rafting together wasn't any different. Hell, Hannah was in the same raft with him and his family."

"Why wasn't she in your raft?"

Nate's eyes narrowed in suspicion. "What's with all the questions? You don't think I'm the one who poisoned Tom, do you?"

If he did poison King, why would he have risked having his daughter in the same raft, where she could have accidentally picked up his bottle to drink from? "No, nothing like that. I was just curious, since I pulled them both out of the river."

Quintana had talked about how the drinks had been passed around. Mandy tried to figure out a way to find out if Nate had handed one to Tom King without divulging that's where the poison was found. "How do *you* think he was poisoned?"

"None of the rest of us who ate Lenny's donuts was poisoned, so I think someone slipped it to Tom before the trip even started. The man didn't have what you call a stable family life. The cops should be looking there."

The realtor gave another snort while Nate downed the rest of his drink. He glared at her.

"Did you eat or drink any of Lenny's snacks?" Mandy asked.

"Yeah, and so did Hannah. Just about everyone took a donut out of the box when it was passed around."

Frustrated that she couldn't get him off the donuts and onto the sport drinks, Mandy asked, "What about the drinks?"

Nate waved his hand in disgust. "What about them? Who cares? As I said, the cops should be looking into Tom's personal affairs, not questioning innocent business rivals. And that's all it was, friendly business competition between Tom and me. I need a refill." He strode off to the bar.

The woman realtor polished off her martini and licked the last trace of gin off her painted lips. "Don't believe a word of what he says, honey. He and Tom were out for each other's blood."

Mandy stared as the woman winked at her and turned to follow Nate to the bar.

Rob approached, holding two bottles of beer. "There you are. I've been looking all over the room for you."

Mandy grabbed one of the beers and chugged down half of it. "And I've been looking for you. I was dying of thirst."

With a frown, Rob said, "You knew where I was, at the bar, but you wandered off."

"I'm sorry. I needed to talk to Detective Quintana and Hannah Fowler. And her father offered to introduce me to some members of the Water Issues Board. Remember, I'm representing Uncle Bill's business here."

Rob wiped beer off his lips. "Speaking of business, we need to talk."

David came up beside Rob and tossed his arm over Rob's shoulders. His flushed face showed he had been hitting the bar a few times. "Good to see you two together. I assume you've told Mandy about—"

"Not yet." Rob's voice held a warning tone. "I haven't had a chance."

Mandy looked from one to the other with growing suspicion. "Told me about what?"

Rob tugged at his collar. "Um, maybe—"

"About the buyer I mentioned," David said. "Isn't it great you two will be working together?"

Mandy glared at Rob. "*You're* the buyer?"

Rob put up his palms. "Now, don't get upset, Mandy. I wanted to break this to you gently, explain what I had in mind."

"It's obvious what you had in mind," Mandy said, anger boiling up. She clenched her hands, and both men took a step back. "You want to finish what you started and steal the rest of Uncle Bill's customers. Might as well, huh, given that his business is going to die along with him."

"Mandy, no—"

"And you." Mandy turned on her brother. "You went along with his scheme, just so you could rid yourself of the whole messy *problem* and get back to Colorado Springs."

David joined the chorus. "Mandy, no—"

"You've had enough." Mandy snatched the beer out of David's hand and shoved both her bottle and his at Rob. "We're going home in your car, and I'm driving." She pulled on her brother's arm and started walking away from Rob.

David shot a look of sympathy at Rob, which made Mandy's blood boil even more. What right did they have to sell off Uncle Bill's legacy, to decide her future?

"Don't be ridiculous," Rob said. "I brought you here. I'll take you home."

"No way," Mandy shot over her shoulder. "I don't want to have anything to do with you right now."

ELEVEN

The man who is swimming against the stream
knows the strength of it.
—WOODROW WILSON, 28TH PRESIDENT OF USA (1856–1924)

THE NEXT MORNING, MANDY stood on the narrow pebbled bank of the Arkansas River right below the Class V Pine Creek rapid in the Granite Gorge. Her heart felt as stony as the huge, dark boulders surrounding her, and her emotions boiled as violently as the furious water in the river. She couldn't decide who she was mad at more, her brother, whom she left snoring on the sofa, or her boyfriend, dangerously close to becoming her former boyfriend. The two had connived behind her back to sell off her uncle's business, with no thought to how she would feel about letting go of her uncle's legacy.

Typical bull-headed males. Why do they always have to be in charge, to assert their control over you, to run roughshod over your feelings?

She picked up a stone and hurled it as far upstream as she could. It plopped into the whitewater, to disappear and never be seen again, possibly to be rolled all the way down to the Pueblo Reservoir. Too bad she couldn't do the same with her problems.

A shoe scraped behind her, clattering pebbles down a trail that snaked into the steep gorge from the bank a few feet above Mandy's head.

She turned, her scowl still deep on her face.

A pimply teenage boy, wearing a FIBArk volunteer T-shirt, halted and started backing up. "Uh, never mind." He returned to the bank and the buzzing crowd of spectators and officials lining it.

Smart boy. He instinctively knew when a woman was cursing his whole sex and decided to steer clear.

Heaving a sigh, Mandy looked up at the sky. Another clear blue sunny day in Colorado. Not a good match for her mood, but good for the first day of FIBArk events, including the Pine Creek Boater X race, which was due to start soon.

Mandy had volunteered to be a shore rescuer below the meanest hole on the meanest section of what some folks called the meanest whitewater river in the American West. Five competitors would race in their kayaks in each heat of the race. They would jostle with each other for the right line through the maze of massive boulders and waves while fighting the river to stay upright and alive.

The crux of the half-mile-long Pine Creek rapid was the gigantic hole in front of her that stopped many competitors cold. If they were lucky, the river eventually spit their boats out. If they were unlucky, that was where the rescuers like Mandy came in.

Over the course of the day, quite a few of the boaters would take an unexpected swim.

Mandy swung the rescue throw bag in her hand, feeling the heft of it, loosening the anger-induced tension in her arm. When thrown at a kayaker who had been sucked out of his watercraft, the rope attached would play out. Mandy would loop the other end across her back, plant her feet, and serve as an anchor to the swinging line after the kayaker grabbed hold.

Her portable radio crackled. "All rescuers be alert at their stations. The first heat has started down."

Mandy looked thirty yards downriver, where another throw-rope rescuer stood waiting. She gave him a thumbs-up. He returned the signal and flashed the same to two volunteers in a rescue raft anchored to shore in a small eddy even further below him.

A cheer went up from the spectators. Soon, the bright primary colors of river-running kayaks appeared upriver. These boats were larger than the sprightly playboats Mandy had watched in the Salida river park. The purpose of these boats was to keep paddlers safely on top of the frothy surface of aerated whitewater and to turn fast in technical rivers instead of facilitating vertical show-off moves like cartwheels and loops. Their bigger cockpits allowed an easier "wet exit" if the kayak flipped and the occupant couldn't flip it back over, forcing them to pop the seal of the spray skirt covering the cockpit and flush out of the boat.

One kayak bounced into the hole and immediately flipped upside down. Mandy tensed in anticipation.

The paddler swept his paddle and swung his hips to right the boat, but the churning water immediately bashed it over again. After two more attempts and some furious power strokes, the kayaker popped his boat out of the hole and rocketed down the river. His elated "whoo hoo" echoed off the gorge walls.

Good recovery. Mandy scanned the rest of the river below the hole and counted five kayaks. All the boats in this group had made it successfully through the rapid.

Her radio crackled again. "Second heat heading down."

When the second group came into view, two kayaks rode the liquid roller coaster side by side, their occupants battling it out for the best position. One paddler's shiny blue helmet and PFD matched the color of his pristine boat perfectly. The other's orange helmet clashed with his sun-faded green PFD and yellow boat. Both the boat and helmet were liberally patched with duct tape.

The blue kayak nudged forward, and the back of the boat tapped the front of the yellow one, pushing it away. The color-coordinated kayaker rode a perfect line down the standing waves along the edge of the hole. The mismatched kayaker plowed straight into the hole and immediately flipped.

He struggled to an upright position one, two, three times, each time rolling over again. On the fourth try, his paddle flushed out of the hole. Spectators above Mandy gasped.

Without the paddle, she knew that flipping the kayak with just his hands would be near impossible. Expert kayakers did practice hand rolls in their kayaks, but that was in calm water. This guy probably was going for a swim.

She ignored the cries of the crowd and concentrated on the rocking bottom of the kayak, searching for the orange helmet to bob up out of the water. She counted ten, twenty, thirty seconds.

Where is he? Can't he get his spray skirt undone?

Finally, he popped out beside his boat, spitting water and flailing his arms. He managed to kick the kayak, which propelled him to the edge of the hole and flushed him out.

"Rope!" Mandy tossed the throw bag underhand and hit him smack in the middle of the helmet. A perfect throw!

The kayaker grabbed the rope, hooked it over his shoulder and rolled onto his back. Mandy loved it when the person being rescued knew how to do his part.

Quickly, she looped her end of the rope across her back. Grabbing tight on either side, she plopped down on her butt and braced one foot against a large rock. When the rope's length played out, the weight of the swimmer smacked the twisted cord against her spine. She leaned back in a body-belay position and dug the heels of her river sandals into the pebbles beneath her.

Her feet shifted as the taut rope pulled her toward the water. The rock bracing her foot loosened and tumbled away. *Shit!*

She scrabbled deeper with her heels, trying to stop her slide toward the roiling water. But the man's weight and the force of the water pushing him downstream were too much for her without good foot leverage. No matter how hard she strained against the rope, she could not stop her slow slide. She was dressed for a swim, in her shortie wetsuit and PFD, but that didn't mean she wanted to surf the rapids. She was about to holler "help" when she spied the rescuer downriver running toward her.

He grabbed the line and started hauling it in hand-over-hand as it swung the kayaker to shore.

Grateful for the release of the pressure off her back, Mandy stood and ran the rope a few yards downstream to a tall boulder. She wrapped the line around the boulder to anchor it then wound the slack around the boulder as the other rescuer pulled in the line.

Finally, the kayaker flopped on the shore like a beached trout, gasping for breath. Mandy and the other rescuer dropped the line and ran over to pull him the rest of the way out of the water. By the time the kayaker was safe, Mandy was gasping as much as he was. She leaned over with her hands on her knees to suck in air.

He sat up and pulled off his helmet. "Where's my boat?"

A bolt of recognition shot through Mandy. *Jeff King, Tom's son.*

"Still in the hole." The other rescuer waved his hand upstream, where the battered yellow kayak churned over and over.

Another kayak flushed into the hole. While its occupant worked to stay upright and exit the hole, his boat bumped Jeff's kayak out. It floated downstream, upside-down, spinning and bobbing in the waves and bouncing off half-submerged boulders.

Jeff slapped his knee. "Damn!"

Mandy's radio crackled. "Next heat's coming down."

"I'll take your place with my throw rope," her rescue partner said, "until you catch your breath."

Mandy nodded and took a few more deep breaths. She had brought three throw bags, but she decided to restuff the wet rope into its throw bag and reuse it. Because of the extra weight, a wet rope could actually be thrown better than a dry one. And, she didn't want to leave the rope on the bank where someone could trip on it.

When she started picking up the rope, Jeff scrambled to his feet, letting water sluice from his PFD and swim trunks. "Let me help you get that. It's the least I can do after you pulled me out."

"You almost pulled me in," Mandy joked.

Jeff peered at her. "You're Mandy Tanner, aren't you?"

"Yep. And you're Jeff King. I feel real bad about your dad."

Jeff stuffed the armload of rope he had picked up on top of the rest of the rope she had pushed into the bag. "I should apologize for Mom's behavior at Dad's memorial service."

Mandy shrugged. "She was upset about your father, I'm sure."

"Still. And she didn't even thank you for trying to save Dad." Jeff stuck out his hand. "Thanks. Gonzo told me what you went through to pull Dad out of the water and give him CPR."

Mandy's face flushed with embarrassment while she shook Jeff's hand. "Just doing my job. I only wish ..."

"He had lived? Yeah, well." Jeff stared down the river.

He didn't say he wished his father had lived, too. Mandy's gaze went upriver, tracking the next heat of kayaks splashing through the rapid. They all made it through safely.

Jeff faced her, a hang-dog expression on his face. "My boat's a goner."

"We've got volunteers at the finish line who should be able to retrieve your boat. Maybe your paddle, too."

"This was going to be the last race for that boat, and for sure it is now. I doubt it'll survive the bashing it'll get. Duct tape won't heal the wounds this time." A sheepish smile teased his lips. "I suppose you saw all the patching."

Mandy nodded. "Gonzo told me you really wanted to win that Wave Sport."

"*Needed* to win it," Jeff corrected. "That was a thousand-dollar boat. I could have sold it, bought a cheaper used one, and had some money to live on. I'm flat broke. Suppose I'll have to get a job now that I've blown the race."

"Working for your father's company?"

"No way. I have absolutely no interest in real estate."

"Will your mom help you out?"

Jeff shook his head and frowned. "She told me I could live at home, but she's not giving me one cent of cash. Dad got to her, won her over to the dark side. Even though he's gone now, she's not budging."

Mandy assessed him. Could he have poisoned his own father? He certainly didn't sound very broken up about his father's death. He hadn't said one word about missing him. "Will you get any inheritance money?"

"I wish! I thought I would, was looking forward to it. But Dad's will locked up my money in a trust. I can't touch it until I'm thirty, and then there's conditions attached."

"Conditions?"

"Yeah, becoming an upstanding citizen, a contributing member of society, and all that bull." Jeff kicked the pebbles at his feet, his mouth curled in distaste. "I'll eat dirt before that happens."

"What're you going to do?"

"Why are you so interested? You don't even know me."

"We've got *some* connection. I just pulled you out of the water."

He stared at her. "Like my Dad."

Mandy's radio squawked, "Next heat coming down."

Seizing this opportunity to extricate herself from the conversation, she said, "Gotta go," and ran to her station on the bank, allowing the other rescuer to return to his station downriver. She shouted to Jeff, "I hope your boat's okay."

He gave her a dismissive wave and started trudging up the trail to the upper edge of the gorge, shoulders slumped. If he had killed his father, the financial outcome certainly wasn't what he expected.

———

After shuffling paperwork all afternoon in the AHRA ranger office, Mandy was more than ready to head outside. She called David at her uncle's office, and he assured her he could check in the afternoon trip without her. So, she could fulfill her promise to volunteer as a river rescuer for the Media Challenge race in the Salida Whitewater Park.

The race was an excuse for spectators to jeer at local media celebrities and reporters for outdoor adventure magazines as they tried to navigate bright blue or yellow inflatable duckies through the gentle rapids. Most of the contestants took it in stride, hamming it up for the crowd.

To make it more difficult for them, ropes were strung across the river, from which hung paired-pole "gates" through which they were supposed to navigate their skittish craft. Since many were neophytes to whitewater, just staying upright and dry was usually the main goal. Mandy expected to have to fish quite a few out of the water.

While she meandered through the milling crowds and past the craft and food booths to reach the river, the tantalizing aromas of cotton candy, kettle corn, and roasted turkey legs reminded her that she'd skipped lunch. Maybe she could grab something to eat after the race.

A Frisbee sailed by, and Ajax leapt up to snag it. Yelling, "Catch, Mandy," he tossed it to her.

She caught it, flipped it back to him and waved goodbye. "Gotta go fishing."

Once she reached the river, Mandy teamed up with Kendra in one of her uncle's rafts. They waited in an eddy below the biggest drop, the most likely place for racers to wash out. Kendra paddled while Mandy grabbed swimmers by the shoulder straps of their PFDs and hauled them in. They often landed right on top of her, so she was soon soaked. She didn't mind, though. The dampness cut the heat of the warm, sunny day. After ferrying the sheepish reporter or news anchor to shore, she and Kendra would head back to their post to catch their next fish.

Everyone along the banks was enjoying themselves, clapping and hollering at the racers, and the beer was flowing as freely as the river. Mandy kept a sharp eye trained on the crowded banks on either side. A drunken spectator stumbling and falling in the fast-moving water, with no PFD or helmet and possibly no inkling of how to swim, was even more of a concern to her than the safety of the race participants.

During a lull between heats, Kendra rested her arms on the paddle across her knees. "What's going to happen to your uncle's company, Mandy?"

Mandy shot her a sharp glance. "Why do you ask?"

"There've been rumors among the guides that the business is in trouble and might close." She held out her palms. "Not that I want it to happen at all, but if it's going to, I need to know. All of us do. We're living paycheck to paycheck, most of us, and gotta start hustling for new work if the moola's gonna stop."

While Kendra talked, Mandy spotted Lenny Preble and a small group of followers passing through the crowd on the opposite bank. The environmentalists were thrusting flyers into people's hands. Often as not, once they had moved on, the flyers were dropped on the ground. Another trash cleanup job for Lenny was in the works—one of his own making.

Mandy looked back at Kendra and saw the deep concern furrowing the young woman's brow. "We don't have plans to close the business anytime soon. David and I are looking for someone to manage it when I can't be there. I promise you, if for any reason we have to close before the end of the season, I'll make sure you guides have at least three weeks' notice."

Kendra blew out a breath. "That's a relief."

Mandy returned to checking the crowd. A tow-headed little boy, about five or six years old, chased a springer spaniel with a Frisbee clenched in its mouth onto a pile of rocks jutting out into the current. Just as Mandy was about to holler, "Get off those rocks," the boy stumbled and fell in the water.

"Let's go," Mandy yelled to Kendra.

As the boy's head popped up out of the water and the current swept him toward the bridge, a man leapt in the water after him with a big sploosh.

A collective gasp went up from the people nearby.

Damn, now there are two of them. Mandy kept her gaze trained on both heads while Kendra shoved on the paddles.

They reached the man first, but he refused to be hauled in. "Get my son!" he sputtered. Before Mandy could grab him, he kicked off from the side of the raft.

Steve's advice after the Tom King incident would point to saving the man first. Given the man's refusal, however, Mandy had no choice but to do what he said. She yelled at Kendra, "Head for the boy."

Not much of a swimmer himself, the man's arms flailed in the current while he strained to catch up to his son.

Kendra's paddle power was more effective, and the raft nudged ahead of him.

After two more strokes, Mandy could reach the boy. She grabbed him under the armpits and hauled back. With his light weight, he almost flew out of the water and landed on the other side of the raft.

He laughed. "That was awesome!"

"Glad you think so," Mandy said with a grin and turned to Kendra. "Let's pick up his father."

Kendra nodded and back-paddled to slow the raft and ease up next to the floundering man.

He grabbed onto the side of the raft. Breathing heavily, he coughed a couple of times. "My son. Is he okay?"

"Yes, sir," Mandy said. "Let's get you in the raft now. When I pull under your arms, kick your legs as hard as you can to help me lift you in."

She rested her knees against the side of the raft, slid her hands under his armpits. "Now."

It took all her strength, but with him kicking, she was able to haul him halfway in. She grabbed his belt and spun his legs into the raft.

He flopped on the bottom of the raft, coughed a few more times, and held out his arms to the boy. "Come here, Ricky."

The boy fell on his father's chest, making the man gag again, and hugged him tightly. The boy seemed to be fine, but Mandy worried about the father, who seemed to be having trouble catching his breath. She observed them both carefully while she and Kendra ferried them to shore.

After the man and his son climbed out and thanked them, Mandy said to Kendra, "I'm going with them. Once I'm sure they're okay, I'll catch up with you."

"No rush," Kendra replied. "We've got plenty of rescuers here hoping for a chance to pull a celebrity out of the water."

Mandy trotted after the wheezing man and his son. "Sir, I'd feel a lot better if you two came with me to the first aid station."

"Why? We're fine. What I need to do is find our dog and get my son home so we can change out of these wet clothes."

Typical macho male. Knowing he wouldn't go for himself, she appealed to his fatherly concern. "I'd like to have the paramedics check your son. Make sure he didn't swallow too much water. Then you can look for your dog. The tent's this way."

To prevent further argument, she took hold of the boy's hand. "I hear they have lollipops, too."

"Cool!"

With the boy skipping excitedly at her side, Mandy started walking toward the first aid tent. He didn't seem to care a whit that he was soaking wet. At least it was warm enough in the sun that Mandy didn't have to worry about hypothermia.

The man followed, though his steps seemed slow and reluctant. He kept looking around, searching for the dog.

One of Lenny's flyers blew across the grass and stuck to Mandy's calf. She pulled the paper off and stuffed it in her pocket. *I've got to get Lenny to clean these up.*

About the time they reached the first aid tent, the family dog ran up to them, its fur drenched. The plastic blue Frisbee was still clutched in its mouth.

The father plopped down on a chair and petted the dog while a first-aid staffer checked out his son and handed the boy his much-anticipated lollipop.

"No problems here," the staffer said to her.

She pointed her chin at the boy's father. "Check the dad."

"I don't need to be checked." The father stood, and his hand went to his chest.

"Did you happen to swallow or breathe in any water when you were in the river?" Mandy asked him.

"Yeah, I think so." He gestured to the boy. "C'mon, son, time to go."

The attendant who had checked the boy was hearing all this, but he didn't seem to have the same alarm bells ringing in his head that Mandy did. He busied himself with stowing supplies.

Am I being overcautious? Am I going to make this father angry for no good reason? Mandy's stomach rumbled. She was hungry, the man wasn't cooperative, and having handed him over to the first aid tent, he wasn't her responsibility any longer. Maybe she should just let him go on his way. Then she could grab something to eat.

The father and son turned to leave.

Mandy bit her lip and reviewed the symptoms in her mind. The feeling that something wasn't right nagged at her again. *No, I've got to stop him.*

She put a hand on the man's arm to prevent him from leaving. "What's it feel like when you take a deep breath?"

The man looked at her with annoyance, but she kept her hand on his arm. "Take one now."

He drew in a deep breath. He promptly started coughing and clenched his chest. When he got his breath back, he said, "It feels like a fire burning in my chest."

"Please sit down."

"Oh, c'mon."

Mandy made her voice more forceful. "Please sit down, sir." She stared at him until he slid back into his chair.

The attendant, who had been listening, pulled Mandy aside, out of hearing of the father. "You think this is a parking lot drowning?"

Mandy nodded. "If we don't get him to a hospital, he could die."

"Keep him here. I'll call an ambulance." The attendant walked over to the phone on the check-in table.

Mandy squatted beside the gasping father. "I'm sorry to have to tell you this, sir, but your condition is serious. We're calling an ambulance for you."

The man's eyes widened. "You've got to be kidding me."

"No, I'm not. You aspirated some water into your lungs when you were in the river. The water's breaking down the surfactant in your lungs that keeps fluids from clogging the airways. So now, body fluids are leaking in, filling up your lungs. Pretty soon, you won't be able to breathe."

"It doesn't feel that bad to me. I don't really need to go to the hospital, do I?"

Mandy had to convince him how serious this was. She appealed to his fatherly concern again. "Only if you want to be around tomorrow to play Frisbee with your son."

TWELVE

So we beat on, boats against the current,
borne back ceaselessly into the past.
—*THE GREAT GATSBY*, FRANCIS SCOTT FITZGERALD

MANDY STAYED TO ENSURE that the man and his son were loaded into an ambulance. When he called his wife, Mandy got on the cell phone to explain the urgency of his case. She didn't hand the phone back until she was sure his wife would take over in nagging her husband to submit to treatment.

The first-aid attendant promised he would watch the dog, which Mandy had tethered to a nearby tree.

Once convinced she had done all she could, Mandy set off through the crowd to find Lenny Preble. She picked up a couple of the flyers along the way. Below a muddy smudge, the title of one read, "Save the Arkansas!" A cartoon below it showed a devil dumping a front loader full of uprooted trees into the river. Over-kill, but it got the point across.

While searching a block lined with vendors of outdoor sports equipment, adventure magazines, freeze-dried hiking foods, and high-tech sun protection products, she spotted Lenny and his gang wolfing down granola samples at a natural foods booth. In addition to the forest green T-shirts, they all wore matching baseball caps emblazoned with Lenny's nonprofit logo. She walked over to them. "Hi, Lenny."

"I see you have some of our flyers," he mumbled, then swallowed his mouthful. "How do you like the devil cartoon? I drew that one myself."

Mandy thought she recognized some familiar features in the devil's face. "Who'd you base the devil on?"

Lenny grinned and sidled up to her. "Can you keep a secret, since I don't want to disparage the dead? The flyers were printed a couple of weeks ago. I modeled the devil after Tom King. Though Nate Fowler's not much better. You think the flyers get the message across?"

"Yes, I do. Unfortunately, a lot of them, like these, are winding up on the ground."

"Stupid tourists." Lenny waved his hand at a nearby trash receptacle. "Can't they see the trash cans all over the park? If they don't want to read about how developers are ruining the river, the least they can do is properly dispose of the flyer."

Mandy nodded. "No disagreement here. I know how much you care about the river, Lenny, with your litter patrols. I was wondering if your group would be willing to do one along the festival grounds." She held out the muddy flyers she had picked up. "Since some of the litter, unfortunately, is indirectly coming from you."

A scowl crossed Lenny's face. He pulled out his car keys and handed them to one of his cohorts. "Go get some of the heavy-duty trash bags out of my car."

He made a point of deliberately walking over to the trash can next to the granola stand and throwing his bowl in there. He glared at all the tourists around him and cleared his throat loudly at two teenage girls who had gotten up from a table and left their bowls.

They sheepishly returned and threw the bowls in the can.

"Thank you very much." Lenny's voice dripped with sarcasm. He took the flyers out of Mandy's hand and dropped them on top of the granola bowls.

"And thank you, Lenny. I knew I could count on you," Mandy said. "Just like you picked up all the trash from the donuts and drinks you served on the trip last week."

"How'd you know about the snacks?"

Rather than reveal that the police now had the trash, Mandy told a white lie. "Gonzo told me. He loves donuts. Were you the one who handed them out, and the drinks?"

Lenny's eyes narrowed. "Noooo, not all of them. A lot of people helped themselves or passed things to others in their family or raft."

"Who gave Tom King his?"

"How the hell should I know?" Lenny said with a shrug. "I wasn't paying attention. Why's it matter to you, anyway?"

"You know that Tom was poisoned, right?"

"Yeah, it was in the paper. How do you think the cops found it? The autopsy?"

Mandy shrugged. *I know, but I'm not telling.*

Indignation purpling his face, Lenny snapped to military attention as if someone had rammed a rod down the back of his shirt. "He couldn't have been poisoned by the snacks. No way. The drink bottles were shrink-wrapped, and the donut boxes still had the tape on them from the store. Besides, I heard he was poisoned hours before the trip started."

"Who said that?"

Lenny waved his long-fingered hand dismissively. "Any of at least fifty people who've accosted me in the past few days. Everyone wants to find out what I know about King's death and to tell me what they think happened. I hope you haven't been listening to people's wild-assed theories."

He thrust out his chin. "Who thinks I killed Tom King?"

Mandy put up her palms. "No one's accusing you, Lenny, especially not me."

Thankfully, his cohort returned with the trash bags and tossed Lenny's car keys back to him.

"I'll let you get to work," Mandy said, backing off. "Thanks again for volunteering to pick up the litter."

Lenny grabbed a trash bag from his friend. "You know, some people in this town deserve to be stuffed in a trash can like the rest of the garbage."

———

Mandy wrinkled her nose at the giant pretzel smothered in warmed-over cheese sauce that she had bought for her dinner. Tentatively, she took a bite, chewed the cloying lump, and swallowed. It wasn't her usual natural fare, but it would quiet the beast growling in her stomach. And it was the cheapest meal she could find among the food booths at the festival. She forced herself to take another bite and looked upstream at the starting line of the Raft Rodeo.

She had wormed her way into a prime spot along the railing of the F Street Bridge spanning the river, so she could watch Rob compete. He and his secret partner, whom he had refused to name to Mandy, had been practicing at the Salida Whitewater Park whenever they could get free in the evenings. The prizes were a joke, because the race was designed primarily to entertain the crowd, but the competition for bragging rights among the outfitters was fierce.

Mandy spied David strolling along the paved path next to the river, his gaze scanning the crowd. She waved to him and yelled his name.

He waved back and headed toward her.

While she waited, she took a few swallows from her water bottle to rinse the glue-like cheese out of her mouth. Even though it was approaching 6:30 pm, the start time of the race, the hot sun was still baking the crowd. The sun wouldn't set for two more hours, so sales of cold beer, sodas, and water bottles were brisk. She smiled at a knot of giggling teenagers who were using the heat as an excuse to rub ice cubes across each other's necks and backs— preferably a member of the opposite sex.

David came up behind her and peered over her shoulder at the paper plate in her hand. "You going to finish that? I'm famished."

Mandy glanced at the half-eaten pretzel, the sauce congealing, and handed it to him. "Take it from me, please."

She waited for him to take a few ravenous bites. "How'd things go today?"

"Not bad. We had some walk-ins. Two couples. So we sent three rafts down Brown's Canyon this afternoon instead of two."

Four was better, even five, but with their fifth raft blown, that wasn't possible. Before Mandy could ask David if he had come across any good news, or more likely, more bad news in her uncle's books that day, the announcer introduced the first heat of rafts.

One team, the "Whitey Tighteys," wore briefs over their poly leggings, and another had a large golden retriever wearing a doggy PFD sitting in their raft as ballast. The dog didn't help much. When the paddlers tried to stand their raft on its end in the play hole above the town launch ramp, all three occupants went for a swim.

The underwear-clad team executed a spin, set their raft on its side in the hole, and surfed back and forth to cheers from the crowd. After peeling out, they stood and bowed while their raft bobbed down the river.

"That'll be a tough team to beat," David said to Mandy.

Mandy grinned back. "Just wait. I bet Rob's got some tricks up his sleeve." Then she remembered she was supposed to be mad at him.

David pushed forward to stand beside her and leaned on the bridge's concrete railing. "You know, Mandy, I'm convinced Rob's motives for offering to buy the company aren't selfish. He's not trying to steal Uncle Bill's customers. He really wants to help us."

"I know that now, after sleeping on it. But that's not really why I'm mad at you two."

David stared at her, puzzle lines wrinkling his forehead. "I don't understand."

"See, that's another symptom of the whole problem. You and Rob are both so wrapped up in taking charge and making decisions that you can't even see when you're stepping on people."

"You think we're stepping on you?" Realization dawned on his face. "Oh, you wanted a say in the decision. But that's why Rob and I wanted to talk to you, to explain his proposal—"

"Dammit, David." Mandy slapped the concrete, making her hand sting. "Rob should have come to me first with that proposal, not you, or at the very least, both of us. I should have been in on it from the get-go. Uncle Bill *did* leave half the business to me, you know."

"Step into Rob's shoes for a minute. You've been so touchy around him lately, then you were grieving for Uncle Bill. He was afraid to approach you with the idea, afraid to approach you at all."

Mandy frowned. "Is there anything about our relationship that Rob *hasn't* told you?"

"Frankly, I don't want to know anything about my little sister's love life, even the fact that you have one. I still like to think of you as an innocent teenager."

He flashed a smile to show he was joking, but when Mandy thrust her jaw out at him, the smile faded. "C'mon, Mandy, we're not trading secrets behind your back."

"No, just conspiring behind my back. Planning my future without my input. Like I'm still a helpless kid, which in case you haven't noticed, I'm not." She folded her arms across her chest and stared at a raft attempting an end-o in the play hole. She barely noticed when it flipped over.

David put a hand on her arm to turn her toward him. "No, you're not still a kid. I'm sorry if I treated you that way. I'm just—" He let go of her arm. "Just trying to make up for … you know."

"No, I don't know."

David leaned forward on the railing and stared at the water rushing under the bridge. "For not helping you more after Mom and Dad died. For palming you off on Uncle Bill so I could finish my degree."

"I never felt like I'd been palmed off."

"Well, I felt damned guilty for doing it."

Mandy threw an arm around his back and talked softly into his ear. "Don't David. I love, loved, Uncle Bill, and he gave me everything—a home, education, security, and a shoulder to cry on whenever I needed it. You couldn't have done all that. You were only nineteen yourself."

"I could have given you that shoulder," David mumbled. "And when I heard Uncle Bill had died, and you were alone again, the guilt came rushing back. I wanted to do a better job of it this time, make up for neglecting you before."

"So that's why you're meddling in my life."

"Meddling!"

When David looked at Mandy, she half-smiled to show she was half-joking.

"Okay, point taken," he said. "Sorry I tried to make decisions for you."

"Apology accepted. Now, if I could just make Rob understand."

"I'm sure you can. He seems like the kind of guy who'll listen. And he loves you, Mandy."

A thrill went through her. "You think so?"

David arched a brow. "Oh, yeah."

Just then, the announcer's voice bellowed over the loudspeaker, "Our next entry is the infamous swordsman, El Zorro, and his voluptuous wife, Elena!"

"That's got to be Rob. Zorro's his hero." Mandy craned her neck to search upriver for Rob's raft.

"Who's the well-endowed Elena?" asked David.

"I have no idea." Mandy spied the raft and pointed.

Rob stood in the front of the raft, flourishing a rubber sword and wearing a black mask, black cape, and black gaucho hat tied over his helmet. His obviously male partner in the back wore a long black wig over his helmet. Two soccer balls jiggled under his extra-extra large red dress, their white hexagons peeking out from the gaping top.

The crowd clapped and hooted.

Mandy giggled. Which of Rob's rafting guides had the gumption to dress in drag? They were still too far away for her to make out Elena's face.

When the raft approached the play hole, Rob tossed the sword aside and hunkered down with a paddle to help his partner. The two slid expertly into the hole and spun the raft a few times. Then they high-sided the raft, slipping one edge under the foaming water while sitting on the high side to keep it from flipping. They slid off to one side of the rapid, let the raft settle onto its bottom, then spun it end-on to the play hole and started paddling toward the center.

"They're going to attempt an end-o!" Mandy yelled to David.

Zorro-Rob and his mock-Elena stood on the upstream end of the raft. They dipped the upstream end under the water while pulling on ropes on either side of the raft to lift the downstream end. It rose, flashing the bottom of the raft to the crowd lining the banks and bridge, until the raft was almost vertical. The raft danced on its tail in the water to the cheers of the crowd. The two men expertly held it in place and upright with one hand each and made small paddle corrections in the water with their other hands.

They could only hold the position for a few seconds, though, until the bottom of the raft came crashing down onto the water, taking both paddlers with it. The false Elena bounced off the raft and into the river. While splashing back to the raft and climbing in, he lost his wig. The black mass undulated in the current like a multi-tentacled octopus.

Mandy recognized the ropy, matted dreadlocks peeking out from underneath the man's helmet. She grabbed David's arm. "It's Gonzo! Elena is Gonzo."

David laughed then put two fingers in his mouth and let out a loud wolf whistle in Gonzo's direction.

Gonzo looked up at the bridge, spied Mandy and David waving at him, grinned and waved back. He shouted at Rob, who had gotten back on his feet and was flourishing his cape and bowing to the crowd along the bank as the raft floated by. The two men looked up at the bridge as they slid under.

Mandy leaned over to wave at Rob.

Her Zorro tore off his mask and threw her a theatrical kiss, but his eyes conveyed a different message—confusion and a question.

———

While Mandy drove home, she reviewed the conversation she'd had with David when he walked her to her car. He said the only way they could keep Uncle Bill's business afloat was to run at full capacity all summer, which was impossible with the cancellations and blown raft. Too exhausted to brainstorm solutions, Mandy had said she wanted to sleep on it.

David had said he would drink on it, this being his last night in town. They could talk more in the morning before he returned to Colorado Springs to put out some fires at work. He promised to return for Uncle Bill's memorial service on Monday.

When he had asked if she would be all right by herself until then, she'd said, "There you go again," and he backed off, but not before Mandy saw the hurt look on his face. Was she being too hard on both Rob and David? Should she just give up on Uncle Bill's legacy

No, I'm not ready to do that yet.

When she pulled the Subaru into the drive, Lucky went bonkers and started barking and jumping up against the chain-link fence. That wasn't normal. Mandy opened the gate to let the dog out into the front yard. When she went in the front door, Lucky pushed past her then ran into the kitchen and ran back, barking continuously.

Mandy followed the frantic dog into the kitchen and turned on the light. Broken glass lay scattered on the sink, counter, and floor. The Venetian blinds over the sink window slapped against the sill.

What the hell?

Mandy stepped back into the living room. "Here, Lucky!"

The dog ran to her, and Mandy checked his paws, one by one. No cuts, yet. She commanded Lucky to sit, then stepped into the kitchen and slid the pocket door between it and the living room shut to keep the dog away from the glass fragments. Lucky immediately started barking from the other side.

"Hush! It's not safe for you in here."

The barking subsided to a whine and snuffles at the door crack.

After stepping carefully over the glass, Mandy pulled up the blinds. Her window glass was gone, except for a few shards. A big hole was punched out of the screen. Mandy searched the kitchen. She spied a large rock under the kitchen table, with a white piece of paper rubber-banded to it.

She leaned down, keeping her knees off the floor, and picked up the rock. She yanked the paper free and spread it out on the kitchen table. Words cut out of the newspaper had been glued to it. They read, "Keep your nose out of the Tom King business or else!"

Or else what? Heart pounding, Mandy checked the kitchen door. Locked.

She walked to the pocket door, took off her shoes in case some glass had gotten embedded in the soles, and pushed past Lucky's inquisitive nose. She locked the front door and returned to the kitchen, closing the pocket door in Lucky's face again.

She put her shoes back on, grabbed the broom leaning in the corner and started sweeping. Nothing like action to drive away some of the panic. But as she worked, she kept glancing at the note.

Everyone she had talked to lately about Tom King had ended up angry at her or suspicious of her motives. She reviewed her conversations over the past few days with Lenny Preble at the Salida Riverside Park, Jeff King at the Pine Creek Boater X, Nate Fowler at the FIBArk Kickoff, and Evie Olson at the Final Touch

Day Spa. They all had potential motives for killing Tom King. None of them had liked her probing questions. And Paula King had yelled at Mandy at her husband's memorial service.

Was one of them upset enough to throw the rock through Mandy's window? Was the rock thrower Tom King's killer? Or could this message have come from someone else? Someone Mandy hadn't talked to yet, but who heard she'd been asking questions.

She swept the glass into the dustpan and dumped it in the trashcan. Then she checked the bottoms of her shoes. Lastly, she wet a paper towel and wiped the floor to pick up any remaining small fragments. With the floor clean and safe for Lucky's paws, Mandy opened the pocket door.

Lucky pushed in and shoved his head under Mandy's hand, begging for petting, for assurance that everything was all right. While staring at Mandy, the dog's eyebrows worked back and forth, a sign he was worried.

With good reason. After calming Lucky with a good rubbing behind the ears, Mandy washed her hands, then unscrewed the cover of her peanut butter jar, dipped her finger in and sucked on a gob of comfort food. It didn't give her much comfort tonight, though.

If someone was threatened by or angry at her enough to throw a rock through her kitchen window, what would they do next? Or would they wait to see what she would do next?

She looked at the window. The glass shards were still there. She stood.

Taking this action to mean they would be going for a walk, Lucky went to fetch his leash.

But Mandy had no desire to leave the relative safety of her home for the streets. Not when the willies were still sending shivers down her back.

"Sorry, Lucky. I've got to get the rest of that glass out of the window. You'll just have to do your business in the yard."

She flipped on the back porch light and peered outside, searching the yard for movement. Nothing. But that didn't stop her from continuing to look for a few more minutes.

Lucky finally scratched at her sneakers.

"Okay, okay." Mandy's hand shook as she reached for the doorknob.

THIRTEEN

Drinking nature is an unquenchable thirst.
—BERRI CLOVE

MANDY DROVE TO HER uncle's place. Friday was her day off from river rangering, but with a business to run, it wasn't going to be a day of rest. She would be working nonstop through the summer. And last night hadn't been very restful either. Even with Lucky beside her in the bedroom, she hadn't felt safe until she heard her brother let himself in.

He hadn't arrived until well past midnight, so she didn't have the heart to wake him before she left. She tip-toed out, leaving him sprawled and snoring on the couch. She left a note on the kitchen table asking him to call or stop by the business before he headed back to Colorado Springs.

She glanced at the passenger seat of her Subaru, where she had tossed the threatening message from last night's rock. She would have to get her window replaced today. And she would have to face Detective Quintana. And when she told him, she would have to admit to her conversations with the suspects.

Which would reveal she'd done exactly the opposite of what he had told her to do.

After she parked in her uncle's lot, she checked her watch. Customers for the morning trip would be arriving in half an hour. No time to call Quintana now. It would have to wait until after she ran the morning shuttle.

Kendra and Dougie were moving around the equipment yard, loading three rafts and handfuls of paddles onto the top of the bus. This was a good sign—the first time in days that they had booked more than a vanload of rafters. But where was the third guide?

Mandy joined them, shielding her eyes from the glaring rays of the morning sun. Though strong enough to make her squint, the sunbeams hadn't cut through the morning chill yet. Dew still clung to the grass and to equipment which had been left outside overnight. "Who's the third guide?"

Kendra hesitated and glanced at Dougie. "Gonzo."

"Where is he? He should have been here half an hour ago."

Dougie shrugged and Kendra bit her lip.

Mandy pulled out her cell phone, feeling a tension headache coming on. "I'll call him."

Just as she finished dialing his cell phone number, Gonzo's car pulled into the parking lot. It screeched to a bouncing halt beside Mandy's. He stepped out, slammed the door, and took a step toward them. Losing his balance, he put a hand on the back of Mandy's car to right himself, then leaned into a sweeping bow, as if trying to cover up his stumble.

"Queen Elena at your service." A giggle burbled out of his lips before he could assume a straight face and stiff posture.

Mandy snapped her phone shut and pocketed it. A fit of giggles wasn't what was burbling up in her gut. She waited while Gonzo stepped carefully toward her. "You're late."

"Hey, after the night I had, I'm lucky I'm here at all." He put a hand to his head. "Woo, I don't know how many beers people bought me. I'll have to dress up as a girl more often."

He started laughing, but when no one joined in, his laughter died out. "Seriously, Mandy, you missed a hell of a party at the Vic. Your brother sure enjoyed himself. Everyone was asking him where you were."

As Gonzo spoke, stale beer fumes wafted toward Mandy. She studied his bloodshot eyes, his unsteady feet, and his shaky hands. *Had Uncle Bill had to handle this before with Gonzo?*

"You're still drunk, aren't you?"

"Nah," Gonzo overshot his wave of dismissal and spun around. "I musta gotten at least three hour's sleep this morning. I'm raring to go." He snorted and rubbed his hands together. "Ready, brave Knight Dougie? Lovely Princess Kendra?"

When Dougie and Kendra just stood there looking at him, Gonzo put his hands on his hips. "Party poopers. I guess I'll have to keep these tourists entertained all by myself."

Dougie and Kendra's reaction bolstered Mandy's confidence. They didn't appreciate Gonzo's behavior any more than she did. She certainly couldn't allow him to lead customers through dangerous whitewater.

"No, you won't. You're not working today." Mandy turned to Kendra. "You got Ajax's cell phone number?"

When Mandy pulled out her phone, Gonzo grabbed her arm. "Hey, I'm here. And I'm ready to work."

"I'm not entrusting the safety of our customers to you in this state, Gonzo. Go sleep it off." She shook her arm in an effort to release his grasp, acting more sure of herself than she felt.

Gonzo's fingers dug in deeper. "But I have to work today. I'm broke."

Mandy knew how close he was to abject poverty. Most of the seasonal rafting guides barely scraped by on the low pay and erratic hours. They were so addicted to the highs from running whitewater that they put up with sleeping in tents and eating peanut butter on saltine crackers so they could be on the river.

But she had a business to run. She couldn't let Gonzo see how much she sympathized with his predicament. Her mouth in a firm line, Mandy pried his fingers loose and pushed his hand off her arm. She took a deep breath to calm her nerves.

"You should have thought of that before you drank all those free beers. Consider this a warning, Gonzo. You show up here for work drunk again, I'll have to take you off the payroll."

Gonzo's face turned dark. His fists balled up. "You can't talk to me like that. I'm one of the best guides on the Arkansas. I can show up at any outfitter's, including your buddy Rob's, and they'd hire me in a heartbeat."

"Go ahead and try," Mandy said. "They won't put a drunken guide in charge of a raft either."

"Screw you. I don't deserve this grief. I quit." Gonzo stomped to his car.

Mandy started after him. "Gonzo, wait. Don't drive like this."

He refused to look at her as he started the engine and peeled out of the parking lot, his spinning wheels spouting gravel.

Kendra came up to stand by Mandy. "You think he'll be safe on the road?"

"At this point, I don't care." Mandy rubbed her throbbing head. "Sorry, I do care, but I'm so mad at Gonzo I could spit fire. I wish he hadn't put me in that position. I hated having to tell him off."

"He deserved it this time." Kendra handed Mandy her cell phone. "Ajax's number is on the screen. Just press the call button."

Mandy called the guide's number and explained the situation to him.

"Gee, Mandy, I sympathize," he said, "but I can't make it in until the afternoon trip. I'm in Buena Vista now, and I don't have my car. I'm waiting for a friend to come pick me up."

Probably went home with some girl last night. "I understand," Mandy replied. "But I could really use you this afternoon."

"I'll be there."

Frustrated and with time running out, Mandy opened the back of her station wagon. She pulled out the extra helmet and set of paddling clothes she always kept in there. "I'll be the third guide this morning."

The first carload of tourists drove into the parking lot, waving in giddy excitement at the solemn threesome.

"Who'll run shuttle?" Dougie asked.

"I'll have to call and wake David and ask him to do it before he goes home."

And she would have to come up with some explanation for the customers as to why the trip was leaving late. And put off her conversation with David about Uncle Bill's business again.

The way things were going, the problem would solve itself. There wouldn't be any business left.

———

After running the shuttle for the afternoon rafting trip, Mandy's arms were sore from guiding the morning trip, but her mood was much improved. Spending a morning creating fun for others had lifted her spirits. She decided it was too nice a day to eat lunch inside. When she got home, she called Cynthia to invite her to an impromptu picnic at the water park. She whistled a jaunty tune while fixing PBJ sandwiches.

Mandy hadn't realized how much she missed guiding trips since she'd started the river ranger job—the thrill of lining up a raft for a perfect roller-coaster ride along a train of standing waves, breaking though the initial shyness of the tourists to get them to open up about themselves and open their minds to relaxing on the river, catching the bright rays of their smiles when it finally happened.

The best part was the camaraderie with the other guides. Mandy smiled, remembering the goofball things they did to make the experience memorable for the customers—starting water fights with the other rafts, the dumbest joke competition on one of the slow sections, leading a cheer fest during the return bus ride, and slipping in a gentle reminder that rafting guides lived on tips.

After tossing the sandwiches and some diet Pepsis in a small cooler, Mandy loaded Lucky into her Subaru. The poor dog had been cooped up too much at home while Mandy split her time between her river ranger duties and the rafting company. And after last night's scare, Lucky probably could use some happy excitement too.

Mandy drove into town, fingers drumming on the steering wheel in accompaniment to her favorite Pink CD, *M!ssundaztood*. She commanded Lucky to heel as they walked to the river. The dog practically danced at her side, panting with excitement and sniffing at everyone they passed. But he only broke his heel once to leave a sprinkle message on a nearby tree and alert other dogs to his presence.

When they reached the river bank, Mandy found a shady spot upriver of the main play hole in the whitewater park. It wasn't the perfect location for viewing the antics of the kayaks competing in the freestyle preliminaries, but it was close and out of the blazing midday sun. She sat on the grass and unwrapped a sandwich.

A Steller's jay, its dark blue plumage and crest glistening, swooped down and landed on the grass. It cocked its head to scan the ground around her for crumbs.

Lucky was well-acquainted with the smell of peanut butter. When he came begging and chased off his competition, she broke off a piece of her sandwich to give to him. She never failed to be amused by the frantic licking that resulted while he tried to scrape the sticky treat off the roof of his mouth.

"Are you feeding that dog peanut butter again?" Cynthia tossed a large bag of potato chips on the ground, sat on the grass next to Mandy and leaned back on her elbows. She reached into the cooler for a sandwich and took a bite. "Not bad. What kind of jelly is this?"

"Blackberry. Rob's mom made it."

And it might be the last jar she would get from Rob's mom, given the state of her relationship with him. To cover up the flash of sadness she felt, Mandy took a big bite and stared at a kayaker surfing a standing wave.

Cynthia didn't seem to notice, however. "Okay, it's not Monday, but here's one for you. How do you make a blonde laugh on Monday?"

"I haven't the foggiest."

"Tell her a joke on Friday." She glanced at Mandy's sad expression. "Sorry, stupid choice. You weren't laughing at anything on Monday, were you?"

Mandy gave the rest of her sandwich to Lucky and hugged her knees. "No, I wasn't. But thanks for trying to cheer me up."

"How could you not cheer up on a day like today?" Cynthia waved her hand in the direction of the river. "Perfect weather and a perfect spot by the river for enjoying it."

A kayaker executed a flawless pivot around a gate pole, his boat making a graceful turn, as if dancing with the pole as partner. The kayaker shouted out a "whoop" that expressed more about the sheer pleasure of playing with the water than about scoring in the race.

Mandy smiled, remembering feeling the same way that morning. "Could you live somewhere without a river?"

"Never," Cynthia said vehemently.

"Me, neither." Mandy knew she'd wither up and die like a neglected houseplant if she couldn't soak up the energy of the moving water and the myriad plants and wildlife it sustained.

Cynthia ripped open the potato chip bag. "Hey, I've got news about Paula King. Apparently, she and Tom King were attempting a reconciliation before he was killed. A neighbor of theirs spotted

Tom carrying suitcases back into the house a few nights before the rafting trip."

Mandy nodded. "That jives with what Evie Olson and her friend Shirley Logan said at the beauty parlor." She summarized the conversation. "It sounds like Evie had more of a motive to kill Tom King than Paula did."

"Unless the reconciliation didn't work." Cynthia eyed Mandy's nails. "You sure didn't get my money's worth out of that manicure."

"I'm hopeless." Mandy held out her fingers and assessed the damage. "With all the work I do with my hands, there's no way I could keep the polish from getting chipped. Trouble is, I don't have any remover to take the rest off. I'm sorry I wasted your money. "

Cynthia sat up. "But you didn't waste it. You found out Evie was no longer seeing Tom King and was upset about it."

"And upset about me asking questions. Maybe really upset. Someone threw a rock through my kitchen window last night, with a message attached, telling me to keep my nose out of the Tom King business."

"You think it was Evie?"

"Or Jeff or Paula King. Or Lenny Preble. Or Nate Fowler." Mandy scooped a handful of potato chips out of Cynthia's bag and paused before slipping one into her mouth. "Or someone else."

Cynthia's brows furrowed. "Have you told the police?"

"Not yet. I know I have to, but I've been putting off telling Detective Quintana, since he requested that I not talk to suspects."

"This is a big deal, Mandy. You've got to tell the police ASAP." Cynthia plucked a stalk of grass to put between her teeth. "Have you fixed the window at least? Someone could get in your house that way."

Mandy snorted. "That house is so easy to break into, no one needs to mess with the kitchen window. I hadn't been worried before, because I don't have anything worth stealing, and Salida's not exactly a hotbed of crime."

"But now someone's after you, not your stuff."

"A rock through my window doesn't mean someone's after me."

Cynthia stared at her.

"Okay, okay, I know." Mandy cringed a little. "But I've been on the river all morning. I'll fix it this afternoon. After running the morning shuttle, David said he would slap some duct tape over the hole in the screen before he left for Colorado Springs. And he made me promise I'd get the glass replaced today."

"David's gone? Bummer. He was a lot of fun at the Vic last night."

Mandy studied Cynthia's face. A blush colored her friend's ears. "Are you going sweet on my brother?"

"No, no, no," Cynthia said too quickly. "He's just fun to be around is all. He even laughed at my oldest, lamest blonde joke."

"Which one is that?"

"Oh, you know, two blondes flip a raft, and one swims to river right and the other one swims to river left. After they climb out of the water, one asks the other, 'How do I get to the other side?'"

Mandy jumped in with the punch line she'd heard umpteen times. "And the second one says, 'You ditz, you're already on the other side.'"

Cynthia snorted a laugh, then took the blade of grass out of her mouth and tickled Lucky's nose with it until the dog sneezed. "David's coming back for your uncle's service, right?"

Mandy shoved Cynthia's shoulder, knocking her over sideways. "You lying sack of pinto beans. You've got the hots for David."

Cynthia arched a brow at Mandy then slowly drew her tongue across her lips.

The two of them burst out laughing. Mandy fell back onto the grass, and Lucky, wanting to be part of the game, jumped on top of her and licked her cheek.

When he went after Cynthia, she playfully pushed him off. "Yuck, get out of my face, you slobbery dog."

Mandy couldn't imagine her staid accountant brother having fun. She wished she had been at the Vic last night to see it. As her giggles died down, she realized she hadn't laughed like this since her uncle died. A flash of guilt hit her, but was just as quickly swept away. Uncle Bill would have wanted her to be doing just this, lounging on the grass by the river and laughing with a friend.

She sent up a silent prayer and hoped he was playing on a sparkling, gurgling river like the Arkansas wherever he was. A gust of wind tossed the tree branch above her, letting a bright ray of sunlight through. Closing her eyes, Mandy smiled and let the warmth soak in.

Until she was attacked by another doggie slurp.

"Come here, Lucky." Cynthia tackled Lucky, pulled him off Mandy, and tossed a stick for him to fetch. Her gaze tracked the dog's path, then she nudged Mandy. "Speak of the devil. There's Paula King herself."

Mandy sat up and scanned the pedestrian path.

Paula saw them staring at her and looked around, as if seeking an escape route. She must have changed her mind, though, because she squared her shoulders and lifted her chin. The high heels she wore under her embroidered capri jeans sunk into the grass as she changed direction and approached Mandy. She stopped a few feet away and lifted her sunglasses to scan Mandy's outfit—an oversized, faded T-shirt and nylon paddling shorts she'd thrown on over a bathing suit.

Mandy bristled under the scrutiny. She felt like shouting, "I just came off the river," but pride clamped her lips shut. She was also curious why Paula had decided to approach them.

Lucky bounded up with the stick, dropped it in front of Cynthia, and walked over to sniff Paula's crotch.

Paula shoved the dog's nose away. "Get this beast away from me."

"Lucky, come," Mandy commanded. When Lucky responded, she grabbed his collar and told him to lie down. She started to rub his stomach, which always made him roll over placidly on his back, begging for more.

"I suppose I should thank you for pulling my son out of Pine Creek rapid yesterday," Paula drawled. She crossed her arms. "You seem to have made a practice of plucking King men out of the Arkansas."

Mandy glanced at Cynthia, who quirked an eyebrow at her. *This is coming from a woman whose husband died a week ago, one she was reconciling with?*

"That's what I do."

"Is it your job to ask so many questions, too?"

Mandy's hand paused in mid-circle on Lucky's stomach, causing the dog to bat it impatiently with his paw. "What do you mean?"

"Jeff said you were asking questions yesterday. Why are you so interested in my husband's will?"

"Will? I didn't say anything about a will," Mandy said. "We were just talking about why he wanted to finish that race so badly. He was pretty mad he blew his chance to win the Wave Sport."

Paula harrumphed and stared at a kayaker cartwheeling in the river. "I must be mistaken, then."

"Was Jeff upset about our conversation?" *Upset enough to throw a rock through my window?*

"It doesn't take much to set either of us on edge these days." Paula started to leave, then turned back. "You have my sympathies over your uncle's death."

"Thank you. And you have mine. For your husband."

Paula stared at her for a moment. She stood as stiff as a military officer at attention, holding something in, something that was clawing to get out. "Thank you." She turned and headed up the hill.

After she left, Cynthia gave a theatrical shudder. "No way is that woman a natural blonde. I bet her hair is as black as evil itself."

Mandy patted Lucky's stomach to signal she was done with his tummy scratch. "She didn't seem to be grieving much, did she?"

"No, I'd say she was just plain mad."

"And her anger's pointed right at me." *Just like at Tom King's funeral.* "What did I do to her?"

FOURTEEN

No one tests the depth of a river with both feet.
—AFRICAN PROVERB

MANDY COULDN'T PUT OFF paying a visit to Detective Quintana any longer. She dropped Lucky off at home and changed out of her rafting clothes into lightweight pants and a short-sleeved shirt with an actual collar.

She tried to figure out how to pull the empty frame out of the kitchen window, but gave up after fiddling with the screwdriver and getting nowhere. Too many layers of old paint had the frame firmly welded into place. She had hoped to drop it off at a glass shop on the way to the Chaffee County building and get them to install new glass. Now, she would have to break down and ask Rob to help her get the frame out.

With hands on her hips, she studied the window. Tomorrow morning the kitchen would be chilly without some kind of barrier.

Maybe she could scrounge up some cardboard. And, as Cynthia said, anyone could sneak into her place through the opening that was now just covered by a screen. Mandy tried not to think about that.

When she arrived at the Chaffee County building, she had to search the sheriff's offices until she found Quintana standing at the copier. She spied an empty paper box next to the machine. "Mind if I take that?"

"No, go ahead." His gaze went straight to the note in her hand. "What've you got there?"

Mandy handed it to him. "This was tied to a rock that sailed through my kitchen window yesterday."

"Were you home? Did you see anything?"

"I was out of the house all day and didn't get home until after eight. It shook up my dog, Lucky, though."

Quintana reread the note. "So where have you been poking your nose?"

Mandy picked up the cardboard box and sighed. "You're not going to like this."

"I suspect not." He grabbed his copies and steered her down the hall. "Let's go to my office."

Once they were seated, Mandy steeled herself and told him what she'd been up to.

Quintana listened quietly, stroking his mustache. When she finished, he folded his arms and looked out the window, as if composing what he was going to say—or composing himself.

Mandy clasped her hands and cringed inside.

Quintana directed a steely gaze at her. "Just like I predicted, your personal involvement in the case stirred up emotions—the killer's. Did you deliberately ignore my advice?"

Morosely, Mandy shook her head. "I didn't ignore it. I thought about it a lot. I just…you know, whoever killed Tom King indirectly killed Uncle Bill, too. I couldn't walk away from these people when I had the chance to question them, when one of them is responsible for my uncle's death."

"And by doing so, you've put your own life in danger. What would your uncle say about that?"

Oh God, that was a low blow. Mandy folded her arms tightly across her chest. "He'd hate it. He'd be yelling at me, ten times angrier than you are."

"And he'd be scared for you. As I am. As you should be. You could have been hurt by that rock. And who knows what this person's next move will be?" He braced his hands on his knees. "You're in danger, Mandy, and I don't have the manpower to put a guard on you. The best thing you can do right now is to obey the message."

Mandy took a deep breath. Could she stay out of this? Whether she could or not, she had to convince Quintana. "Okay."

Quintana stared at her for a moment, then seemingly satisfied, he said, "Okay. Now, do you suspect anyone in particular of throwing the rock?"

"Unfortunately, I left every single one of them pissed at me in one way or another. Though it's hard to imagine Paula King flinging the rock. It seems to be beneath her. But her son, Evie Olson, Lenny Preble, or Nate Fowler?" Mandy shrugged. "It could have been any one of them."

"Right now, I'd lay odds on Jeff King, at his mother's direction."

"What makes you say that? Have you found out something? Something I can put in my case report or tell the park managers?"

Quintana picked up one of the papers he had brought back from the copier. "This is a search warrant for Paula King's house."

"What are you looking for?"

"I have two eye witnesses who saw her hand a sports drink bottle to Tom King. And no one who saw anyone else hand one to him. Given that we found aconite in one of the bottles in your uncle's trash, we're going on the assumption, for now, that that's how the poison was administered. So, I'm going to look for evidence at her house and in her cars."

"You mean Western monkshood plants?"

"Or the dried roots. I consulted a plant expert in the agriculture department at Colorado State University. He said the roots can be dried and stored for up to two years, then ground into a poisonous powder. We'll look for any suspicious powders, too."

He handed her a couple of the sheets of paper. "He emailed some pages out of a plant guide, so we'll know what we're looking for. We won't see those bluish flowers, because they bloom later in the summer. But they grow pretty tall, two to six feet high, and the leaves are what the guy calls palmate."

"Like a palm tree?"

"No, like the palm of your hand and how your fingers spread out from that. He told me the best example is a maple leaf. We all know what one of those looks like."

"Can the poison only be made from the roots?"

"The whole plant's poisonous, but the biggest concentration is in the root, especially a young one dug up in the spring. And he said making a powder out of the stems or leaves is a lot more difficult and messy than using the root."

She pointed at a picture of what looked like a stunted brown carrot. "That's what this photo is of?"

"Yes. The guy said the root can be mistaken for wild horseradish."

He almost had to pry the pages out of her hands. She craned her neck to get another look at the photographs as he stapled four sets of them together. He tapped down the packets, put the search warrant on top, and stood.

Realizing he must be planning to execute the warrant right then, Mandy rose, too.

A woman poked her head in the office. "Deputy Rogers can't come with you. He got a call that his wife is in labor." Just as quickly, she exited.

"Great," Quintana said. "That means I'm short one on my search detail. I need a four-person team, two pairs, and there's no other deputy available."

Mandy felt a stir of excitement. "Could you use some help from a fellow law enforcement officer, the one who initiated the case?"

He stared at her for a moment, as if weighing the pluses and minuses. "If you could remain impartial, follow my directions to a T. Think you can?"

"You bet."

"I'd much rather have you snooping under my tutelage than on your own." When she opened her mouth to protest, he held up a hand. "Now, if Paula or Jeff King object to your presence, it would be best if you went back to your car."

"I understand."

He opened a desk drawer and pulled out a rumpled, laminated clip-on badge, with the Chaffee County Sheriff's logo and the words "Official Observer" on it. He handed it to her. "We use these for fellow law enforcement officers and plain folks who are doing ride-alongs with us. Gives you the appearance of a little more authority."

Quintana gathered a couple of patrol officers and introduced them as Deputies Mansfield and Thompson. He gave them the handouts on Western monkshood. He described what they were looking for, reviewed the search procedure and made assignments. Then the four of them trooped out to their cars. After stashing the cardboard box in the back of her Subaru, Mandy followed the two police cruisers to the flanks of Methodist Mountain south of Route 50, far from her own small cottage and the close streets of town.

Here, widely spaced paved and gravel roads wound among new developments with large lots and names like Fawn Ridge and Cherokee Heights. Set far back from the road, luxury homes peeked through stands of gnarled pinion pine and juniper, what the rangers called "PJ forest." Quintana turned his cruiser into a long cul-de-sac and parked in front of a huge custom-built home of Douglas fir post-and-beam construction perched on the top of a ridge line. A covered breezeway led from the house to a detached three-car garage.

Mandy followed Quintana up the drive, then took a few steps into the side yard. She looked past a gazebo containing a hot tub to a panoramic view of the town of Salida, fronted by the curving highway and the sparkling creek alongside it, the South Arkansas, which joined with the main river south of town.

"Quite a place they've got here," she said to Quintana when she rejoined him on the porch.

"Yep. Nice view, huh?" He rang the doorbell.

And cooler and quieter than town. The only other sounds were the soft rustle of the light breeze blowing through the trees and the creak of stiff shoe leather as Deputy Mansfield beside her shifted his weight. The scent was clean, too, of pine and juniper needles baking in the sun.

Jeff King opened the door, his eyes wide with surprise. Barefoot, he was dressed in jeans and a stained Red Hot Chili Peppers T-shirt. He held a half-empty soda bottle. When he spied Mandy standing beside Quintana, he frowned. "What's this?"

Detective Quintana handed him a copy of the search warrant. "We have a warrant to search your home for evidence related to your father's murder case."

"My mom's not here." Jeff's hand was still on the door, blocking them from entering.

"She doesn't need to be," Quintana said. "We still have legal authority to enter. You can call her, if you wish. Either you or she or both of you can be present, but you cannot impede the search in any way."

Jeff pointed at Mandy. "Why is she with you?"

"Ranger Tanner initiated the case," Quintana said, his tone calm and smooth. "The Sheriff's Department often works cooperatively with other law enforcement officers whose agency is directly involved in an investigation. The team approach saves taxpayers' resources."

Mandy kept her mouth shut. She noticed Quintana didn't offer Jeff the option of objecting to her presence.

"Now, if you'll excuse us, we'll begin on the ground floor." Quintana stepped forward, forcing Jeff to step back and release the door. "Where would you like to remain while we conduct the search?"

"The kitchen, I guess."

"Deputies Mansfield and Thompson will go with you to the kitchen and search there." Quintana nodded to Mandy. "You'll stay with me."

"I'm calling my mother," Jeff said as he and the two officers headed for the kitchen.

"Fine with me," Quintana replied. "Deputy Mansfield, when she gets here, tell her I'd like a word with her."

He slipped on a pair of latex gloves and handed a pair to Mandy. He checked that Jeff was out of earshot then said, "Don't want to take the chance of getting any aconite on our skin."

A chill went up Mandy's spine while she donned the gloves and checked for holes.

She followed Quintana through the master bedroom, with its heavy cherrywood furnishings, into the master bathroom. A glass-block walled shower stood in one corner and a Jacuzzi soaking tub in another, under a picture window overlooking the river below. Under a long mirror on one wall was a granite countertop with two sinks. One was cluttered with makeup pots and tubes and perfume bottles, and the other was completely bare except for an electric shaver plugged into an outlet. Either Tom King had been a neat freak, or Paula had already disposed of all of his things except for the shaver.

Quintana pointed toward the medicine cabinet. "You look in there, and I'll search the lady's cosmetics and ointments here. Tell me if you find any suspicious-looking powder or something that might be a piece of Western monkshood root." Quintana pulled out a drawer under the sink counter and leaned over it.

Mandy opened the medicine cabinet. She felt a little guilty, like a party guest snooping on her host, then reminded herself she was part of a law enforcement team. Who would have thought that a former whitewater river guide would be sorting through someone's medicine bottles?

She went through all the bottles, opening them one at a time, but found only pills inside, mostly over-the-counter painkillers, cold medicine and stomach remedies, and a prescription for a cholesterol-lowering statin. At first, given their body types, she was surprised to see the prescription was written for Paula and not Tom. Then it hit her—Paula was the epitome of a Type A personality.

"Nothing here," she said to Quintana.

"Okay, start on the clothes closet while I finish going through the drawers, sink cabinets, and linen closet."

Mandy stepped into the walk-in closet and let out an appreciative whistle. "My bedroom could fit inside here."

Quintana gave a snort and pulled out another drawer.

In the closet, head- and waist-high rods across two walls held pants, skirts, shirts, and blazers. A high rod against the back wall held dresses, floor-length gowns, and men's suits. Interspersed between sections of rods were shelves stacked with folded clothing, about a third of it men's clothing.

So Paula hadn't gotten around to removing Tom King's clothes yet.

Mandy looked at the floor. In front of all three walls of the huge closet, except for one small area containing about a dozen pairs of men's shoes, two rows of women's shoes were lined up, most pairs sitting on top of shoeboxes. Every color of the rainbow was represented, as was every style—boots, mules, stiletto heels, pumps, you name it. Mandy popped the lid off one shoebox and spied another pair of shoes inside.

The woman could give Imelda Marcos a run for her money.

Mandy searched the shelves first, even dragging a chair in from the bedroom so she could see all the way to the back of the top shelves. Then she patted down the clothing, searching pockets.

"I'm going into the bedroom," Quintana announced.

"I'll be here awhile." Mandy sat on the floor and started opening shoeboxes and checking them one by one. A pair of lime-green strappy heels, liberally studded with rhinestones, made her pause. She took one out of the box, stood it on her palm and stared at it.

What possible event in Salida would you wear these to?

A shadow fell over her.

"Nice to know you're enjoying my shoes." Her voice dripping with sarcasm, Paula King stood in the closet doorway, arms folded across her chest. She swiveled to face Detective Quintana, who had come up behind her. "What is she doing here?"

"She's part of our investigative team."

"Oh, no. You're not pulling one over on me. She's a river ranger, not a sheriff's deputy. I want her out of my house. Now!"

"Fine," Quintana said smoothly. "She can search the grounds outside. If you'll follow Deputy Mansfield back to the kitchen, you can wait with your son there while we finish."

Silently simmering, Mandy returned the shoe to its box and stood. Yes, she and Detective Quintana had discussed this possibility, but instead of leaving, she would much rather tell this uppity woman where she could stuff her lime-green, rhinestone-studded shoe.

After Paula left the room, Quintana quirked an eyebrow at Mandy, sympathy and humor conveyed in that simple gesture. "We'll switch partners. You and Deputy Thompson can search the grounds while Deputy Mansfield and I finish the house. Show me where you left off in the closet."

Mandy pointed out which shoeboxes still needed to be searched then gave him a curt nod and left. While she walked toward the kitchen, Paula's shrill voice preceded her as she gave Deputy Mansfield not just a piece, but a large, jagged chunk of her mind.

In the kitchen, all the cabinet doors gaped open. Mansfield had taken everything out from under the sink and was now shoving the haul back in, under Paula's watchful eye. Thompson had pulled spice jars off a large spice rack onto the granite countertop. He was opening the jars and sniffing them, then returning them to the rack, probably out of order. Jeff King sat slumped at the kitchen breakfast counter next to his mother. His cheek rested on one hand, while the other hand spun his empty soda bottle on the smooth gray granite.

Mandy quickly explained to Deputy Thompson what Quintana wanted them to do. As she made a hasty exit out the back door, Paula King's glowering stare seemed to drill a hole into her back.

Thompson followed, carrying a small duffle bag. "I feel sorry for Mansfield, having to babysit those two."

Mandy walked to the breezeway and surveyed the grounds. "Where should we start?"

Deputy Thompson pointed to the garage. "How about there?"

When Mandy opened the door, the warm, musty smells of potting soil and fertilizer greeted her. Two luxury automobiles sat parked in the front of the garage, just inside the closed automatic doors, but at least ten feet of space was available in front of them. The third, empty bay and the space in front of all three seemed to serve as a garden shed. Shovels, rakes, hoes, and brooms hung between pegs on one wall. A hose snaked across the floor and more hoses hung looped on racks. Along the back wall stood a built-in worktable, with shelves above and below it. A jumble of pots, seed packets, gloves, bulbs, smaller tools, and gardening supplies filled the shelves.

Mandy gawked at the huge space. "My whole cottage would fit inside this garage." *And I'm repeating myself.* Through the windows on the garage doors, she spied Jeff's battered pickup truck on the driveway. He probably wasn't allowed to park his undignified transport inside.

Thompson laughed. "Tom King knew how to make money, that's for sure."

"And his wife knows how to spend it. You should have seen Paula's shoe collection." Mandy headed for the worktable. "This looks like as good a place as any to start."

Deputy Thompson poked his gloved finger into a pile of misshapen tubers out of which grew blade-like stalks that had been trimmed to about six inches. "Could this be what we're searching for?"

Mandy peered at them. "Those look like iris rhizomes. I've got some irises in my yard. Someone must have been dividing them, getting them ready to replant."

She shuffled through the pile, spreading them out. One root looked different from the others. It was longer, more carrot-shaped, darker in color, and had no bladed leaves attached. Mandy's mouth went dry. "You have that handout Detective Quintana gave you?"

Thompson took the folded papers out of his pocket and spread out the picture of the Western monkshood root next to the odd-looking live root.

Mandy studied them both. "Sure looks like the same thing."

"I'll bag it." Deputy Thompson pulled a lunchbag-sized paper bag out of his duffle.

As he was nudging the root into the bag, Mandy stayed his hand. "Wait. See that? One end's been ground off."

She looked around the worktable, spied a small black plastic 35mm film case next to the rhizome pile, and picked it up.

"Why would a film case be in a garage?" Thompson asked.

"Why indeed." Mandy gently pried off the top.

FIFTEEN

*Men are afraid to rock the boat in which they hope to
drift safely through life's currents, when, actually,
the boat is stuck on a sandbar. They would be better off
to rock the boat and try to shake it loose.*

—THOMAS SZASZ

THE CASE WAS HALF-FILLED with a fine white powder. Deputy Thompson let out a low whistle. After he bagged the film case with its mysterious white powder, he said, "I need to tell Detective Quintana."

They found Quintana in the Kings' living room, systematically searching the bookcases. Thompson quietly told him what they had found.

Quintana gave a curt nod. "Search the grounds. See if you can find any of the plants."

Mandy and Deputy Thompson went back outside and searched the large flower garden behind the garage then all the decorative planting beds placed strategically around the house. They found no plants that fit the profile of Western monkshood. After twenty minutes with no results, Mandy stood in the middle of the King family's back yard, wondering where else she and Thompson could look.

Deputy Thompson joined her. "You know, it's even more suspicious that there's no monkshood in the yard. They can't claim they cut a root by accident if they had to bring it in from somewhere else."

"I can't think of where else the flowers might be growing," Mandy said. "The rest of their land is native forest."

"Okay. Time to report to Quintana."

They returned to the house. Quintana had moved on to the dining room, and was on his knees in front of the china hutch. When he saw them, he rose. "Find anything?"

"No," Deputy Thompson replied. "There's none around. Not unless it's growing wild in the forest nearby."

Quintana smoothed his mustache, then approached Paula King in the kitchen. "Mrs. King, could you come with me into the living room, please? Deputy Thompson, bring the evidence bag."

Mandy followed Thompson into the living room but held herself back, deeming it best that Quintana and Thompson, the official Sheriff's Department representatives, do all the talking.

Quintana led Paula into the room and indicated she should take a seat on the sofa. He stood directly in front of her, leaning over in a slightly menacing pose. "Now, Mrs. King, who is the gardener in the family?"

Paula shot a suspicious look at Mandy. "I am. Why?"

"When was the last time you used the workbench in the garage and what did you do there?"

"This morning. I was dividing up irises, getting them ready to replant."

Quintana took the evidence bag containing the film canister from Deputy Thompson's hands, opened the bag, and showed the canister to Paula. "My team found this on the workbench. What can you tell me about it?"

"I've never seen it before. Is that a film canister?"

"Yes." Quintana handed the paper bag back to Thompson, who re-stapled it and labeled it with the time it was opened.

"I have a digital camera." Paula said. "I don't use film."

"Many people still use the plastic canisters for storing things, buttons and such. You do that?"

With a shake of her head, Paula said, "That's what Tupperware is for. What's so important about a stupid film canister anyway?"

"It's not the canister. It's what's inside it. What do you think we found in that canister?"

"I have no idea. Dirt?"

Quintana stared her down for a moment, then asked, "What kind of camera does your son have?"

Paula gave a snort. "Probably none. I bet he pawned the one we gave him for Christmas a few years ago."

"What kind of camera was it?"

"Digital."

"Has Jeff ever used the gardening workbench?"

"I can't get him to mow the lawn since he moved back in. Why would he want to mess with flowers?"

Quintana signaled Thompson. "Why don't you go ask Jeff King these questions directly? And fill out a receipt, inventory, and return sheet for that evidence to leave with Mrs. King."

Paula watched the deputy leave. "What's this all about? What does gardening have to do with my husband's death?"

"We're not sure yet, Mrs. King. Maybe you can tell me. Your husband was poisoned, remember?"

Understanding dawned on Paula's face. "Did you find poison in that canister? You can't suspect me. I know nothing about poisons, and I already told you that I loved my husband."

"Yes, you did." Quintana didn't sound convinced. "We still need to test the contents of that canister. In the meantime, I'm going to have to ask you to come down to the station with me. You're a person of interest in the case now, and I need to ask you some questions."

"What if I decide I don't want to answer your questions?"

"You have that right, of course. But if you don't cooperate, I'll be forced to arrest you, and neither one of us wants that. I'm sure you wouldn't want word of something like that to get out."

Paula glared at Mandy. "And I wonder how that would happen?" Sarcasm iced her words.

Quintana held up a palm. "We're professionals, Mrs. King, all of us, and we don't divulge information about cases to the public. But the media has access to the police blotter."

"Fine! I'll come with you, but I'm not missing Bunko tonight." Paula spun on her heels.

As they followed Paula to the front door, Quintana whispered to Mandy, "They're going to be one short in that Bunko game."

Jeff King entered the hallway with Deputies Mansfield and Thompson. "Where are you taking Mom and why?"

"She's coming down to the station with us." Quintana pulled Deputy Thompson aside and had a short conversation before turning back to the rest of the group.

"Your mother is a person of interest in the death of your father now," he said to Jeff. "I need to ask her some questions. And you need to stick around. Based on what she tells us, I may question you next."

Jeff's eyes went wide. "You think she killed Dad?"

"I didn't say that."

A red flush crept up Jeff's cheeks. "Don't go with them, Mom."

"If I don't, Detective Quintana said he'll arrest me." She picked up her purse. "I've decided to cooperate for now."

"I'm calling our lawyer." Jeff stalked back into the kitchen.

Detective Quintana walked with Paula King down the driveway and put her in the back seat of his cruiser. Then he accompanied Mandy to her car.

"This looks promising." He smoothed his mustache. "If she did it, we've got her in custody. And if Jeff King killed his father, we've got him running scared and off-balance, wondering what's going to happen to his mother. We'll be watching him."

Mandy glanced at her watch. "I've got to drive the afternoon shuttle for our Brown's Canyon raft trip. Do you need me anymore?"

"No, go ahead."

"I want to know if what we found is aconite, though."

"I'll keep you posted." He turned and looked at the back of his cruiser. Paula sat as stiff as a statue of an Egyptian pharaoh inside.

"I'm not sure Jeff is capable of murder," Mandy said, "but that lady sure fits the profile of a black widow."

———

Mandy pulled the bus into the parking lot for the Hecla Junction takeout for Brown's Canyon. She managed to turn the bus around so its back and the attached trailer faced the river just before Kendra, Dougie, and Ajax arrived with their charges. Mandy had been worried she would be late, but the guides must have let the customers relax and play Geronimo, jumping off a cliff into the water, longer than usual at the rest stop. When she climbed out of the bus, the three guides were pulling a raft up on the bank and telling customers to throw their PFDs and paddles into it.

After directing the customers, squishing in their muddy shoes, onto the bus, Mandy went to help the guides load the rafts in the trailer. Two rafts sat piled on the trailer, with the paddles and PFDs sandwiched between them in the lower raft. Dougie and Ajax clambered like monkeys over the pile, tying it down.

When Ajax spotted her, he stood and shot Mandy a pained look. "Uh, Mandy, I've got a problem to report."

"Wait a minute," Mandy said. "Where's the other raft?"

Kendra put a hand on Mandy's shoulder. "It's pinned on the second rock in Raft Ripper. Ajax's bunch was from Japan, and they didn't understand English very well. He couldn't get them to follow his commands and was fighting their mixed-up paddling the whole way down the river."

"I'm really sorry." Ajax fumbled the knot he was tying and loosened it. "I know how tight things are for the company. I hate to add to your problems."

Being another raft short was a *big* problem. Mandy needed four rafts the next day. With the torn raft, she was out of spares, and Saturday during FIBArk was the biggest day of the season. All the other outfitters would be busy Saturday, too, so finding a loaner raft would be impossible. Her head whirled as she tried to think of a solution. Then she noticed Ajax's hang-dog expression.

"I'm sure you did your best under difficult circumstances, Ajax. No reason to be sorry. Was anyone hurt when you pinned?"

"No. They all washed downstream, and Kendra and Dougie picked them up."

"That was part of the problem," Kendra said. "Ajax didn't have anyone to help him high-side the raft."

"Did you try to pull it off?"

"Of course. We roped it up and worked on it for almost an hour. Even had the customers helping us pull on the line from the bank. It's really wedged."

A frustrated sigh escaped Mandy's lips.

Ajax jumped down from the trailer. "We plan to come back with more ropes and pulleys, but we decided we'd better send these folks on their way home first. They were getting pretty impatient while we worked on the raft."

Mandy glanced up at the back bus windows and saw a couple of glum faces staring down at her. *Great. The customers had a bum time. That doesn't bode well for repeat business.*

"It must have been a cramped ride the rest of the way," she said, "with everyone in two rafts. At least it happened toward the end of the trip. Did you get many complaints?"

"Some," Kendra replied, "but a couple of the kids had gotten tired of paddling, so we put them in the middle—along with Ajax. He kept them entertained."

Ajax rolled his eyes.

Mandy knew what that meant. Pulling out all the old knock-knock jokes and hand games. Increasing the self-deprecating banter to put the blame on himself and off the customers. Trying desperately to convince them that they were still having a good time.

"Okay." Mandy rubbed her hands to convey more self-assurance than she felt. "Damage control time. Put your smiles on and chat them up on the way back. By the time I get the bus to home base, we need to convince them they had more fun today than if they'd gone to Disneyland."

As they neared the front of the bus, she clapped a hand on Ajax's back. "I've got the emergency package of chocolate chip cookies in my duffle bag. Why don't you be the one to pass them out?"

———

An hour later, Mandy waved goodbye to the last carload leaving the rafting company parking lot. She dumped a stack of coupons for "ten-dollars-off your next ride" on the office counter. She had passed them out to the customers along with a cheery speech encouraging them to come back. As her hand dropped to her side, pessimism soaked in. Very few of the customers looked like they had been convinced.

She still had the closing-out paperwork to do, and she needed to prep for the next day's trips, but first that raft had to be retrieved.

And it was already almost six thirty. There wasn't much daylight left for the long task ahead.

She donned her wetsuit and grabbed some power bars from the kitchen. After locking the front door, she went out back into the equipment yard to see what she could do to help the guides. The rafts and paddles had been stowed. The customers' wetsuits, booties, helmets, and PFDs were collected, washed out, and hanging up to dry.

Kendra, Dougie, and Ajax were all still dressed for the river. Kendra had added a wetsuit to her ensemble, and the guys had put on spray jackets. If the sun went down while they were still working on the stuck raft, the air would get chilly fast. Dougie was tossing ropes and carabiners into the back of his pickup truck, and a raft lay nearby.

Mandy handed out the power bars. "What's the plan? Walk up from the takeout?"

"That's all we can do," Ajax answered glumly. "There's no other access point."

Rob's truck pulled into the side parking lot. He climbed out and looked into the bed of Dougie's truck.

"Hi, Rob. What brings you here?" Mandy asked, trying to sound casual in front of the others.

"I'll tell you later." His glance at the guides conveyed that what he had to say was private. "What's going on?"

Kendra dumped an armload of paddles into Dougie's truck bed, causing a metallic clatter. "We've got a raft pinned at Raft Ripper."

"Ouch," Rob said. "I've got some extra rope and pulleys in the truck, if those will help."

"Thanks," Mandy said. "I'll be sure to get them back to you tonight or tomorrow morning."

Rob shot her a quizzical look. "I'm coming with you."

"But—" Mandy began, then realized the sensibility of Rob's offer. An extra person, especially one experienced in swift water rescue, would help get the job done quicker. "I hate to ask you. I'm sure you've had a long day."

"You're not asking, I'm offering." Rob grinned and took her arm. "C'mon, you can ride with me."

All of sudden he seemed to take charge of the retrieval operation. After they tied the raft onto the back of Dougie's truck, he led the caravan back down to Hecla Junction. On the way, he quizzed Mandy for details about the stuck raft's position. She couldn't tell him much since she hadn't been there and felt more and more frustrated as he shot questions at her and analyzed strategies out loud.

When they reached the river, Rob hoisted ropes out of his truck and handed the pulleys to Dougie, who added them to a duffle bag stuffed with throw ropes, a first aid kit, and hardware that he slung over his shoulder. With Ajax carrying the company ropes, that left Kendra and Mandy with the raft stuffed with extra paddles, which they pulled on a line up the river behind them.

After forty minutes of bushwhacking and climbing over rocks, Mandy's arms ached and trickles of sweat ran down the inside of her wetsuit. When they reached the bank opposite the two huge knife-edged rocks in the channel that formed Raft Ripper, she stopped to catch her breath. The sounds of heavy breathing and water being sucked out of water bottles surrounded her as the others rested, too.

Mandy swiped her brow while she studied the scene. Ajax's raft still lay plastered sideways against the upstream side of the second rock, three-quarters submerged. Roaring water slammed against it, but the raft never budged. It was definitely stuck and stuck good.

"There's more water going over the far side of the raft," she said. "So the first thing we need to do is get across the river so we can angle a rope from that bank to peel the raft off from this side."

"Like a banana skin, right." Rob grabbed a paddle. "Dougie and I will paddle the raft across while you and Ajax ride. Kendra should stay on this side with a throw rope downstream just in case. Rescue's easier from this side. Everyone got whistles for signaling?"

He's taking over again. Mandy simmered as she led the group further upstream to get a safe distance above the rapid. Sure, Rob had more years of raft guiding experience than she did, but she was the river ranger here, she knew the capabilities of her team best, and the raft belonged to her now. She quickly formulated a revised plan. It was time to reassert her authority.

"Kendra's our best rigger so she should be in the raft instead of Ajax."

Rob stopped and gave her a quizzical look. "But she's not as strong as him. Three men pulling on the rope should be enough to get the raft unstuck."

Mandy put her hands on her hips. "No, it won't. Kendra said they had a bunch of customers pulling on a rope before and it didn't come off. Right, Kendra?"

Kendra nodded. "But we were pulling from this side."

"Still. We need to rig a Z-drag to give us a three-to-one mechanical advantage, and you're the best one to do it."

The others bounced a few looks of confusion between Rob and her, then Rob shrugged. "I guess this is Mandy's operation."

She avoided looking directly at him. "It *is* my company's raft, after all."

She bit her lip as a sudden wash of sadness swept over her. Just four days ago, it had been Uncle Bill's company and his raft.

The others loaded the raft silently, probably thinking the same thing.

When they were ready, Rob and Dougie ferried the raft across the river. As soon as they reached the bank, Mandy hopped out and walked up to a big ponderosa pine. She slapped the bark, releasing a slight scent of vanilla. "We'll use this tree as our anchor."

They worked swiftly to construct the Z-drag line using the pulleys under Kendra's direction. Once it was done and Kendra had inspected it, Mandy said, "Okay, I'll paddle into the eddy below the raft and attach the line while you three stay here."

Rob sat on his heels and looked from Mandy to the stuck raft and back again. "I'd like to make a suggestion. Whoever's connecting the line to the pinned raft needs to be tall, in case he has to reach a D ring far underwater. Also, the stronger that person is, the better, to tug the line taut. I think you and I should swap jobs. With the Z-drag, you don't need as much strength here."

Mandy hated admitting it, but Rob was right. Besides, she could tell he was itching to get out there and be a hero. "Okay, cowboy."

Rob flashed a smile and hopped in the raft. He paddled out to the center of the river, rode the current past the stuck raft and executed a perfect eddy turn to slide his raft behind the rock. He tied his raft's bowline around the prominent tip, then scrambled onto the rock.

Mandy winced. She would have tried to work from the anchored raft, which was safer than the slippery rock. She couldn't tell him what she thought, though. The roar of the rushing water was too loud for anything but hand signals and whistles to pass between Rob and the three on the shore.

Rob lay on the rock and reached down along the sides of the pinned raft to attach a rope to D rings on the raft's sides. When he had a three-point formation, he attached that rope to the Z-drag line and tugged it tight. He signaled Mandy to start pulling.

Mandy, Kendra, and Dougie pulled in line easily for a while, then strained as the tension picked up. Their progress slowly ground to a halt, as the battle between the mechanical force of the three of them multiplied three times and the pressure of the moving water reached a balance.

Mandy blew on her whistle to get Rob's attention. She signaled with a hand swiped across her throat that their efforts hadn't worked.

Rob nodded and signaled for them to release the tension some.

After they did that and Mandy whistled back, he lay down on the rock and groped underwater between the rock and the raft.

What is he doing? Then Mandy realized he was trying to find a pressure valve to release some of the air in the raft.

Rob slid down, his head splashing under the water. Both arms plunged into the churning water. He started to slip and one leg flailed in the air.

Mandy held her breath. Finally, Rob brought a hand out to clutch the surface of the rock, stopping his slide, and raised his head back up out of the water, shaking it to fling drops off his hair. The air left her aching chest with a whoosh of relief.

Apparently Rob succeeded in expelling some air from the raft, because he signaled Mandy to start pulling again.

This time, the gang pulling on the rope made slow, painful progress. All of Mandy's back and arm muscles strained as the rope crawled through the pulleys. Soon Rob let out a cheer. He pushed against the far side of the raft. Slowly, slowly, it peeled back from the rock.

Suddenly the raft popped free and came sailing toward the bank.

When the raft bumped against the river bank, Mandy scrambled down to pull the raft up on the shore. A quick inspection didn't show any damage. *Thank the river gods.*

By the time Rob returned to their side of the river and, with Mandy's help, lined his raft back up the bank, Kendra and Dougie had dismantled the Z-drag line and coiled all the rope.

Rob swept Mandy up in a hug and yelled, "Success?"

"Success!" After planting a big kiss on his lips, Mandy high-fived Kendra and Dougie and shot a few whistle blasts to Ajax, who jumped up and down on the other shoreline.

After that, it was a straightforward matter to ferry to the other side, pick up Ajax, and paddle the two rafts down the river to the takeout. By the time they loaded everything into the two trucks, the sun had dipped behind the mountains to the west. Mandy shivered in the evening chill, and her stomach wouldn't stop rumbling.

From the guides' talk about celebrating over burritos and beers, Mandy could tell that they were hungry, too. It was almost eight thirty, after all. Poor Lucky would be looking for his dinner at home and wondering where his mistress was.

Mandy climbed back into the passenger seat of Rob's truck, and he cranked the engine. When she remembered she still had paperwork to complete, as well as unloading all the equipment, she slumped in her seat and leaned her head against the window. She felt utterly drained of energy, but somehow had to come up with more.

Rob peered at her. "You okay?"

"I still have the trip closing-out paperwork to do, and I'm sure Lucky is starving. I know I am."

He pursed his lips as he steered the truck up the bouncy dirt road. "How about if the guides and I unload so you can do the paperwork? Then I'll pick up a pizza and meet you at your house."

"You don't need to do that."

"No, I don't, but I want to." His voice was tight, strained. "We have to talk, Mandy. That's why I came by after work."

Rob's hands clenched the steering wheel. His jaw muscle bulged with tension.

Mandy just wanted to eat and fall into bed, but it had been two days since she had walked away from Rob at the FIBArk kickoff, saying she didn't want to have anything to do with him. His confused stare as he drifted under her position on the bridge at the raft rodeo had torn at her heart.

"You're right. We need to talk." He deserved some answers. Problem was, she wasn't sure what they were.

SIXTEEN

In matters of style, swim with the current;
in matters of principle, stand like a rock.
—THOMAS JEFFERSON, 3RD PRESIDENT OF USA (1743–1826)

WHEN MANDY GOT HOME and climbed out of her Subaru in the dark, Lucky leapt up against the fence, rattling the chain links and barking repeatedly at her. A sense of déjà vu flashed in Mandy's head. *Was another rock thrown through a window? Or something worse?*

Then she realized that this was Lucky's angry bark, not fear. Rightfully so. She had left the poor dog alone in the yard for over thirteen hours.

She let the dog inside, immediately fed him, and refilled both his inside and outside water bowls. After he finished eating and drinking, she gave him a good brushing to get back in his good graces.

Soon Lucky was nudging her hand for ear scratches, everything forgiven.

If only dealing with people was so easy.

Lucky ran to the living room window to look out and barked. He had heard Rob's truck crunching into the driveway before she did. Mandy quickly set plates, two cans of beer, and napkins on the table, then opened the door for Rob.

When he lifted the lid of the large pizza box in the kitchen, releasing hot steam filled with the tantalizing aroma of cheese, ham, and pineapple—her favorite toppings—she felt faint.

By mutual unspoken agreement—or starvation—they plowed into the food without talking. Mandy ate four slices, twice her usual, and Rob polished off the other eight. Sated, she downed the last of her beer.

Rob reached into the fridge for a second beer for himself. "Another?"

Mandy shook her head. "I'm ready to burst. Thanks for the pizza."

Rob popped the top of the beer can and took a few gulps. "Thanks for the beer." He put down the can and gazed at her.

Oh no, here it comes.

"I know you're going through a really tough time, Mandy, with your uncle's death and trying to run his business at the same time you're starting a new career, but ..." He seemed unsure what to say next, or unsure of her reaction.

Mandy tried to help him along. "But?"

Rob ran a finger up and down the beer can, leaving a trail in the condensation. "Every time I try to help you, you end up mad at me. You've got me wound up tighter than the whirlpool in Maytag rapid. Like today, what was that business on the river?"

Mandy blew out a breath. "You don't just help, Rob. You take over. That raft was my responsibility, and I knew what I was doing. I knew how to retrieve it."

His expression had wounded animal written all over it. "I didn't say you didn't."

"But you implied it, by assuming leadership of the operation. I felt like I had to wrestle it back from you."

He lifted the beer can to his lips then set it down again. "So I insulted you? Injured your pride?" His tone was incredulous.

"Yeah, frankly. Why's that so hard to believe?"

"Well, because—" He stopped, as if he knew what he was going to say next was a big mistake.

Mandy leaned forward. "Because I'm a girl?"

Rob nodded, his face drawn down in pure misery.

"What if I'd been a guy? Would you have taken over so fast?"

After a pause, he said, "I guess not."

"See, that's what bugs me, Rob. You don't treat me like an equal." She leaned back in her chair and held out her hand. "Like with the offer to buy Uncle Bill's business. You went to David, not me."

"Dammit. You had me so confused by then, I was afraid to talk to you about it. I thought you'd blow up in my face."

Mandy gave a half-smile. "I probably would have."

"See?" Rob jabbed a finger at her. "I went to David looking for advice on how to approach you."

"Trouble is, he doesn't know any better than you do. I was mad at David, too."

Rob raked his fingers through his hair as if he felt like tearing it out. "What am I supposed to do? I can't go tip-toeing around you like you're surrounded by broken glass."

Like I was last night. "I'm not that fragile, Rob."

"Every time I try to do you a favor, take care of you, you blow up in my face." Rob's tone grew faster and louder. "It's damn frustrating!"

"I don't want to be taken care of. I can do that for myself." Mandy leaned forward and looked straight into his eyes. "Can't you just care for me without feeling you have to take over my life?"

"But that's how a man cares for a woman. At least that's how it is in my family. Mom said Pop didn't have to say he loved her. He showed it every time he tuned her car, unplugged the kitchen drain, or weeded her garden. She *liked* it and said I should treat my woman the same way." His hand slapped the table, making their cans bounce. "How am I supposed to show you I love you?"

A warm glow suffused Mandy, and a goofy grin split her lips. "You love me?"

Rob gulped the rest of his beer and crushed the can. "Yeah, you infuriating little she-devil." He grinned back at her.

She rose, pushed the table aside and sat on Rob's lap. She slid her fingers into his hair, following the tracks he had made earlier, then trailed her hands slowly down the sides of his face to cup his chin.

"*Mi querida* is back," he whispered.

She bent her head and teased his lips with hers.

His breath caught, and he hardened beneath her.

She trailed kisses up his cheek and ran her tongue along the edge of his ear. "I've got a better way for you to show me you love me," she whispered.

With a grateful growl, he put his arms around her and ground his lips against hers, parting them to let in his hungry tongue. His hands roamed under her T-shirt, over her back, hunting for the clasp of her bra. When she tugged at his T-shirt, tucked into his jeans, he stood, taking her with him.

They whirled, hands tearing at clothes, fingers inching under to caress warm skin, until her rear end bumped up against the sink. She lifted her arms so Rob could pull off her T-shirt. They locked lips again while she rolled the bottom of his shirt up to his armpits.

He leaned back and tore off his shirt. "Right here, on the counter?" Passion hoarsened his voice.

Her response was to throw her arms around him and grind her hips against his.

A cold blast chilled her back. The breeze tossed the window blinds, clattering them against the frame.

Rob reached behind her. "I'll close the window."

Mandy leaned away. "You can't. It's gone. Someone threw a rock through it last night."

"What?" He raised the blinds to reveal the screen patched with duct tape. "Who did this?"

Mandy rubbed her chilled arms. "Who knows? Forget about it." She pulled his face down for a kiss.

After kissing her lips, he trailed kisses down the side of her neck then stopped.

"Don't stop now." Mandy groaned and peeked at him.

Rob was staring at the window. "You must have pissed off someone."

She sighed. "I've been talking to people who might have killed Tom King, and I seem to have pissed them all off. It could have been any of them—or someone else. A note was tied to the rock."

Rob grabbed her shoulders and moved her away from the cold breeze. "What did the note say?"

"'Keep your nose out of the Tom King business or else.'"

Worry furrowed Rob's brow. "Or else what?"

"I don't know." The mood had been shattered. Disappointed, Mandy reached for her T-shirt.

Rob stepped toward the window to take another look at the screen. With an "oof," he staggered back against the table, banged into it and slid to the floor.

Mandy dropped to her knees beside him. Blood poured out of his shoulder.

"My God, what happened?"

Rob clutched at the wound and grimaced. "I think I've been shot."

———

At the Heart of the Rockies Regional Medical Center, Mandy screeched her Subaru to a halt outside the emergency walk-in entrance. She cut the engine, then ran around the car to open the door for Rob.

His face was pale, and the T-shirt wrapped around his shoulder was soaked through with blood. A groan escaped his lips when he rose from the seat. He staggered back to lean against the car while Mandy slammed the door shut.

She dipped her head under his other arm and helped him stand. "Lean on me."

He gritted his teeth and took a small step forward.

She put an arm around his back and pushed, trying to hurry him to take the few steps needed to get inside. His passivity scared her. *What if he doesn't make it inside? Should I have called an ambulance?* Taking Rob herself had seemed quicker, since the hospital was so close to her house, but if he lost consciousness and started to fall, she couldn't hold him up.

Rob leaned more heavily on her with each agonizing step toward the emergency room door. Mandy began to pant from the exertion—and fear. Rob's weight and wooziness reminded her of pulling Tom King out of the water.

And that rescue attempt had ended in death.

Finally they reached the foot mat. The door swished open. She spied an empty plastic chair just inside the doorway and slid Rob into it. Mandy yelled to the startled receptionist at the registration counter, "My boyfriend's been shot. He's bleeding—he needs help NOW."

The stocky, middle-aged woman stabbed the intercom button. "Wheelchair STAT."

Within seconds a large male orderly rushed into the lobby, pushing a wheelchair.

Mandy directed him to Rob and hovered, feeling useless, while the orderly helped Rob into the chair.

Rob's face was as pale as whitewater foam. As the orderly pushed him through an automatic door into a hallway leading to examining rooms, Rob's gaze lit on Mandy, but he seemed to be having trouble focusing.

When Mandy tried to follow, the orderly stopped her with a hand. "You need to stay here, miss, do the paperwork. We'll take good care of him."

The door closed behind them, and Mandy bit her lip to keep the tears from flowing. Panic had twisted her gut. Her late dinner of pizza and beer rumbled ominously.

What if Rob's lost too much blood? What if the bullet's done too much damage for him to be able to use that arm again?

"Miss? Miss?" the receptionist called. "I need you over here. Hello, Miss?"

Finally Mandy stepped to the counter. "When can I see Rob?"

"Soon, but we need some information first." The woman pushed a clipboard toward her.

Mandy scanned the form. "I don't know what insurance company he has."

"Don't worry," the receptionist said. "Fill out what you can, and we'll get the rest from him. He probably has the card in his wallet. Now, for gunshot wounds we have to call the police. You know that, right?"

"When you call, tell them to notify Detective Quintana," Mandy said. "This is related to a case of his. He needs to know that the bullet came through Mandy Tanner's window."

With a nod, the woman wrote down both the detective's name and Mandy's. "You can take a seat to do that paperwork."

When Mandy faced the waiting room, she finally noticed the other occupants. A young mother held a whining toddler with a red face and a weak cough on her lap. An overweight middle-aged woman looked at the wall clock, checked her watch, and repeated the ritual. Anxiety was etched in the deep worry lines on her face.

Mandy could relate.

She went to an empty chair and started filling out the forms. She knew the basics, Rob's address, phone number, and so on. But when it came to next-of-kin, she couldn't remember any more than the names of his parents, that they lived in Pueblo, and that Rob had dinner with them every other Monday. In fact, Rob had hinted lately that she should go down to Pueblo with him soon.

Mandy moved on to the next line of the form. She had no idea if he was allergic to anything. What if they gave him an antibiotic that he reacted to? She vowed to trade medical information with Rob as soon as possible. Neither one of them had family now in Salida. They had to look out for each other, now that they were a true couple. Rob said he loved her.

A realization hit her like a slap. Her pen clattered to the floor. *I never told him I loved him back.*

The urge to see him became overwhelming. She couldn't let him go on thinking she didn't love him, not after he took a bullet that must have been meant for her.

She bent down to pick up the pen, but a noise made her raise her head. The orderly had come back out with a rag and a bottle of antiseptic. His hands encased in latex gloves, he went to work cleaning the chair Rob had sat in. Blood covered the chair's arm and drops stained the floor.

A chill went through Mandy.

The orderly saw her staring. "Can't be too careful about body fluids these days."

"I know he doesn't have AIDS," Mandy said. "He was just tested." They had done the responsible thing a month ago, gotten tested for STDs and traded the results. It was embarrassing, but with both of them being trained first-aiders, they knew it had to be done.

The orderly nodded but kept on cleaning. "Name's Ed Lindeman, by the way. What's yours?"

"Mandy Tanner."

"Well, Mandy, your friend looks like he's in pretty good shape, athletically."

"He's a whitewater rafting guide."

"Done some rafting myself," Ed said with a nod. "You know, folks in good shape have a much better chance of surviving a medical emergency. I think he'll pull through just fine."

"Thanks." Mandy hoped he really knew what he was talking about.

Finished with his task, Ed smiled, then walked back through the automatic doors.

Mandy finished what she could of the forms and turned them in to the receptionist. "Will you call me, please, as soon as Rob can have a visitor or when you know something?"

"Sure thing, dear," the receptionist replied. "Try to relax. He's in good hands now."

Too edgy to sit, Mandy paced the length of the room. She checked the clock at the end of each circuit. When the mother and her child were called in, Mandy stepped aside.

The mother gave Mandy a wan, sympathetic smile when she passed, and Mandy tried to respond in kind. "I hope your little one feels better soon."

She resumed her pacing.

Mandy was wearing a groove into the carpet when the receptionist called her to the desk. "We're going to admit Mr. Juarez for the night at least. As soon as the doctor's done with him, he'll come out to talk to you, but I'll warn you that he said it would be awhile."

Relief flooded through Mandy, making her clutch the counter for balance. "So Rob will be okay?"

"Of course, honey." The woman patted Mandy's hand and looked at her with sympathetic eyes. "He's just weak and in a lot of pain right now. Not a happy camper. He'll need some TLC later. I assume you can provide that."

She gave a playful wink and turned to her computer screen.

The outside door snicked open, and Quintana stepped through. He was still dressed in his uniform, even though it was approaching eleven o'clock.

Mandy ran toward him then stopped, hesitantly twisting her hands. When he opened his arms, she stepped gratefully inside their circle. The tears she'd been holding back started flowing. Suddenly the enormity of all she had been through in the last few days hit her—losing her first rescue victim, then the devastating death of Uncle Bill, followed by an attempt on her own life which had almost succeeded in taking Rob's.

"Rob. Oh, God. Someone shot Rob in the shoulder."

Quintana patted her back. "Is he going to be okay?"

"I think so. I want to see him. I *need* to see him, but they won't let me."

"I'm sure they have their reasons. Let's go outside and talk in my cruiser." Quintana dug a packet of tissues out of a pocket and handed them to her. "It'll be more private there."

Mandy told the receptionist where she would be, then let Quintana steer her outside while she fumbled the tissue packet open and blew her nose.

Quintana pointed to her Subaru, still parked right outside the door. "Is that your car?"

"Oh, yeah, I forgot to move it."

"Give me your keys, and I'll put it in a parking space. My car's right over there." He pointed to a police cruiser parked a few yards away in the emergency parking lot.

Once they were both inside the cruiser, Mandy told Quintana the whole story of how the bullet had come through her now-glassless kitchen window and hit Rob.

He listened carefully and took notes, then flipped his notebook shut. "I'll get the bullet from the ER. They'll save it for me. Then I'll search all our suspects' homes for guns, check them against the bullet. If anyone doesn't give me permission, I'll ask for a warrant."

"All the suspects?" Mandy said. "I thought you'd narrowed it down to Paula and Jeff King."

"The bullet came through your window about half an hour ago, right?"

"Right. Rob brought in the pizza about nine thirty, and we'd finished eating it and were talking."

"I just finished saying goodbye to Paula King and her lawyer. About the time that shot was fired, I was at the station's front desk, signing her out. I was on my way home when I got the call over the radio about Rob."

Mandy felt a twinge of guilt that he hadn't had a chance to see his family yet after an already long day. "So you don't think Paula killed her husband?"

"I didn't say that," Quintana replied. "The only thing we know for sure is that she didn't fire that bullet through your window. That was someone else. Could have been an accomplice of hers—like her son. Or someone other than King's killer, who for their own reasons doesn't like the way you've been snooping around."

"Did you find out anything from Paula?"

"She kept insisting she knew nothing about the root and the powder you found. Then her lawyer showed up and said if we didn't have anything more to go on, we had no basis for holding her. He was right, frankly. We won't have the lab results for two or three days, and with no proof that what we found was aconite, we had to release her."

Dejected, Mandy leaned her head back against the head rest. "We're not getting anywhere, are we?"

"On the contrary," Quintana said. "I'll have a bullet to match, once they dig it out of Rob's shoulder."

As she imagined how painful that would be for Rob, Mandy winced in sympathy.

"And potentially, we may have our hands on some of the poison," Quintana said. "Lastly, you've made someone very nervous. I like nervous suspects. Though, I'd much prefer them to be nervous because of me than a young river ranger."

He stroked his mustache. "You need to lay low for a while. This escalation from a rock to a bullet through your window is worrisome. Do you have somewhere other than your house, or your uncle's place, where you can stay for a few days?"

"I'll spend the night here with Rob. I don't know what I'll do after that. I don't know how long they'll want to keep him here.

And if they release him, I don't know if he'll need someone to take care of him."

Or if I can do it. She wasn't even sure she and Rob were far enough along in their relationship for her to move in with him and become his caretaker, even for a few days. In the meantime, there was Lucky to think about. Mandy decided to call Cynthia and ask for her help.

"The hospital should be safe enough. Let me know where you decide to stay after tonight. I wish I could provide protection for you, but we don't have the manpower." Quintana gave her an assessing look. "You ready to go back in there?"

Mandy scrubbed at her tear-stained face. "I guess so."

He opened the car door. "Let's see if they've gotten that bullet out of Rob's shoulder. Then we've both got work to do."

SEVENTEEN

You could not step twice into the same river,
for other waters are ever flowing on to you.
—ON THE UNIVERSE, HERACLITUS OF EPHESUS (540–480 BC)

A RAY OF MORNING sunlight shone through the venetian blinds across Rob's hospital room window and lit on Mandy's face. Even with her eyes closed, the brightness made her squint. As she slumped, curled in a ball, in the chair beside Rob's bed, pains started reporting in from various parts of her body. Her tailbone twinged, her cricked neck ached, and she felt like some sadist was stabbing a serrated knife under one of her shoulder blades. With a groan, she straightened out her stiff arms and legs, flexed her back, and leaned over to check on Rob.

His face was in repose, and he breathed deeply, still in a drug-induced slumber. A huge mound of bandaging encased his shoulder.

His arm was bound to his body. He tried to shift his position, failed, and grunted in his sleep.

Mandy wanted to touch him, reassure herself by feeling the warmth of life coursing through him, but she didn't want to wake him. She tried to be satisfied with gazing at him, counting his breaths, watching his eyelids twitch.

The sun's rays slowly traveled across the floor until a nurse rattled in with a cart. The moveable shelf on top held a breakfast tray, and the stationary shelf below held a tray of medical supplies. She picked up an ear thermometer and fitted a disposable cap on it.

"Do you have to disturb him?" Mandy whispered.

"We've got to make sure he doesn't have a fever," the nurse said. "That's a sign of infection, and we don't want that. I'll need to wake him to check his dressing anyway."

When she poked the thermometer in his ear, Rob grimaced and stretched out his legs under the covers. His eyelids fluttered. One opened, revealing a malevolent eye peering at the nurse. "What kind of way is that to wake someone?"

The nurse smiled and extracted the thermometer. "Ninety-nine. Not bad."

Mandy leaned in. "How're you feeling, Rob?"

"Lousy." He scanned her rumpled clothes and tousled hair. "Have you been here all night?"

"Yeah." She gave his hand a squeeze, then held on. "I didn't want to leave you alone, in case—" She gave a little shrug. "In case you woke up and needed something."

"Sorry to break up this tender moment, but I need to get in there and check that bandage." The nurse stood next to Mandy with the tray of bandaging supplies and a bemused smile.

Mandy rose, then grabbed the side of the bed for support. Her left leg felt like bees had moved in and were humming an angry chorus together. "My leg's gone to sleep."

"Wiggle and stomp it," the nurse said, and put the tray of supplies on the nightstand next to Rob's head.

Mandy hobbled toward Rob's feet, held on to the bed rail and shook her leg until the buzzing died down.

The nurse slowly unwrapped the outer bandage on Rob's shoulder, revealing a blood-stained inner bandage, then a row of stitches along an angry, purple wound.

Suddenly light-headed, Mandy looked away.

The nurse shot her a glance. "Why don't you go freshen up, wash your face?"

"I do need to pee," Mandy mumbled.

She backed out of the room and fled down the hallway, looking for a public restroom. The one in Rob's hospital room was too close. She had to get away—from the wound, the smells, the too-knowing nurse, and Rob, so he couldn't see how much his injury disturbed her. When she found a restroom, she headed straight for the sink and splashed cold water on her face until her hands stopped shaking.

How am I going to take care of Rob if I can't stand the sight of his wound? She leaned on the sink and looked at her reflection in the mirror. *You'll just have to get over it, you wimp.*

She plastered on a brave smile and dried her hands. When she returned to the room, the nurse had finished rebandaging Rob. She cranked up his bed so he was in a half-sitting position.

The nurse pushed the top of the cart holding the breakfast tray over Rob's lap and peered at Mandy. Apparently liking what she saw, she gave a little nod. "Okay, how about if you help your friend here eat his breakfast? He tells me he's right-handed. Since the left shoulder is injured, you should only need to take the lids off and cut his food for him." She picked up the tray of bandaging supplies and left.

Glad to have something useful to do, Mandy set to work uncovering Rob's scrambled eggs and slicing his ham.

He took a few bites. "This tastes pretty good. I'm surprised how hungry I am."

Mandy brushed back a lock of Rob's hair that had fallen over his forehead. "I told Detective Quintana what happened. He came in and got the bullet from the doctors last night."

"Does he have any idea who did it?"

"He knows Paula King didn't, since she was with him. He's going to search everyone else's houses and cars for the gun."

"Lenny Preble and Evie Olson, too?"

"And Nate Fowler and Jeff King. Those are the people I pissed off with my questioning. If he doesn't find anything at their homes, Quintana may search the property of some other folks who were on the trip."

"What's he going to do to protect you?"

"Not much. He can't. There aren't that many cops on the Chaffee County Sheriff's rolls."

Rob put down his fork and frowned at her. "Until he finds out who did it, this person could take another pot shot at you. That bullet wasn't meant for me. You need to hide out."

Suddenly feeling shy and unsure of herself, Mandy looked up under her lashes at Rob. "I was kinda hoping to invite myself over to your place after you check out of here—just for a few days, you know, to help out. To show you … like you were saying your Pop showed your Mom."

Understanding bloomed in Rob's eyes. He reached over with his good hand to cup her cheek and stroke it with his thumb. "I'd like that, *mi querida*."

"Knock, knock. You decent?" Cynthia came through the doorway with a stuffed teddy bear that held a miniature paddle in one hand, and in the other, a helium-filled Mylar balloon proclaiming, "Get Back To Work, You Slug."

Rob grinned. "What would you have done if I wasn't decent?"

"Enjoyed the view." Cynthia leered at him. "How's the patient? Not feeling any pain, I hope."

"The doc has me pretty drugged up," Rob said. "In fact the world's looking downright rosy. I could get used to this stuff."

"Good." Cynthia kissed Rob on the cheek, put the bear on his nightstand, and gave Mandy a hug. "I fed Lucky for you this morning. That dog misses you."

"Thanks. Poor Lucky's had to put up with a lot lately."

Cynthia rubbed her hands together. "Okay, here's the latest blonde joke to cheer you both up. Why did the blonde nurse bring a red marker to work?"

"You've got me," Rob said.

"In case she had to draw blood!"

Rob tilted back his head and laughed. "Good one. Just what I needed. Now you need to talk Mandy into taking a break."

"No way," Mandy said, buttering his toast. "I'm sticking with you."

"The nurses are taking good care of me, and you look bushed."

Cynthia scanned Mandy's face. "Dark eye circles aren't exactly your look, girl. If you were going for sultry, you missed and wound up with haunted."

Haunted by the threat to Rob's life, by the fact that I caused it. Mandy opened the jelly container and picked up a knife to spread some on Rob's toast. "But you need me to help you eat. I want to take care of you."

She wanted to tell Rob why, that she loved him, but Cynthia was in the room. Why didn't she say it before, when she had the chance, rather than make that lame reference to his Pop?

Rob took the knife out of Mandy's hand. "I hate grape jelly."

Mandy looked at the packet label. "Dammit. I knew that."

"I don't intend to be here very long anyway," Rob said. "I'm going to talk the doc into letting me sign out today."

"Today?" Cynthia asked. "That's so soon."

"I've got a business to run."

"With one good arm?"

"My staff will help me. And Mandy will be there to help at the house."

Cynthia crossed her arms, lifted a brow and looked from Rob to Mandy. "Oh? I hadn't heard about this new arrangement."

"It's temporary," Mandy said.

Rob grinned at her. "I'm looking forward to you scrubbing my back."

Mandy could tell from his grin that he wasn't just thinking about his back. A flush warmed her cheeks.

"All right, you two," Cynthia broke in. "If you're going to go all moony-eyed, I'm out of here."

"Could you *please* take her with you?"

As Cynthia said, "Sure," Mandy said, "But, I thought—"

"You need to get cleaned up and get some rest." Rob picked up the keys on his nightstand and tossed them to Mandy. "You can move some of your things, my car, and Lucky to my place. I'll call you when they release me, then you can drive me to my office."

Realizing debate was futile, Mandy stood.

At that moment, Gonzo walked in the room. "Hey bro, I hear you lost a lot of blood. Where's a guy line up to donate around here?"

When his gaze fell on Mandy, his jaw hardened and he took a step back.

"Please stay, Gonzo," she said. "I'm just leaving, and I'm sure Rob would like your company."

He gave a silent nod, then stood aside while Mandy and Cynthia left the room.

In the hallway, Cynthia asked, "What's up with Gonzo?"

"I had to pull him off a trip yesterday, and he got mad and quit." Hurt by the shocked expression on Cynthia's face, Mandy felt the need to explain. "He showed up late and drunk. His drinking has gotten out of hand. It's affecting the safety of the customers."

"You're talking like a boss. I thought you were his friend."

"Yes, I am. I'm hoping he'll cool down enough that we can talk about it, and he'll come back to work for me." Mandy pushed open the doors to head out into the hospital parking lot. "But only if he'll do it sober. I am a boss now, Cynthia, and I owe it to Uncle Bill to run the business the best way I can."

Cynthia frowned. "Maybe we can do some kind of group intervention for Gonzo."

"Maybe. But I'd wait awhile. He's still pretty pissed." Shading her eyes against the sun, Mandy scanned the lot, then remembered that her car was around the side in the emergency parking lot. She pointed in that direction. "My car's over there."

"I'm at the end of the next row. I'll wait there for you and follow you home. You could probably use some help packing, right?"

"Yeah, thanks." Mandy looked at her watch. "I'm due in at work in half an hour."

"I'm sure Steve will understand. Rob's shooting was in the paper this morning." Cynthia laid a hand on Mandy's arm. "You two seem to be moving pretty fast. You sure you want to move in with him?"

"It's only until he can take care of himself. I can't leave him to struggle on his own, especially since he got shot at my place. He needs me."

Cynthia peered at her. "And maybe you need him, too."

———

When Mandy called Steve to tell him she would be in late, he asked her to meet him at the Salida Boat Ramp. He was volunteering as a standby rescuer for the kayak slalom race. After the call, she and Cynthia ran a complicated shuttle to move some of her things, Lucky, and both Mandy's car and Rob's truck to his place.

She felt odd being in Rob's house without him there, but Cynthia's bustling presence made her forget her awkwardness. The previous owner had had a couple of dogs, so the yard was fenced. After some liberal sniffing, Lucky seemed to settle in, especially when Mandy gave him a rawhide bone to chew. By nine thirty, she was ready to report to Steve.

"I'll come with you," Cynthia said. "I want to watch the races myself."

After parking a couple of blocks from the river, Mandy threaded through the crowds with Cynthia in tow. When one of Cynthia's regulars offered to buy her a beer, Mandy continued on toward the banks of the Arkansas River. She spotted Steve sitting in his kayak in an eddy below the boat ramp and knelt on the rocks beside him.

"How's Rob?" was the first thing out of his mouth.

"He lost a lot of blood but seemed okay this morning," Mandy replied. "He won't be able to use his left arm for a while, though."

"Bummer. He'll hate not being able to paddle." Steve shaded his eyes and studied her. "You stayed up all night with him, didn't you?"

"Do I look that bad?"

"Just bushed. Look, why don't you take today off? Most of the rangers are out on the river, some in a volunteer capacity like me. We can probably limp along without you for a day while you catch up on your sleep."

"I already took last Friday off. I hate to do it again so soon. What will the other rangers think?"

"They haven't had to deal with two deaths and a near-miss in the space of ten days, Mandy. Why was someone shooting through your window anyway?"

"Detective Quintana and I think it's because I've been asking too many inconvenient questions about Tom King's death."

"So he thinks Tom King's killer is out to get you, too?"

Mandy bit her lip. "Maybe."

Steve's brows furrowed. "Damn. How's he going to protect you?"

"He can't. Doesn't have the manpower. I'll just have to lay low for a while. I won't be sleeping at my house for a few nights. Hopefully, Quintana will find the killer by then."

"You going to stay with your brother in the Springs? That's an awfully long commute to work."

"No, I can't abandon Uncle Bill's business. Or Rob. He needs me to take care of him."

"Ah." Steve gave a knowing nod. "So you'll be at Rob's."

"It's not what you think. And don't tell anyone." Mandy spotted a kayaker working his way through the slalom gates hanging over the river. His orange helmet and sun-faded green PFD looked familiar. "Isn't that Jeff King?"

Steve peered upriver. "Yep."

"Where'd he get a kayak? His was bashed up in the Pine Creek Boater X Thursday."

"He came by my place last night. Talked me into loaning him one of the demo boats that we use for rescue drills."

As Jeff executed a tight turn around one of the gate poles, the bottom of his blue kayak rolled up out of the water.

Mandy spotted a familiar white patch. "The one that went through Royal Gorge by itself. It got pretty bashed up. Doesn't it still leak?"

"Not that much. The duct tape Jeff patched the holes with should hold for the length of the race. He's desperate for either a prize boat or money and kept begging until I finally gave in. He agreed to clean out our boat garage in exchange for the loan."

An image of a muddy floor, dusty shelves, spider webs, and muddled gear popped into Mandy's mind. "He really is desperate."

Then a realization hit her. "You said he came by last night. What time?"

"A little after nine."

"How long did he stay?"

"He was on a rant about the unfairness of life, how the river gods were against him. Not just for crunching his boat, but also for what he claimed was the false arrest of his mother. He was incensed by that, called Quintana an incompetent boob. It took me a while to get him to say what he really wanted. Then, by the time we got the kayak out of the boat garage, it was after ten."

"And you were with him the whole time?"

"Yeah." Steve raised a brow at her. "You suspect Jeff of killing his father and shooting Rob?"

"Well, from what you've just told me, he certainly didn't shoot Rob."

Mandy stood and watched Jeff King negotiate the last two gates in the course. As far as she could tell, he had nailed every gate, even the next-to-last tricky red one that had to be navigated in an upstream direction. If his speed was good, he might actually place in the money.

When Jeff passed Steve's kayak, he flashed a thumbs-up at them, his wide grin showing he was satisfied with his performance.

He sure isn't acting like someone who orchestrated a shooting last night. An image of scowling Paula King sprang into her mind. *Hiring a shooter would be more Mama's style.*

EIGHTEEN

My great-grandfather was but a waterman,
looking one way, and rowing another.
—JOHN BUNYAN

WHEN CYNTHIA WANDERED UP with her free beer, Mandy said her thanks and goodbyes to Steve. After walking away, she pulled Cynthia aside to fill her in on what Steve had said about Jeff King, finishing up with, "So that means Nate Fowler, Lenny Preble, and Evie Olson are the top suspects for shooting Rob now."

"And for killing Tom King?" Cynthia asked.

"Likely. Do you know if any of them own a rifle or go hunting?"

Cynthia thought for a moment. "I remember Evie saying her dad took her hunting a few years back with some goofy idea of it being a bonding experience. Evie totally hated the whole trip, from sleeping on the ground, to overdosing on Dinty Moore stew and jerky, to shooting innocent animals."

"But did she learn how to shoot? Does she own a rifle?"

"I really don't know."

"Okay, let's try another tack. Do you think Evie knows enough about plants to make—" Mandy stopped. She wasn't supposed to reveal what type of poison Tom King was killed with to anyone, not even Cynthia.

Cynthia drank the last of her beer and crumpled the plastic cup. "To make what?"

"A poison of some type."

With a shrug, Cynthia said, "I wouldn't be surprised if she was into gardening, but do you think she's sophisticated enough to figure out how to make poison? Isn't a bunch of chemistry involved?"

Cynthia's reference to gardening gave Mandy an idea. "I don't know why I didn't think of this before. I should check out everyone's garden, see if any poisonous plants are growing in them."

"I didn't know you were such an expert on poisonous plants." Cynthia cocked her head and studied Mandy, as if she could sense that Mandy was keeping something from her.

"Detective Quintana showed me literature about them. I can recognize some of the common ones, I think."

"So you think Tom King's killer had been planning to kill him for months, long enough to grow the plants?"

"No, not necessarily. Quintana told me some of the most common garden flowers are poisonous, so the killer may have already had the plants handy. They may even have given him or her the idea of using poison." Mandy grabbed Cynthia's crushed cup and tossed it in a nearby trash can. "C'mon. I have a phone book in the car. You can look up addresses for me, so we can scout out these people's gardens."

With a wistful glance at the slalom course on the river, Cynthia said, "There goes my plan to enjoy the races this morning."

When they reached Mandy's car, Cynthia looked up Evie Olson's address in the telephone book, and Mandy headed off in that direction. She hadn't driven more than five blocks when she came upon a line of red traffic cones blocking the next intersection. Two police cars glided slowly past them with lights flashing and sirens blaring. The mobile van from the KBVC radio station followed, blasting a jaunty tune.

Mandy groaned. "Oh no, I forgot about the parade."

"Maybe we can turn around."

Mandy looked in her rearview mirror. Already, two cars had pulled up behind her, side-by-side. Their occupants were climbing out to watch the FIBArk parade. "Too late."

"Well, if I can't watch the slalom races, at least I can watch the parade." Cynthia opened her car door.

With her fingers drumming on the steering wheel, Mandy considered asking the other drivers to move their cars.

"Those flower gardens aren't going anywhere," Cynthia said. "Might as well enjoy the parade. It's never very long anyway."

Mandy let out a sigh and followed Cynthia to the cones.

Clowns and a gaggle of energetic pre-teen cheerleaders followed the radio van. A motley collection of floats motored by. Their occupants ranged from Collegiate Peaks Anglers to the local chapter of the Red Hat Society, the ladies on board dressed in purple and sporting all manner of clashing red hats. Many of the makeshift rafts that would compete in the Hooligan Race that afternoon had been hauled onto flatbed trucks. Their costumed crews tossed candy and waved enthusiastically to the crowds lining the route.

Cynthia hollered encouragement to all of them and jumped up and down while begging for candy. About fifteen minutes into the parade, she grabbed Mandy's arm. "Look, there's Rob's gang. They went for a pirate theme this year."

A chorus of hearty "Avast, mateys!" greeted Mandy's ears. Among the guides in swashbuckler costumes, she spied Gonzo in his well-endowed Elena costume, now transformed into a well-endowed pirate wench. When she waved at the float, one of Rob's rafting guides recognized her. He held up a hand-lettered sign that read, "Win one for the Robster."

"Rob's going to hate missing out on the Hooligan race," Mandy said. Wondering if he had been successful in convincing his doctor to discharge him, she checked her watch. It was still midmorning, ten thirty, so maybe Rob's doctor hadn't come by to see him yet. She pulled her cell phone out of her pocket to make sure she hadn't missed his call, since it was set to vibrate, but there was no message.

A shower of hard objects pelted her head. Mandy instinctively ducked and threw up her arms. "Ouch. What the heck are those?"

"Jolly Ranchers," Cynthia answered as she bent down to scoop the colorful hard candy off the ground. "Though, since pirates are throwing them, maybe they're supposed to be Jolly Rogers."

Mandy looked up and saw Gonzo grinning at her, an evil glint in his eye. Did he hit her on purpose? She soon received her answer when he pulled his arm out of a bag and pitched a handful straight at her face.

Mandy spun and ducked again. The hard candies pinged off her back. "Gonzo's obviously still mad at me."

"Nah, he's just having fun." Cynthia stuffed candies in her pocket with one hand and waved at Gonzo with the other.

Mandy rubbed her sore head. "Some fun."

Soon, the appearance of the Salida high school marching band signaled the beginning of the end. Sweat poured down the faces of the tuba players. A horse troop followed them, and a street sweeper brought up the rear, cleaning up whatever the pooper-scooper duo missed.

Mandy headed back to her car.

Cynthia followed, unwrapping one of the Jolly Rancher candies. "That was nice of Gonzo to throw us so much candy."

Yeah, right. Not wanting to voice her disagreement and upset Cynthia, Mandy just climbed in the car and started it up while she waited for her friend to get in. "We should hurry to Evie's house. Hopefully, she's out watching the parade, too, and we can check her garden before she gets back."

A volunteer came by and picked up the traffic cones, and Mandy stepped on the gas. A few minutes later, they were parked on the street beside Evie's small, two-storied clapboard house, which sat on a corner lot.

Mandy approached the four-foot slatted wood fence surrounding the back yard. A vegetable garden was staked out on the other side of the yard. Next to the fence on the street side, a long flower garden had been planted. Funky sunflower sculptures made out of brass with a mature green patina stood among the real things. However, the staked, nodding heads of the real sunflowers didn't have the disturbing facial expressions of twisted fear, anger, and gaping pain that their brass cousins did.

Mandy slowly stepped toward the rear of the lot, studying the varieties of the flowers in the bed as she went. She recognized daisies, Indian blanket flowers, coneflowers, and lupine. Then she stopped.

Next to a bunch of blooming foxglove, also a poisonous plant, stood some plants about three feet tall with palmate leaves. She crouched down to get a closer look. A few buds had appeared. One had a sliver of blue petal peeking out from underneath the bud casing. *Bingo!*

"Find anything?" Cynthia had come up behind Mandy and spoke right in her ear.

Mandy started. "Jesus, Cynthia, you spooked me."

To throw Cynthia off track, Mandy pointed at the foxglove. "You familiar with that flower?"

"Yeah, foxglove, where digitalis, the heart medicine, comes from." Cynthia drew in a breath. "Oh, that could be poisonous, couldn't it?"

A car drove by, and the occupant stared at the two women.

"Let's go," Mandy said. "We don't want Evie's neighbors getting suspicious."

After they got back in the car, Mandy said, "Now look up Nate Fowler's address."

After they arrived at Fowler's home, Mandy slowly coasted past it. She parked in front of a house two doors down. Nate's home had no fence, but it sat between two houses on either side, all facing a park across the street. The three homes looked quiet, with no cars outside, no one in the yards, and no discernable movement in the windows.

Mandy peered out the windshield at the large, stucco-and-tile Southwestern-styled home. "There are a few flowers out front that we can check from the street, but to see the back yard, we'll have to walk around."

Cynthia leaned forward to stare at the house. "What if someone's home and catches us snooping around in the yard?"

"That would not be a good thing."

"So what do we do?"

"We certainly can't go up and ring their doorbell and ask permission to search their yard."

"What about ringing the doorbell and running, just to see if anyone comes to the door?"

"If Nate's home and if he's the one who shot Rob, the last thing I want is for him to see me."

"I'll do it, then. Keep the car door open for me." Cynthia climbed out before Mandy could object.

Mandy held her breath while Cynthia sauntered nonchalantly up to the stoop, looked around to check that no one was on the street, and rang the doorbell. She loped across the lawns and dove into the car. "Get down!"

While Cynthia awkwardly pulled the car door shut from her slumped position on the seat, Mandy slid down in the driver's seat. Slowly, she raised her head enough to see the front door. After counting to ten, then twenty, then thirty, she let out a slow breath.

"Looks like no one's home. Let's go."

Cynthia followed her to the front yard and kept a lookout while Mandy examined the flower beds below the front windows.

"Nothing," Mandy said. "Let's check the back yard."

She led the way around the side of the house. A number of large urn-shaped planters filled with flowers were stationed around the colored concrete patio. Two tall blue spruces flanked a long rainbow-shaped flower bed between them at the far end of the lot. While Cynthia headed for the flower bed, Mandy checked the urns but saw no monkshood. She joined Cynthia, and again none of the flowers had the right characteristics.

Mandy pointed toward a garden shed in the far corner of the lot. "Might as well search around that." She circled the shed to check for more flowers. As she was rounding the far corner, she heard the door of the shed creak open.

Cynthia let out a low whistle. "Check this out."

Mandy hurried to the doorway and looked in. Cynthia stood next to the left wall and lifted a rifle by its barrel, holding it up for Mandy to see.

"Put that down!" Mandy yelled. "Don't you know not to touch evidence?"

Eyes, wide, Cynthia let the rifle drop back onto its stock to lean against the wall. "Evidence? What do you mean?"

"What if that's the gun that was used to shoot Rob?"

"Criminy!" Cynthia stepped away from the rifle.

"Let's get out of here. Now!" Mandy wheeled. She had just started toward the house with Cynthia when she heard the sound of a car pulling into the driveway and a garage door opening. "Shit," she whispered.

Cynthia froze. "What do we do?"

"Run for the spruces and hide." Mandy took off for the nearest one.

Cynthia panted behind her. They both ended up squatting behind the same spruce, but it was large enough to cloak them from the view of anyone in the house.

"I'm so nervous, I'm about to pee my pants," Cynthia whispered. "How are we going to get out of here?"

Mandy spread apart a couple of the spruce's lower limbs and peeked in the house windows. Nate's wife was unloading grocery bags in the kitchen. "I think it's only Nate's wife, not the man himself, but I still don't want her to see us. Let's wait a bit and see where she goes."

"Okay, while we're waiting, here's a blonde joke apropos to our situation."

When Mandy shot Cynthia a derisive look, Cynthia said, "Hey, might as well make the best of things. Anyway, a brunette and a blonde are walking along in a lovely park, like this yard here. The brunette says suddenly, 'Awww, look at the dead birdie.' The blonde stops, looks up, and says, 'Where?'"

Mandy chuckled, then looked up. "I hope there aren't any birds sitting in this tree, preparing to drop a bomb on us."

"Lovely thought."

They waited until Nate's wife had finished her task and left the room.

"Where's she gone to now?" Cynthia asked. "My legs are cramping."

A window was raised in the second story then came the faint sound of running water. A toilet flushing? A shower? The sink? Mandy counted to sixty and listened again. The water was still running.

"I think she's taking a shower. Now's our time to make a run for it. Go!"

The two of them shot out from behind the tree, through the yard, across the front lawns, and into the car.

Mandy fumbled the keys out of her pocket and started the engine.

Just then, Nate's wife ran out of the front door of the house. "Hey! What were you doing in my yard?"

Mandy slammed the car into gear and stomped on the accelerator. As she drove away, she checked the rearview mirror. Mrs. Fowler stood in her yard, shading her eyes and staring at the car. Mandy hoped the woman wasn't reading the license plate.

Mandy didn't stop until they were entirely out of the neighborhood. Then she pulled over. She took a big breath, which felt like her first since they high-tailed it out of Nate Fowler's back yard.

"Whew, that was close," Cynthia said. "Do you think she could tell who we were?"

"I sure hope not." Mandy looked at Cynthia. "You up for one more, or have you had enough?"

"Enough? Heck no, I haven't had this much fun since we pulled that panty raid on Kendra and her pal's tent when we all went camping at the Sand Dunes."

"Their payback was tough, though. I had to wash my sleeping bag twice to get all the sand out." And payback on this expedition could be much tougher. Their adversary had a gun and had shown a willingness to use it. "You're sure? Whoever we're looking for has killed one person and tried to kill another."

"I can't let you do it alone, Mandy. And I know you will." Cynthia folded her arms and set her jaw.

Mandy looked at her a moment longer, then put the car in gear. "Okay, find Lenny Preble's address."

Lenny lived in a one-story cottage, not unlike Mandy's, also with a small yard contained by a chain link fence. But unlike Mandy's, Lenny's yard was meticulously groomed and contained a large vegetable and flower garden along the length of the back fence. Mandy stepped into the alley behind Lenny's yard to walk along the fence. Cynthia trailed behind, her head swiveling from side to side to check for observers.

Against the fence, a bank of corn stalks rustled in the warm breeze. Past them, plump green tomatoes hung on staked bushes. Mandy's mouth watered as she imagined dipping slices into cornmeal and frying them up. Fried green tomatoes had been a favorite dish ever since her uncle had introduced her to the southern delicacy. She shook her head. *Can't think about him now.*

The next section of Lenny's garden seemed to be devoted to herbs. Mandy recognized the curly parsley heads, stalks of chive, and delicate thin leaves of dill plants. She had moved on to the flower bed when her cell phone vibrated in her pocket. A flash of panic hit her before she realized it wasn't ringing and no one could hear it.

When she answered, Rob said, "I convinced the doc to release me, but he wants the nurse to talk to you when you pick me up to make sure we're both going to follow instructions. Can you be here in a few minutes? She can't wait very long."

"Sure. See you soon." Mandy pocketed the cell phone and turned to Cynthia. "I've got to pick up Rob."

"Want me to finish up for you?" Cynthia asked. "I know what foxglove looks like, and I can walk to my place from here. In fact, I think that's foxglove right there." She pointed to the left side of the flower bed.

Mandy didn't want to tell Cynthia that she was looking for the wrong plant, so she scanned the whole flower bed, as if she was having trouble finding the foxglove. After spotting some plants about three feet tall with palmate leaves, she peered at them to check the buds.

"Not there," Cynthia said. "Over to the left."

"Oh, I see now." Mandy did indeed see the foxglove, but couldn't make out any color on the unopened buds of the palmate plants. They looked like Western monkshood plants, but without climbing the fence into Lenny's yard, she couldn't be sure. She stepped closer.

Cynthia pulled on Mandy's arm and hissed, "Someone's coming."

"We're out of here, then." No way did Mandy want a repeat of what had happened in the Fowlers' yard. Trying for an air of nonchalance, as if she belonged in the neighborhood, Mandy led the way back to the car. She nodded at the teenage kid walking a prissy little poodle that must have belonged to his mother, given the embarrassed glance he cast their way.

When they reached the car without the kid saying anything, she let out the breath she'd been holding and said to Cynthia, "I'll drop you off on the way to the hospital."

While Mandy drove Cynthia home, she nibbled on her lip. *How extensive are these instructions going to be? Am I really up to nursing Rob?*

———

Mandy stood at Rob's kitchen sink a couple of hours later and took a long drink of water. She had just finished loading the dishwasher after she and Rob had eaten the ham and cheese sandwiches she'd fixed for lunch. She made a note to swing by her house sometime later to get her peanut butter and blackberry jelly, so she wouldn't go into PBJ withdrawal.

A glance at the pile of bandaging supplies on the counter caused a heavy sense of dread to settle on her. Tonight would be the first time she'd have to redress Rob's wound by herself. She remembered the nausea she had felt when the nurse described signs of infection to her—the green pus, the smell. The last thing Mandy wanted to do was get her nose anywhere near the angry red scar.

She plunked the glass on the counter and turned away from the medical supplies. *You'll do it because you have to do it, girl. For Rob.*

The subject of her mental conversation sat ensconced in his easy chair, with his feet up and remote in hand. After watching him flinch and groan whenever he moved during lunch and seeing his face grow paler, Mandy had forced him to swallow a couple of his pain pills. Now, his eyes were drooping. He was having trouble focusing on the baseball game on the set.

Fine. He can use a nap. When Mandy's cell phone rang, she snatched it up and opened it, hoping to avoid startling Ron out of his doze. *No luck.*

He sat up and looked expectantly at her.

The caller was Quintana. "Where are you?"

"At Rob's house."

"I'll be right over."

Mandy closed the phone and sat in the chair next to Rob's. "Detective Quintana's coming."

Rob raised an eyebrow. "He must have something to report. Maybe he arrested whoever did this." He pointed with his chin at his bandaged shoulder.

"I hope so." And she hoped he wasn't coming for another reason.

A few minutes later, a knock sounded at the door. Rob clicked off the TV, and Mandy let the detective in. He walked into the living room with a decided bounce to his step and waited for Mandy to resume her seat. He seemed too excited to sit himself.

"We found the gun that matched the bullet they cut out of your shoulder, or at least we're pretty darn sure. The CBI ballistics lab will confirm that when they compare the rifling marks."

"CBI?" Ron asked.

"Colorado Bureau of Investigation."

"Whose gun?" A sinking feeling stole into Mandy's stomach.

Quintana turned to her. "Nate Fowler's."

Of the five top suspects, she would have pegged him as having the least volatile personality. But maybe that was the problem—he held it all in until he exploded.

"The bullet came out of a Winchester hunting rifle," Quintana continued. "We found one in Fowler's garden shed no more than an hour ago, and it had been fired recently. Still smelled of cordite. None of the other suspects had weapons in their homes."

He sat on the edge of the sofa. "Nate kept claiming the rifle wasn't his, that he'd never seen it before. That made him even more suspicious in my mind, so I arrested him. But I'm having CBI run an ownership search and look for fingerprints, too."

"Oh, hell." Mandy put her head in her hands.

"I thought you'd be happy," Quintana said.

When Mandy lifted her head, the detective was staring at her with a quizzical gaze. She cleared her throat. "You aren't going to like what I have to say."

Quintana and Rob shot glances at each other.

Mandy shifted uncomfortably in her seat, feeling the heat rise in her cheeks. "Cynthia touched the barrel of that rifle."

"What! How do you know that?"

"Because I was there when she did it." Before she could lose her nerve, Mandy blurted out, "We were searching the Fowlers' yard for Western monkshood plants. And Evie Olson's and Lenny Preble's."

"Hell, Mandy, what part of 'you need to lay low for a while' did you not understand?" Quintana jumped to his feet and started pacing. "You two could have botched my whole investigation by tampering with evidence."

"I'm really sorry. I knew better, but Cynthia had already picked up the rifle before I saw her with it."

"Damn. I'll have to fingerprint her. And if her prints show up on the gun, Nate can make the case that Cynthia was the one who fired it at Rob, not him."

"Why would Cynthia do that?" Rob asked.

Quintana slapped his thigh. "Who cares? All Nate has to do is throw suspicion on the story that he fired it." He stuck his chin out at Mandy. "And did you even consider that while casing out suspects' gardens, they could have been casing you out from inside their homes? Aiming a gun at you?"

"You just said the other suspects didn't have weapons at their houses."

Quintana's face reddened. "But you didn't know that! And what if Fowler had his gun with him inside the house instead of in his shed? Both of you girls could be dead now. What am I supposed to do to keep you out of trouble, tie you up?"

With a broad leer, Rob said, "Now that I'd like to see!"

"You stay out of this, buster." Mandy glared at him, then focused on Quintana. "I have to take care of Rob. Now that he's out of the hospital, I'll be sticking close to him. You don't need to worry about me anymore."

Quintana pointed at Rob. "Make sure she stays with you. I expect you to call me if she gets another idiot hankering to do any more sniffing around."

Rob grinned. "You've got my word on that."

After rubbing a hand across his forehead, Quintana glared at Mandy. "And I know what your license plate number is."

"Oh no, did Mrs. Fowler report us?"

"Damn right."

"Did she know who we were?"

"No, but she will soon. When you go over to apologize. Not only that, you'll have to convince her to drop the case if you don't want to face trespassing charges."

"Lovely." For Cynthia's sake, Mandy would have to grovel to Mrs. Fowler until she dropped the charges. "When?"

"I have to lay the groundwork first. Gauge her mood. Right now she's probably feeling the need to strike out at someone, since we just took her husband away in cuffs."

Mandy leaned forward. "Cynthia and I didn't see any Western monkshood plants at Nate's house. Did you find aconite powder or monkshood roots?"

"No, though we searched thoroughly. I only arrested Nate for firing the rifle at Rob. I don't have any evidence that he's the one who killed Tom King. That could have been a completely different person, for a completely different reason, but my gut tells me the two incidents are linked."

Mandy's gut agreed with Quintana's. Could that rifle have been planted in Fowler's unlocked shed by someone else? "I think both Lenny Preble and Evie Olson have Western monkshood growing in their yards."

Quintana frowned. "Did anyone see you at their houses?"

Mandy took a deep breath. "No one at Evie's house, but a teen-age boy walking a dog saw us at Lenny's. I don't think he suspected we didn't belong in the neighborhood, though."

"Good. You two have given me enough messes to straighten out."

"Speaking of messes, why aren't you questioning Nate? Where is he now?"

"He's refusing to talk without a lawyer present. Trouble is, his lawyer's in Pueblo, so I have to wait for his return. Thought I'd give you the good news in the meantime. I never imagined what a barge full of bad news you had to give me."

Quintana's radio crackled, the dispatcher saying something about legal counsel. He keyed the mike. "I'll be right there."

He turned to Mandy. "Nate Fowler's lawyer has arrived. I need to get back to the station. No more investigating on your own, you hear? Or I might just have to put you in a cell next to Nate's."

NINETEEN

If you sit by the river long enough,
the bodies of all your enemies will float by.
—CHINESE PROVERB

MANDY CLOSED THE DOOR behind Quintana, then leaned her back against it to think. He had said the two crimes might not be connected, but she thought the same person was responsible for both. The problem was that Quintana hadn't found any signs of aconite at Nate Fowler's home. Could it be obtained in some other form? Was there some other way someone could get their hands on aconite without growing the plants?

"I recognize that look," Rob said. "You're hatching some plan. You better not be thinking of leaving here after what Quintana just said."

"No, I'm just thinking of doing some surfing." She sat down at Rob's computer. "Some Internet surfing."

"I suppose that's harmless." He tried to stifle a yawn.

"Why don't you take a nap?" Mandy said. "I promise I'll stay right here."

"Wake me in a couple of hours. I want to watch my crew run the Hooligan Race." Rob lay back in the easy chair and cranked up the footrest.

Mandy typed "aconite" into the Internet search engine and scanned the results. As she paged down, she soon found a reference to a homeopathic remedy catalog and clicked on the reference. The website named a long list of ills that the toxin supposedly cured, from flu and chills to feelings of apprehension or fear. *Yeah, fear that someone's planning to poison you.*

For a mere thirteen dollars, one could buy thirty tablets, and for nineteen dollars, the economy 200-tablet bottle. It was also available as a skin liniment. Mandy doubted any business would sell a poisonous dosage, so she clicked on 'dosage and potency guidelines' to see if there were any warnings about how much was too much, but found nothing. Of course not. The guidelines were deliberately vague to keep someone from suing the company for giving out dangerous advice.

She scanned the list of homeopathic remedies and found other toxins listed—belladonna, digitalis, arsenic. Could someone gather enough of a poison by ordering it from these websites to come up with a lethal dose? Or were the toxic properties of the poisons somehow neutralized before they were made into homeopathic remedies? While Rob slept, Mandy scanned all the information she could find. By the time four thirty rolled around, when she figured she should wake Rob and get him ready and down to the river for the five thirty race, she had a headache and strained eyes, but no real answers.

———

While Mandy drove Rob to the Salida Riverside Park, a suspicion kept nagging her, like an insistent child tugging at her mother's skirt. She and Detective Quintana were missing something. Even though she had just met Nate Fowler, she hadn't seen anything suspicious in his behavior. She doubted he would have become incensed enough at her questions to fire a bullet through her window. Nor did she believe he was the type to poison his competition.

Though it was impossible to know what lurked in the minds of people who behaved reasonably on the outside, Mandy still expected some kind of crack to appear in the facade of sanity. You have to be at least a little insane or obsessed to kill someone.

Mandy drove the streets near the park for a while, but the closest parking space she could find was still two blocks away. She came around to the passenger side of the Subaru to give Rob a hand in getting out, though she could see his jaw harden at the reversal in their roles. Without comment, she tucked herself under his good arm so he could lean on her while they walked to the park. She smiled up at him and squeezed his waist, pretending that she just wanted to be close to him.

Their progress was slow, because locals who knew Rob wanted to ask him how he was faring, or if they hadn't heard about his injury yet, what had happened to him. The story was getting pretty darn old by the time they reached the full bleachers near the boat ramp. A couple of townsfolk sitting on the edge of the third row waved Mandy and Rob over and gave up their seats for them. When Rob protested, they pooh-poohed his concern, saying they needed to get a beer and find some shade anyway.

Mandy thanked them, then pulled a bottle of ice water out of her backpack and handed it to Rob. The sun was beating down on the bleachers unmercifully. She worried that the heat, combined with his painkillers, might get to him before the race was over. His face was already pale from the walk.

The shores of the Arkansas teemed with masses of people who probably had begun lining up an hour ago to watch the most popular event at FIBArk. Ice cream and popsicle juice dripped down kids' sticky fingers and faces. Adults held plastic cups of beer and iced soda against their cheeks to cool off.

A raft floated downstream, then took up position in an eddy on the other side of the river, ready to assist in rescues. Mandy recognized Kendra and one of the other seasonal river rangers inside.

She pointed out the raft to Rob. "You see Kendra?"

"Yeah. How many swimmers do you think we'll have this year?"

"From the looks of some of the contraptions in this morning's parade, a lot."

He turned to her in surprise. "You saw the parade?"

"Cynthia and I got stuck on a side street crossing the route on our way to look at people's gardens. We saw your pirate crew."

Rob cast a wistful gaze upriver, where the Hooligan Race rafts were gathering in heats around the bend. "Wish I could be out there with them."

"I'm sorry, Rob." She gave his thigh a squeeze.

He covered her hand with his. "I'm not. Better me than you."

A roar went up from the crowd as the first heat of six home-made rafts appeared in the river. Everyone in the bleachers stood. Mandy helped Rob to his feet so he could see, too.

A giant turtle constructed out of inner tubes lashed together and covered with green tarp roiled in the water, pushed along by enthusiastic paddlers straddling the turtle's legs. The gangly reptile was flanked by a woman in a fat bee costume paddling a bathtub and Fred Flintstone and Barney Rubble look-alikes in a makeshift Flintstones car. Surrounding them, Vikings, Hawaiian-shirted surfers, and grass-skirted Polynesians slapped paddles in the water from a motley collection of homemade watercraft.

Rob laughed. "I predict the Flintstones car goes down in the boat ramp rapid."

"I doubt the bathtub will survive it either," Mandy said. "What happens when it fills up with water?"

But mishaps were exactly what the crowd wanted and was hollering for. The winner of the race was not the boat that finished first or in the best shape, but the one that put on the best show for the onlookers.

The noise increased as the rafts hit the rapid and floundered in the whitewater, spilling occupants and shedding pieces. The turtle lost its tail, but the rest of the body survived. The bathtub filled and rolled over, so the bumblebee occupant had to hang on to the bottom. Amazingly, the Flintstones car remained upright, eliciting a congratulatory roar from the crowd.

Mandy grabbed Rob's arm. "Oh look, it's a Viking funeral!"

The Vikings were standing up with arms and paddles crossed over their chests, while one blew mournfully on what looked like a steer's horn. Their wooden raft slowly disintegrated around them, while the "body," which looked suspiciously like a collection of soggy pillows lashed together, slid into the current.

Rob gave out a hoot. "A funeral for the raft or the deceased?"

When the rafts, or what was left of them, had passed, Mandy sat next to Rob and wiped tears of laughter out of the corners of her eyes. It felt good to laugh. Really good. She realized she'd had way too much sorrow in her life lately.

Rob gave her a squeeze. "Your Uncle Bill would have loved this."

Mandy nodded. "The Hooligan Race was the highlight of his year."

"Maybe he's here."

Mandy looked out at the sparkling waters of the Arkansas River flowing past them. "Maybe he is." She leaned into Rob's hug.

"Well, if it isn't Mandy Tanner and her lover boy."

Evie Olson stood next to the bleachers with Shirley Logan, the two dolled up in sherbet-colored capris, spaghetti-strap tops, and matching floppy straw hats. Evie had accessorized with a spangly, sheer shawl in a rainbow swirl of colors draped over her capris and tied at the hip. She took a noisy slurp of her beer.

"Hello, Evie," Rob said in a cautious tone.

Evie took a step closer to Mandy and swayed. She obviously had drunk one too many beers. She jabbed a finger in Mandy's thigh. "I don't appreciate you siccing Detective Quintana on me after you pulled a fast one in the Day Spa."

Mandy swept Evie's hand away. "I didn't sic him on you. He's conducting his own investigation."

"With your slimy help. Fat lot of good it's done. The idiot can't decide who to arrest next for what. First he goes after Paula King then he lets her go and picks up Nate Fowler."

Shirley laughed and slapped Evie's arm. "He'll be coming after you next. Better get your lawyer lined up."

"That's not funny!" Evie glared at her friend, who dunked her nose in her beer glass and stepped away.

Evie swung her evil eye toward Mandy. "You and Quintana should move to Summit County. You'd fit right in at Keystone, since you're a couple of Keystone Kops."

Shirley snorted out a hysterical laugh. Titters came from a few folks in the bleachers around them.

"You obviously rehearsed that line," Mandy said with a sneer. "Couldn't you come up with something more imaginative?"

While Evie drew herself up to her full height, as if preparing for another round, Rob stood. "You're spoiling a good time for everyone, Evie. And you're drunk." He signaled Shirley. "Take her home so she can sleep it off."

Pointing a menacing finger at Rob, Evie said, "That's an insult. I am not drunk." She stumbled, causing the folks in the stands to titter again. She frowned at the group, then turned her wrath on Rob again. "I can make life very difficult for you, Robbie boy. Remember, my daddy's a councilman, and when I tell him—"

Her words were drowned out by the roar of the crowd, signaling that another group of rafts had started down the river course. Everyone else in the bleachers stood and craned their necks to see.

When Evie realized she had lost her audience, she threw down her beer cup and stomped off. Shirley picked it up and scurried after her.

"Good timing, there," Rob said in Mandy's ear. "Don't worry. She'll probably forget all about this by tomorrow."

Mandy worried her lip as she watched Evie gesturing angrily at her friend. "I'm not so sure." The woman sure had a temper when she got drunk. Could she build up enough anger to kill someone, someone who jilted her?

Rob nudged her and pointed upstream. This group included a raft shaped like the roof of a house with "FEMA sucks" painted on it.

"Oh, I get it," Mandy said. "They're Hurricane Katrina victims."

The drowning house was followed by a raft with upright, open plastic garbage cans lashed to the sides. Grinning passengers stood in the cans, their hips even with the water level. They squirted the crowds lining the banks with Super Soakers and hoses. Squeals of delight followed them down the river. One of the men wielding a hose was Lenny Preble. Mandy read the sign on the raft, "Save Arkansas River Water."

"Lenny and his gang don't miss an opportunity to spread their message, do they?" Rob said.

"You've got to admit that using the river water itself to make their point is creative." And just how far would Lenny go, Mandy wondered, to keep development interests from sucking up all the Arkansas River water rights? Would his radical views push him to commit murder?

"That's it!" Rob shouted before she could muse further. "That's the winner."

A large wooden platform straddled two commercial rafts, and a huge hoop decorated in red, white, and blue stood on one end.

At the other end, a young man dressed as an Evel Knievel–look-alike in a sparkly white jumpsuit straddled a bicycle.

Mandy's jaw dropped. "No, he's not—"

Rob chortled. "Yes, he is."

Just as the lumbering platform approached the boat ramp rapid, the man pushed off and peddled furiously. He and the bike sailed through the hoop and splashed separately into the river below the rapid. When his head popped up out of the water and he waved to the crowd, they whistled and clapped their approval.

Mandy grabbed Rob's arm. "That's Jeff King!"

"He's a risk taker all right," Rob replied, "but what a show. His raft deserves to win."

A risk taker. Was he capable of murdering his own father to get access to the money he needed to keep on living as a river rat?

As Mandy resumed her seat next to Rob to wait for the next heat of rafts, she began to think Evie was right, that Quintana had the wrong suspect in jail.

———

Hours later, Mandy poked her head through Rob's bedroom doorway. He was snoring peacefully, in the deep sleep of sheer exhaustion. After watching his guide crew's homemade pirate ship disintegrate in the river, the heat and painkillers finally got to him. He, too, had disintegrated. He had tried to insist on staying for the finals, but Mandy forced him off the viewing stand and into the car.

She couldn't get to sleep herself, however. The question of how Nate Fowler could have gotten his hands on the poison nagged her. She grabbed the peanut butter jar from the kitchen and sat down on the sofa. She dipped in her finger to fetch a glob out and sucked on it.

If Nate couldn't have gotten his hands on enough aconite via homeopathic remedies and he had none growing in his yard, Mandy wondered how else he could have gotten it. She snapped her sticky fingers. By stealing the plants from someone else's yard as easily as Cynthia and she had sneaked in and out of all but one of the yards they investigated. Or by finding Western monkshood plants growing in the wild.

But Mandy still wanted to rule out the homeopathic remedies source. She remembered Kendra was into homeopathic remedies, and she probably would be watching the Pine Creek Boater race footage at the Steamplant Theater that night. Maybe Mandy's rescue of Jeff King had been taped. She could learn something from watching it—and from talking to Kendra.

She wrote a note to Rob that said she was going to watch the race footage, then she let Lucky outside to do his final business of the day in Rob's yard. After grabbing her windbreaker, she softly closed the door behind her and started up her car, pushing Quintana's admonishment not to do any more sniffing around to the back of her mind.

During the ride over to the Steamplant, she conjured up lots of sound reasons why this excursion wasn't really sniffing around. She wasn't planning to talk to any of the suspects. This was for her own educational benefit in evaluating her rescue technique. Besides, she would drive herself crazy if she stayed at Rob's. And if she happened to see Kendra, what was the harm in asking her about homeopathic remedies?

When she entered the theater, the race footage had already begun, but the houselights were only dimmed to allow people to find each other. As much socializing as watching was going on, and the sound of the race was a lot less interesting than the visuals anyway. Mandy spotted Kendra talking to a couple of other rafting guides and worked her way through the rows of seats to get to the group.

Kendra's brows rose in surprise. "Mandy! I thought you'd be nursing Rob. How is he?"

"He's sound asleep and has been for hours. I doubt he'll wake up until morning, so there's not much nursing to be done now. I wanted to see the footage of my rescue of Jeff King. Has it come on yet?"

"Nah, they just started playing the tape about half an hour ago."

"Can I ask you some questions in the meantime?" Mandy pointed to a cluster of empty seats toward the back of the room, where hopefully she could ask her questions without being overheard.

"Sure, I guess." Kendra excused herself from her friends and followed Mandy to the seats in the back. "What's up?"

"You know a lot about homeopathic remedies, right?"

Kendra nodded. "Is this for you or Rob?"

"Neither. It's more of a general question." Mandy leaned close to Kendra and lowered her voice to almost a whisper. "Actually, it has something to do with the King case. You know he was poisoned, right?"

"Right, but you don't think he got a bad batch of homeopathic medicine, do you?"

"No, not exactly. I know a lot of homeopathics are actually tiny doses of what would be poisonous in a much larger amount. What I'm wondering is if someone could order enough of a homeopathic remedy to somehow create a fatal dose out of it."

Kendra thought for a moment. "I really doubt it. You see, homeopathic doses are diluted way too much. A usual dose is 6X, which means the substance is diluted to one part in ten multiplied six times, which results in one in a million parts. To get a strong dose, you somehow have to distill out that one part in a million. Otherwise, someone would have to drink gallons of the stuff to get enough to cause harm."

"Are they just diluted with water?"

"Not all the time. Depends on the substance and what it does in water. Sometimes it's diluted with alcohol or sugar or something else." Kendra shifted. "Even if someone could figure out the chemistry of how to get rid of all the water, alcohol, or sugar and concentrate it down, there's the matter of cost. You'd have to buy thousands of bottles of medicine to get enough for one fatal dose. Who's going to spend that much money?"

Especially when you can just grow the plant in your back yard. Mandy nodded. "Okay, thanks. You've convinced me."

Kendra made her way back to her friends.

Think, girl. No one, not she and Cynthia nor Quintana and his cops had found any monkshood plants or aconite powder at Nate Fowler's house—or dozens of trash bags full of homeopathic remedy bottles either. And Nate didn't come across to her as money-grubbing enough to kill for it. Someone else must have planted the rifle in his unlocked garden shed, just as they easily could have planted the monkshood root and powder in the Kings' detached garage. Someone who was trying to throw suspicion away from himself or herself.

That left Evie Olson and Lenny Preble, both of whom had Western monkshood growing in their yards, and Cynthia had said Evie had hunting experience. Mandy tried to recall if she had heard anything about Lenny Preble and hunting. Given his environmental leanings, she doubted it.

But Lenny was the one who brought the sealed sports drink bottles to the rafting trip. Two witnesses saw Paula give Tom King his bottle, but how did the bottle get from Lenny to Paula? Did he or Evie unseal one, drop in the aconite powder, reseal it, and hand it to Paula along with hers, asking her to give one to Tom? Again, to throw suspicion on her? If so, how could the killer be sure the right bottle got to Tom? And how could he or she have done all that unnoticed?

Mandy spotted Paula King in the crowd watching the race footage. She could ask Paula if she remembered who had given her the sports bottle. But Paula would probably refuse to answer and accuse Mandy of trying to cover up her own incompetence again.

"Hey, Mandy," Kendra shouted and pointed to the screen.

There was Mandy, tossing a throw rope to Jeff King, floundering in the Pine Creek rapid. When it hit him on the head, Kendra shouted "Bingo!" and a few guides clapped in appreciation at the perfect throw.

Mandy watched herself haul Jeff to shore, her feet scrabbling for purchase in the gravel. Maybe she should have tried to belay the rope around that nearby boulder instead of doing a body belay. Would there have been enough time to run the rope around the rock before Jeff's body weight started tugging on it? *Probably not.*

She got the crawly feeling that someone was staring at her and took her focus off the screen to search the audience. When her gaze swept over Paula King, the woman jerked her head forward. She said something to the person sitting on her far side, then glanced at Mandy again.

It's now or never. Mandy stood and made her way forward to Paula's row, then bumped past knees until she reached the empty seat next to Paula and sat down.

Mandy nervously cleared her throat. "I hope you'll grant me a small favor after seeing how I rescued Jeff. I'd like to ask you a couple of simple questions about the raft trip."

"Why the hell should I talk to someone who thinks I killed my own husband?"

"Because I don't think you did. You couldn't have shot Rob because you were with Detective Quintana at the time, and I think whoever shot Rob also killed your husband. Look, I'll keep it short. Then I'm out of here. I won't bug you ever again."

Paula's lips twitched. "Promise?"

"Promise."

She gave out a little sigh. "I guess I can answer some little ol' questions from the person who saved my son from that ugly rapid. Too bad you couldn't have saved his boat, too."

Will the woman's complaints never cease? Mandy took a deep breath. "Okay. On the morning of the rafting trip, who handed you the sports drink bottle that you gave to your husband?"

"I don't know." Paula waved a hand in the air. "As I told Detective Quintana, it was chaotic, people milling around, trying to figure out who was going in what raft. And I certainly wasn't going to share a raft with the Olsons."

"Please. Could you try to remember? Could it have been Evie Olson?"

With a derisive snort, Paula said, "I'd never take anything from that floozy."

"How about Lenny Preble, then? Did he hand you the bottle?"

Paula pursed her lips. "Yeah, maybe."

"Did you see him take it out of the box?"

"I thought you said a couple of questions." Paula folded her arms across her chest.

"Okay, I want to discuss just one little ol' topic, the sports drink bottle. And it's important. Please, think hard. Try to remember what happened that morning."

While Paula stared at Mandy her eyes went unfocused as if she was replaying the morning in her mind. "Okay, I'm picturing Lenny coming over with the box in his hands. He asked me to take two bottles, one for me and one for Tom, since Tom was still messing with his lifejacket."

Mandy's shoulders slumped in disappointment. If Lenny left the choice of bottles up to Paula, he couldn't have poisoned one already. *Am I sitting here talking casually to a woman who murdered her own husband? No, she wouldn't be so open with me if she did, especially given her past animosity.*

"What happened after you gave Tom his bottle?"

"We put them in the raft next to where we were going to be sitting."

Someone must have gotten to that bottle sometime. Mandy mentally reviewed the process of getting a pod of rafts on the river—paperwork, hand out gear, divvy the group up into rafts, introduce the guides, safety talk, load the rafts . . .

"Wait, when did the safety talk happen, before or after you stowed your bottles?"

Paula was silent for a moment. "After, I think."

"How far away from your raft did the safety talk take place?"

"Just a few steps upstream, by the last raft. Ours was the first."

Someone could have slipped the poison in Tom King's bottle then—or exchanged his bottle with one that had been doped already. "Did everyone go to the safety talk?"

"Not the other guides. Or Lenny. When we got back to our raft, he was in his seat. Said he'd heard the talk so many times already that he didn't need to hear it again. I wish I'd done the same and not suffered through Gonzo's lame jokes."

"Did Detective Quintana ask you any questions about the safety talk, like who attended and when it happened?"

"No."

"Were your drink bottles disturbed or moved in any way when you got back to the raft?"

"Not that I could tell." Paula eyed Mandy. "You can't be thinking that skinny dip killed my husband. He wouldn't hurt a fly, and if he saw you swatting one, he'd read you the riot act. My money's on that evil bitch, Evie. I have my doubts about Nate Fowler being the culprit."

"So do I."

"Now, I can't imagine a single other thing I can tell you about those stupid sports drinks other than they tasted like puke. That's it. End of story." Paula turned her back to Mandy to say something to her friend.

End of story is right. Mandy stood and made her way across the row and up the aisle to the back exit. Once in the lobby, she dug her cell phone out of her pocket. She had to call Quintana.

Just then the back exit door banged opened. Lenny Preble strode out of the theater into the lobby.

TWENTY

*A woman is like a teabag—you never know how
strong she is until she gets in hot water.*
—ELEANOR ROOSEVELT

MANDY STIFFENED. *WHERE WAS Lenny sitting? Did he hear me
talking to Paula?*

Lenny walked toward her, his steps echoing in the empty lobby.
The open black and red flannel shirt he wore over his T-shirt and
jeans flapped like a sinister cape behind him. With each step, Mandy's heartbeat ratcheted up a notch.

Two teenage girls came out of the theater into the lobby and
scurried past him, making him pause and frown at them. They
continued on, whispering and giggling to each other on the way to
the ladies' restroom.

"Hello, Mandy," Lenny said casually when he reached her. "I
heard about Rob. How's he doing?"

"F-fine. He's sleeping now."

Lenny nodded. "Good. I heard Quintana locked up Nate Fowler as a suspect. Looks like our two developers are both eliminated. One's dead, and the other one will be going to prison."

"Could be." Mandy unclenched her clammy hand from around her cell phone.

Lenny cocked his head. "Why just 'could be'?"

He's behaving naturally. Maybe he didn't see me with Paula. Mandy tried to make a nonchalant shrug. "You know. Innocent until proven guilty."

"Right, you keep on believing that, even after they found the rifle that shot Rob in Nate's garage."

The hair bristled on the back of Mandy's neck. Quintana wouldn't have allowed that to become public knowledge, would he?

Lenny hitched up his jeans and stood straighter. "The important thing is that the Arkansas is safe for now. And there'll be another buyer for those water rights."

"Another buyer? Who? Aren't you worried?"

"No, because the other buyer will be my nonprofit corporation. This travesty of developers fighting to the death over water rights will convince the good citizens of Chaffee County that they need to contribute to a fund to buy those rights for our children's future."

Two of those children, the pair of giggly teens, crossed the lobby again to return to the theater.

Mandy ached to follow them, back to the crowded room, back to the safety of numbers. She stepped toward the theater, then realized her action wouldn't make sense. Why would she have walked out into the lobby just to return to the theater again? She couldn't make Lenny suspicious.

She altered course. "Good luck with that, Lenny, but I've got to go now. I was headed for the ladies room."

Mandy rushed toward the restroom, feeling Lenny's gaze on her back the whole time. Unfortunately the restroom was empty. *Will he follow me? I've got to make it sound like others are in here.*

She ran into a stall and flushed a toilet, then into a second stall and flushed its toilet. Then she scurried to a sink, turned on the water, and reached over to crank the knob on the paper towel dispenser. She checked her cell phone. No signal. With all the metal construction in the Steamplant, it wasn't a surprise. She'd have to wait for Lenny to leave, then go outside to call Quintana.

Standing there with a handful of paper towels, she waited, muscles wadded up as tightly as the towels in her fist.

Nothing. No one came in. She turned off the sink faucet and waited some more. Again nothing.

Mandy let out the breath she'd been holding and threw the paper towels in the trash can. She cracked open the door and peeked out. An older couple chatting amiably with each other was exiting the lobby. She quickly walked to the outside door and followed them. As they crossed the street, she headed for her car, opening her cell phone. *Yes, a signal!* She found Quintana's cell phone number in her directory, selected it, and put the phone to her ear. The phone rang a couple of times, then it clicked as someone picked up.

Too late, she heard running footsteps.

"Not so fast." Lenny snatched the phone from her as Quintana was saying hello. He threw it into the sculpture garden next to the

Steamplant, then grabbed her arm and whipped her around. All semblance of casualness was gone. His jaw clenched and his dark brown eyes burned into her.

"You're hurting me!" Mandy squirmed and pulled, but she couldn't release her arm from his grasp. The man was thin, but he was strong.

He twisted her arm behind her back and jerked her against his bony chest. "And you're hurting the river. Why couldn't you leave well enough alone?"

His hot breath against the back of her neck made her tremble. "Help!" she screamed, hoping the couple would hear.

Lenny clamped his free hand over her mouth. "No one's out here to hear you. They're all inside the theater."

A car door slammed shut. Probably the couple's, engrossed in their conversation. So Lenny was right.

When he pulled her into the sculpture garden, away from the street, she fought him, panic rising in her throat as she heard the couple's car drive off. *The self-defense class! What did I learn that can get me out of this?* She madly kicked her legs, then looked down, took aim and stomped hard on his instep.

He gasped. His grip lessened.

Mandy broke free. She bolted toward the back of the Steamplant building facing the river, now closer to her than the front door. She hoped to get in the rear entrance and find someone, anyone to help her.

When she reached the brick patio, she glanced back. Lenny was only a few yards away. It was too late to climb the steps and open the door. He would be able to grab her first.

She kept running. Her shoes pounded across the wooden footbridge over a small creek. Her heart pounded against her ribcage, as if trying to escape her chest as desperately as she was trying to escape Lenny.

Mandy leapt down to the concrete boat ramp. When she turned to head up the street into town, she saw Lenny had run alongside the creek and crossed it further up. He had cut off her escape route and was running straight for her, his teeth bared.

With nowhere else to go, she did an about-face and sprinted onto the path paralleling the dark, seething river.

Lenny caught up and body-slammed her, throwing her off the path and onto the boulders below.

Mandy's hip and shoulders whacked the rocks first. Sharp pains shot up her nerves, stunning her, making her see stars.

With an "oof," Lenny landed on top of her.

She kicked and scratched and screamed.

Grunting and punching, he rolled, bringing her with him. When she was unpinned, he hurled her into the river.

Mandy splashed into the cold water. Gasping, she tried to breathe, but her chest muscles seized up.

Again, Lenny leapt on top of her and pushed her under.

The river pulled them downstream, toward the F Street Bridge. Mandy's lungs screamed for oxygen. She shoved against the madman and clawed her way to the surface.

She gulped a quick breath before he pushed her head back underwater.

The deadly current slammed her against one of the bridge supports. Mandy kicked off with all her might.

That action broke her loose from Lenny's hold. She bobbed up to suck air. Another adversary snatched her—the river current. It swirled her around the support, scraping her against the bricks, and flushed her under the F Street Bridge.

She came out on the downstream side and tried to spot Lenny, using the light of the moon. Splashing drew her attention. He'd been sucked around the other side of the support and now floundered toward the town side of the river.

Mandy swam for the opposite side, the one with no buildings, just deserted railroad tracks.

When she felt rocks under her, she scrabbled toward the shore. But her grip slipped, and she was swept downstream again. She swam back to the shore and pulled on rocks until she could bring her feet under her. Half-crawling, half-slithering, she inched her battered body up the bank until she lay on the grass, her chest heaving.

The next bridge across the river was a mile downstream, and Lenny was bound to come across the F Street Bridge looking for her. In fact, she could hear his wet sneakers slapping against the concrete as he sprinted for her side of the river.

Mandy pushed herself up to her hands and knees. *Hide!*

She crawled between a pair of cottonwood trees and the river, but she was still visible from the bank. With no other option, she slid into the icy river again and hunkered down among the jumbled rocks and roots under the cottonwoods.

Cold seeped through her cotton jeans and T-shirt. She pulled her windbreaker around her, but shivers shook her frame.

If Lenny doesn't kill me, hypothermia will.

The rattling of her teeth sounded like tap-dancers. She clamped her mouth shut and hugged herself tightly, but the shivers continued. She waited with her ears tuned for the sound of movement along the river bank.

A great horned owl hooted. Mandy searched for a pair of yellow eyes in the branches above, but couldn't spot the large tufted bird. To some Native American tribes, the owls were carriers sent to fly the souls of the dead to the spirit world. The thought sent another tremor coursing through her.

A pebble clattered on the path upstream, then a shoe scraped and stopped suddenly, as if Lenny had lost his balance and caught himself. "Sh-shit," he stuttered.

Mandy realized he must be shivering, too. Maybe if he got too cold, he would give up looking for her. She held her breath as steps scrunched on the path past the other side of the cottonwoods. She prayed they'd keep moving.

They stopped.

Lenny stepped down onto a boulder. His black silhouette loomed no more than twenty feet from her. He peered into the darkness downstream, then turned and looked upstream.

Feeling his gaze sweep over her, Mandy froze and held her breath. But she couldn't contain the violent shiver that spasmed her whole body.

"Got you, you water witch." Lenny sprinted toward her.

Move! Move! Move!

Mandy's cramped muscles were slow to obey. By the time she clambered out of the roots, Lenny was upon her.

He shoved her back into the river. Icy tendrils swirled around her, sapping body heat and what little strength she had left. The current tugged her toward the deep water in the middle of the channel.

Lenny jumped in after her and clamped his hands around her neck. He squeezed tight.

Her vision dimmed. *This is it. I'm going to die.* Giving up was so tempting, so easy, and she was so tired of fighting. Her arms sagged.

Fight, baby girl. Fight!

Mandy's eyelids fluttered.

Live!

A surge of energy mustered deep within her. Her hands rose out of the water. She shoved her thumbs into Lenny's eye sockets.

"Aaaagh!" He released her neck and smacked her hands.

But she had already balled them into fists. She punched one into his throat, then the other.

Lenny gagged and kicked against her body. The river carried him away.

Mandy thrashed toward the shore on the town side, her arms and legs uncoordinated and sluggish. But she kept moving, sheer desperation driving her toward the shallows.

Her knee banged against a rock. Her hand slapped another. She tried to grasp the rock to pull herself toward the river bank, but her stiff fingers couldn't grab hold.

She kicked down and hit bottom. The momentum carried her forward. She shoved against the bottom again and gained another few feet. Clawing with hands that felt like frozen oven mitts, she fell gasping on the bank, half of her body still in the water.

Get out of the water!

Mandy shoved her feet and rolled, then rolled again up onto grass. Violent shivers racked her body. She coughed up Arkansas River water and spit it out.

She lay not far from the band shell in Riverside Park. No one would be in the park that late, but a light glimmered in a building across the street on the other side of the park.

Can I make it there? Where's Lenny?

Mandy lifted her head and searched the river, expecting to see Lenny climbing out onto the bank to come shove her back into the cold water. But no specter of death appeared. Only silence, and the gurgle of ripples stirring the surface of the Arkansas River.

The only movement was a log slapping against the rocks beside the bank.

A log?

Mandy crawled toward it, her elbows sinking into the mud. The log was Lenny, lying face down in the water. The motion of his body was caused by the eddy swirling around him, rocking his arms and legs.

My punches must have collapsed his throat.

Good. Leave him there to die.

A siren wailed in the distance.

I can't leave him. I'm a whitewater river ranger.

He tried to kill me.

The sirens came closer, approaching the Steamplant Theater.

I'm supposed to rescue people.

I'm half-dead myself. I don't have the energy.

Car doors slammed and people began shouting. Flashlight beams pierced the night sky.

Do it, Mandy. You won't be able to live with yourself if you don't.

She crawled down to the bank, braced her feet against the rocks, and grabbed hold of Lenny's arms. Leaning back, she pulled. His body moved a few inches.

Mandy bent her knees and grabbed him under his armpits. She pulled, and pulled, and pulled. A massive groan escaped her lips as she fell back, Lenny's body flopping onto her legs. She slid out from under him, pushed on a shoulder and rolled him onto his back.

She placed a couple of fingers against his neck and felt a weak pulse. But no air escaped his lips.

Mandy shuddered. *No, I can't do it. And what if he revives? He'll try to kill me again.*

The people with flashlights were down at the river, crossing the F Street bridge. Mandy could make out some of their shouts now. They were men. They were calling her name.

"Here." The word came out as a strangled bark. She cleared her throat and took a deep breath. "Here!"

Someone shouted in reply.

While dark shapes ran toward her, she pulled on Lenny's chin to open his airway. She bent her head to breathe life into his mouth, to do what she was trained to do.

TWENTY-ONE

Let us cross over the river, and rest under the shade of the trees.
—MAY 10, 1863, LAST WORDS OF
THOMAS JONATHAN (STONEWALL) JACKSON

SEATED IN THE FRONT pew of the First Baptist Church, Mandy mumbled, "Amen," after the pastor's prayer, along with the rest of the memorial service attendees. Uncle Bill hadn't been a regular churchgoer, but he was a registered Baptist, so Mandy had arranged for his service to be held here. This was the public tribute, where her uncle's friends, employees, and business associates could say their goodbyes and speak a few words in his honor if they wished. The private ceremony would be later.

She shifted her weight, trying to ease the aches from the myriad bruises and scrapes she had collected during her fight with Lenny Preble in the Arkansas River two days before. In response, David and Rob, the two men left in her life after Uncle Bill's death-seated on either side of her, bent their heads to check on her. David looked perfectly at ease in his gray pinstriped suit, but Rob tugged again at the collar of the crisp light-blue shirt he had taken out of the package along with its matching tie that morning.

She gave her protectors a quick nod to show she was okay and sat up straighter. She had had a chance to dry her tears after David's eulogy. As the recessional music started, she fortified herself for the next heart-rending task—shaking everyone's hand and accepting their murmured condolences.

With a hand on her elbow, David helped her stand, and the three of them moved toward the aisle. She stumbled while exiting the pew.

With his good arm, Rob caught her. "Are you up to standing in the receiving line?"

"I'm just stiff. And I'm not used to these heels." Like Rob, she rarely needed to dress formally, and here this was the third time in a week she'd worn a skirt, starting with Tom King's funeral. She squeezed Rob's left hand, which poked out of his shoulder sling, and turned to follow her brother up the aisle.

———

Two hours later, she sat on Rob's sofa with a plate of potato salad and ham that someone had fixed for her. She couldn't bring herself to eat any of it, or of the multitude of casseroles, salads, and plates of cookies crowded on the dining room table, the kitchen counter, and all the other horizontal surfaces in the house. They'd need to borrow space in friends' freezers and refrigerators to store all the leftovers.

Lucky was in dog heaven, slurping up dropped crumbs and offerings from the soft-hearted. Mandy spotted Cynthia slipping him a cube of cheese and casting a guilty look in her direction. Mandy waved her hand to show it was all right.

Savoring a brief moment of solitude, she leaned her head against the back cushion. Most of the guests had already come around to give her a pat or a hug and now stood eating and talking and drinking in every room of Rob's home.

Detective Quintana sat next to her on the sofa. "Here, give me that plate. You weren't going to eat that food anyway, were you?" He set it on the end table.

"I can't stomach anything now. Maybe later, after the river ceremony."

"The river ceremony?"

"Gonzo and Kendra volunteered to paddle a raft so Rob, David, and I could throw Uncle Bill's ashes in the Arkansas. That's where he wanted to be."

Where he already is. She thought back on her battle with Lenny and the surge of strength that seemed to come from nowhere, the admonition to live.

Quintana nodded. "Makes sense. Bill spent most of his life on the Arkansas."

Mandy cast a worried glance at him. "I'm not doing anything illegal, am I?"

"Not if I don't know about it." He winked. "There's so much noise in here. What was it you said?"

Mandy smiled. "Oh, nothing."

"How're you doing? Frankly, you looked terrible when I saw you Saturday night."

"I feel like I've gone seven rounds with a boxing kangaroo, but I'll recover."

"Good." He looked around to see if anyone was listening, then bent his head to speak softly to Mandy. "We found a mortar and pestle with aconite powder on them in a trashcan in Lenny's workshop. And the plants you spotted in his garden were monkshood."

"So you've pegged him for Tom King's murder. What about for shooting Rob?"

"Also in the workshop was a box of bullets that matched the shape and caliber of the one in Rob's shoulder. We found some used bullets and shells in his back yard."

"Why were they in his back yard?"

"Target practice. One of his pine trees was missing some big chunks of bark, and we dug two bullets out of the trunk. I'm confident the rifling marks on them will match those on the bullet we took from Rob and the barrel of the rifle we found stashed in Nate Fowler's garage. With that evidence and your testimony that he knew the rifle was there, the attempted murder charge for shooting Rob will stick. Then, there's the attempt on your life. Lenny knows his goose is cooked."

"Did he confess to poisoning Tom King?"

Quintana nodded. "Said he rode in the same raft with King, right behind him, so he could watch for when he got woozy enough to not be able to save himself. Then Lenny planned to push King out of the raft when they hit a turbulent spot."

"But the Number Four rapid did that for him."

"That it did."

Nate Fowler approached the sofa and held out his hand to Mandy. "I owe you my profound thanks. Without you, I might still be sitting in jail accused of Tom King's murder."

Mandy shook his hand. "I'm sure Detective Quintana would have figured out you weren't the killer."

"I'm not so sure of that." Quintana stood and put a hand on Nate's shoulder. "I hope you know how bad I feel about locking you up. My gut was telling me you weren't capable of murder, but all the evidence pointed to you."

"That was Lenny Preble's doing, not yours." Nate stuck his hand out. "Apology accepted. The food's not half bad in your jail, either. I haven't eaten beans and wieners since I was a kid."

Quintana threw back his head and laughed. He grabbed Nate's hand and shook it vigorously. "Sometimes I sneak a plate of those myself."

"And now Lenny's eating them." Nate turned to Mandy. "I want you to know that when I get my mitts on those water rights, I'll be donating some for recreational use in your uncle's name."

"He'd like that." Mandy swallowed the lump in her throat. "Thanks. And speaking of apologies, I owe you and your wife one for trespassing in your yard."

With a wave of his hand, Nate said, "Water under the dam, so to speak. We had a good laugh over it. At least you two weren't Peeping Toms." He winked. "Hey, can I get you some food?"

Mandy pointed at the full plate Quintana had taken from her. "Thanks, but I've got plenty."

She spied Rob leaning up against a door jamb watching her and signaled for him to come over. "Do you mind?" she asked the two men.

They turned and saw Rob's approach. "I could use a refill on my beer," Nate said to Quintana. "Care to join me?"

"I'm drinking iced tea, myself. There's some great lemon pie out in the kitchen, though."

After they moved away, Rob settled next to her on the sofa and put his good arm around her. "How're you holding up?"

"I'm bushed. I'd like to get all of this over with, and go out on the river with Uncle Bill's ashes."

"David and I thought so. He's going around giving folks the 'thanks so much for coming' signal. The crowd should clear out soon. But there's something I need to tell you before we leave for the river."

Mandy's heart skipped a beat. "Nothing bad, I hope."

"Something good. Gonzo asked me to talk to you." Rob grinned. "I think he's a little intimidated by his boss lady. Anyway, when he stopped by the hospital and I saw how he reacted to you, I asked him what was up. He told me about quitting after you threatened to fire him. He tried to boast that he could find another outfitter to work for easily, but I squelched that. I told him he had a reputation for being a drunk, that if he wanted to find guiding work, he had to dry himself out."

"How did he react? Is he pissed off at you, too, now?"

"No, I scared him good. We had a serious talk, and I suggested he join AA."

"Did he?"

"He's attended two meetings so far. He has a long way to go, but he asked me to let you know what he's doing. He's hoping for a second chance, but what he really wants is to be your friend again."

"He's always been my friend, Rob. When your friend is screwing up his life, you tell him." Mandy leaned her head on Rob's shoulder. It felt good, like she belonged there. "And I'll support him in this as much as I can. If he can stay sober for the next two or three weeks, I'll rehire him on a provisional basis. But I'll keep a close eye on him."

Rob hooked a finger around a tendril of her hair that had worked loose from her ponytail. While tucking it behind her ear, he ran his finger along the rim of her earlobe, sending tingles down her neck. "And I'm going to be keeping a close watch over you in the next few days, *mi querida*."

Mandy smiled up at him. "But I'm supposed to be taking care of you."

"I've gotten pretty good at doing things one-handed. In fact, you and I are going to head over to your place with my toolbox tomorrow to fix your broken window and that overzealous toaster."

"And the ghost-flushing toilet. But I want to fix them myself."

Rob opened his mouth, then closed it and pursed his lips. "Okay, but I'll lend you my tools—and my expertise."

"And my hands will do the work, so you don't strain your shoulder."

"Hey, about all I need help with is driving—and taking off my pants."

"Rob!"

Rob leered then the grin faded. "You gave me quite a fright you know, when Detective Quintana woke me up pounding on the door and asked where you'd gone. Thank God you wrote that note so I could tell him. I was sure Tom King's killer had finally gotten to you. I've never been so scared in my life."

"I felt the same way taking you to the hospital."

Rob pulled her toward him and kissed her on the tip of her nose. He aimed for her lips, but she drew back.

"Not in front of everyone," Mandy whispered.

"Who?"

She looked around. While they were talking, the room had emptied. The sound of some folks saying goodbye to David at the front door filtered in, but otherwise the house was quiet. So when Rob turned his attention to her lips, she responded willingly.

David walked in rubbing his hands. "Now that's what I like to see. My little sis getting kissed good and proper. Ready to get this show on the road?"

———

After running a shuttle, the five of them slipped a raft into the riffles under Stone Bridge north of Salida. After negotiating the tame Squaw Creek rapid, Gonzo and Kendra paddled silently, befitting the mood of the solemn occasion, while Mandy cradled the small box of ashes on her lap. She sat in the front of the raft, facing David and Rob in the middle.

In this section of the Arkansas, the river took a rest from its mad plunge down five thousand feet of elevation in its first 125 miles and meandered around Big Bend. Cobble bars had formed where the slowing river, no long able to transport rocks and pebbles, dropped its load. The gentle, gurgling current allowed cottonwood trees and large bushes of alder and red-tipped willow to flourish and droop their heavily laden branches in the water. A red squirrel chittered at them as they drifted by. With a gentle plunk, a muskrat slid into the water.

David leaned back and tilted his face toward the sun. "I can see why Uncle Bill loved being on the river. It drains the tension right out of you."

"Why don't you move out here?" Rob asked.

David shook his head. "Too entrenched in the firm back home. I'll have to come visit Mandy more often, though. Plus there's an added attraction."

This statement piqued Mandy's interest. "Oh?"

"Your friend Cynthia's a sweet little number. Lotta fun, too. She told me this great blonde joke. You should hear it, Mandy."

Mandy laughed. "Are you her proxy now? Since she couldn't come with us, she gave you a joke to plague me with?"

A look of disappointment crossed David's face. "You don't want to hear it?"

With a smile, Mandy said, "No, go ahead."

David shifted in his seat. "Okay, I hope I remember this right. Two blondes drove by a wheat field and saw another blonde in the middle of the field rowing a row boat. The driver blonde turned to her friend and said, 'You know, it's blondes like that who give us a bad name!' The other blonde replied, 'I know it, and if I knew how to swim, I'd go out there and drown her.'"

Everyone in the raft chuckled.

"With the ice broken, maybe now's a good time to talk about the future of Uncle Bill's business, Mandy. You and Rob seem to have kissed and made up, so why don't you hear him out on his plans for a merger?"

Rob raised an eyebrow at Mandy.

She ran her hand across the top of the box. Would Uncle Bill have approved of a merger? A sense of calm descended on her. "I'm listening."

Rob leaned forward, elbows on his knees. "This wouldn't just be a merger of two river outfitters, Mandy. I've wanted to branch out for a while—into leading adventure travel trips. We could offer all kinds of experiences. In the summer, horseback riding, climbing, and mountain biking, as well as rafting. And in the winter, ice climbing, cross-country skiing, snowmobiling. We could even combine two or three activities into week-long trips."

He paused, looking hopeful. After Mandy gave him a nod, he continued, "You got into ice climbing last winter, and with your ski patrol background, you'd be ideal to lead adventure trips in the winter when you're not working as a river ranger. And, by adding the other activities, we could extend our trips into the spring and fall, too. Offer adventure trips year-round. And offer full-time jobs to some of our guides."

"You know I love horseback riding, Mandy," Kendra said.

"And I'm getting certified to lead climbing trips," Gonzo added.

"What is this, a conspiracy?" Mandy joked.

"Yes," David said, with a pat to her knee. "A conspiracy for your future, a happy future."

Mandy stared at the box in her lap. A warm glow suffused her.

She looked at the others' expectant faces and smiled. "Uncle Bill would approve. I'll do it."

Kendra and Gonzo cheered while Rob grasped her hand and squeezed it.

David looked relieved. "I'll start on the paperwork tomorrow."

A puffy cloud that had skittered across the face of the sun moved away, allowing its rays to blaze through again. The sunlight striking the water made tiny sparkles shimmer across the surface, as if someone had strewn diamonds across the water. Mandy's gaze followed the sunbeams west. There, on Mount Shavano, glistening snowfields formed the figure of a snow spirit, the Angel of Shavano, which Ute legends said brought their tribe good fortune.

"This is the spot," Mandy said.

Kendra and Gonzo pulled their paddles out of the water.

"Do you want to say something?" David asked Mandy.

She nodded, a huge lump suddenly swollen in her throat. She swallowed it down and looked out over the water to compose herself.

"I'll miss you, Uncle Bill, every single day of my life. But every time I paddle on the river, I'll feel your presence—and your love."

She stood and Rob steadied her. She removed the box's lid and handed it to David. Then she held the box out over the river, slowly tilted it, and let the ashes fall out in a gentle stream.

A slight breeze made them dance and glitter in the sunlight until they drifted onto the surface of the water. There, they dissolved and disappeared, becoming one with the Arkansas River, where Uncle Bill belonged, where he had always belonged.

And where she belonged, too.

"Rest in peace, Uncle Bill."

Beth Groundwater was an avid "river rat" in the 1980s, running whitewater rivers in the eastern United States in an open-boat canoe. She has enjoyed reacquainting herself with that subculture and its updated boating equipment while researching the RM Adventures mystery series. Beth lives in Colorado and enjoys its many outdoor activities, including skiing and whitewater rafting. She loves to speak to book clubs about her books. To find out more, please visit Beth's website at bethgroundwater.com and her blog at bethgroundwater.blogspot.com.